S0-AEU-770

AKA JANE KICKS 'A'!

more ...

"I enjoyed Jane's panache and her upbeat, woman-takes-all story in the James Bond tradition."
—*Poisoned Pen*

"Crisply written ... frothy and fun."
—*Kirkus Reviews*

"Richly plotted, swift paced ... vividly clear ... a sensational opener for what promises to be a thrilling series."
—*Drood Review of Mystery*

MAUREEN TAN

A K A
JANE

WARNER BOOKS

A Time Warner Company

WARNER BOOKS EDITION

Cover design by Rachel McClain
Cover illustration by Mike Racz

Warner Books, Inc.
1271 Avenue of the Americas
New York, NY 10020

Visit our Web site at
www.warnerbooks.com

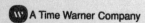 A Time Warner Company

Printed in the United States of America
Originally published in hardcover by Warner Books.
First Paperback Printing: April, 1999

10 9 8 7 6 5 4 3 2

To Mom and Richard, who are always there for me.
To Terri and Mary, the best sisters a writer ever had.
To Morgana, Jessica, and Dick, my good friends and fellow travelers.
To Mark, Marie, and Marguerite, who handle
Mom's obsession with tolerance and humor.
And especially to Peter, for his unflagging faith and
invaluable technical expertise.

threats took turns disappearing beneath the black ones.

PROLOGUE

Berkshire, England

The damp odor of logs, newly stacked beside the fireplace, mixed with the smell that the Christmas tree spread through the Great Hall. Mulled cider simmered in a copper pot on the kitchen stove. Each time the cook and her helpers rushed by, they left the smell of apples, oranges, and cinnamon in their wake.

I sat curled into a wing-backed chair near the fireplace, idly examining the contrast between my hands and the white woolen skirt I wore. I was almost seven. Three years in Greece had tanned my fair skin golden and streaked my brown hair with blonde.

A shadow fell across my chair as my grandfather stepped between me and the fire. He leaned over, planted a brief kiss on the top of my head, then engulfed both my hands in one of his. He held his other hand behind his back.

More questions, I thought. *They* gave up, so they sent me here. Now it's his turn. I curled my hands into tight fists, shifted my eyes to the tapestry pattern woven into the fabric of my chair. I concentrated on the way the red and yellow threads took turns disappearing beneath the black ones.

I was there, they kept saying. I had seen my parents and the driver killed. I was too small, they said, so I was left alive. They were sure I'd seen something important. If only I would answer their questions.

I focused on a single red thread, followed it with my eyes, cast my mind back, *tried* to remember. I had been sitting in the front seat, next to our driver . . .

Stavros hauled on the steering wheel, but the car skidded out of control anyway. It crashed through the twisted branches of the olive trees bordering the road. I was thrown from the seat, slammed against the padded dashboard. The car stalled, rolled to a stop. I landed in a heap on the floor, my face just inches from Stavros' polished black boots. His right foot moved frantically as he tried to restart the engine.

Behind me, the door opened.

I had forgotten to lock it.

I glanced over my shoulder. A man leaned into the car, a stocking mask hiding his face. He held a gun, fired it. Stavros' head exploded. Something warm and sticky hit my cheek and neck, my shoulders and arms. The man pointed the gun into the backseat.

My father shouted, "No, not my—"

The man fired twice. His second shot silenced my mother's screams.

I tried to get away, to claw my way past Stavros' legs. But the man grabbed the back of my dress, dragged me from the car. He dropped me to the ground, aimed his gun.

"Sorry, love. You weren't supposed to be here."

I yanked my hands from my grandfather's grasp, tore my gaze from the red thread. That was all I had seen, all I could remember.

Think! they kept saying. There must have been something.

A crime against the Crown. Didn't I want to help them catch the bad people? Then they would look angry and ask me more questions.

My grandfather sighed and straightened. His eyes were hazel, like mine. Like my father's. I bent my head, concentrated once again on the contrast between my hands and my skirt.

"Merry Christmas, Janie."

"Merry Christmas, Grampa."

"I miss them, too. But you and I . . . We'll manage, won't we?"

"Yes, sir."

He was being nice now, but soon *he* would be angry. Maybe if I just tried harder . . .

"I've brought you a wee gift."

I shook my head. I didn't want the brightly wrapped packages that waited beneath the Christmas tree. I wanted to remember.

He moved his left hand from behind his back, dropped a grey kitten into my lap.

"Yours. Someone to talk to."

He walked away. No questions this time.

I picked up the kitten, pressed my face into its soft fur.

I would not cry.

1

Rome, Italy

The plastique was molded into a thin, even layer against the stiff inner walls of the oversized leather bag. Well-used American bills of large denominations were packed tightly into its false bottom.

Tony ignored the explosives and me. He concentrated on the money.

We were in the workroom of a leather-goods shop located on a narrow, littered street in one of Rome's seedier tourist areas. Inside, narrow aisles and shelves jammed with merchandise promised bargains to unwary shoppers. The shop had been crowded with tourists when I arrived. Tony's assistant was locking the front door behind the last of them.

A doorway, hung with a dust-laden velvet curtain, separated the clutter of the shop from the workroom's clutter. The curtain, probably once dark green, was a muddy olive color. Opposite the doorway was a battered metal desk, in an equally unattractive shade of green. Its surface overflowed with paper and open ledgers. Ceiling-to-floor wooden shelves filled with damaged luggage covered the wall to the right of the doorway. To the left,

Tony bent over a long, wooden workbench. Scraps of leather littered the floor, scattered there when he had cleared the bench with a sweep of his arm.

I leaned against one of the rough shelves, idly pushed a triangular scrap of leather around with my toe. This was my sixth delivery. Tony, I knew, would not be rushed.

One by one, he lifted the neat packets from the bag, broke the narrow brown wrappers, counted the bills onto the bench. He was a big man, slow-moving. The short walk from the cash register at the front of the shop had left him breathing heavily. Perspiration beaded on his upper lip, his shirt clung to his flabby body, he smelled of sweat and garlic.

I tried not to breathe too deeply.

The shop assistant pushed aside the curtain, let it fall into place behind him. He brought with him a whiff of familiar cologne and a draft of fresh air. On my first visit, he'd introduced himself as Roberto. Like Tony, his hair was dark and curly and his eyes were brown. But Roberto was tanned and wiry and built like an athlete. He wore a white cotton shirt open at the throat and rolled up at the sleeves.

"*Signorina*," he said. He nodded curtly as his eyes swept past me. This was business. The pretty Irish stewardess with dark hair and blue eyes was insignificant compared to the merchandise she delivered.

"Is the shipment complete?" he asked Tony.

"Patience. I'm not finished counting." Tony picked up another bundle, then said: "What's this?"

Secured beneath the brown wrapper was a strip of yellow paper. Two stylized Japanese characters were printed along one edge. Tony freed the paper, glanced at it, then crushed it and tossed it aside.

"A greeting from Chicago." He shrugged, returned his attention to the money. Finally he said, "Everything is correct, Roberto. *Grazie, signorina*."

Beside me, Roberto exhaled as if he'd been holding his breath.

I turned my head, flashed him a smile. You worry too much, I thought.

Suddenly, Tony groaned. He clasped his hand to his chest and staggered toward the back of the room. A row of dusty ledgers tumbled to the floor as he sagged across the desk.

"*Signore*, are you ill?" I said.

I took a step toward him.

Tony straightened, swung around. A Luger was in his hand. The barrel end of its silencer pointed unwaveringly at me.

I backed away. Roberto was behind me. He grasped my upper arms.

"Tony, this makes no sense," he said in rapid Italian.

Tony's finger tightened on the trigger.

Roberto pushed me violently aside.

The bullet, meant for me, hit him. He fell backward through the doorway, into the shop.

I dove for the floor, rolled as I wrenched my knife from the sheath on my thigh, flung it as Tony fired again. His bullet tore through my right shoulder. My knife caught him in the throat. At first, he stood motionless, looking bewildered. Then the Luger slipped from his fingers. His empty hand drifted upward toward the knife, toward the hilt that jutted from beneath his jaw. He never reached it. He pitched forward, collapsing into the center of the room.

From where I lay, I could see his face. His eyes were stretched wide, his mouth gasping and bloody. Seconds later, he was dead. Then, except for the sound of my own breathing, there was silence. Silence, and the smells of blood and cordite and leather. No sounds from the shop.

"Brian," I called out urgently, using Roberto's real name for the first time in weeks. "Brian!"

No answer.

Unconscious, I told myself. He was on the other side of the curtain, bleeding and unconscious. That's why he wasn't answering me.

I struggled to my feet. If I moved slowly, I could make it to the doorway and Brian. I took a step, then another. The room wavered, shifted out of focus. The floor heaved. I grabbed the nearest shelf, wedged my elbows into its clutter, rested my forehead against a dusty black valise. I had to stay conscious, had to stay on my feet.

When I lifted my head again, the room was back in focus. I straightened, one hand still clutching the shelf, and noticed a heavy smear of blood. It was from a jagged hole above my right breast. I tipped my head to one side, watched the blood soak into the jacket's woolen fibers. Someone else's shoulder. Someone else's blood. I wondered if the cleaners would be able to remove the stain.

That jerked me back to reality. Concentrate!

Three more steps, maybe four. The room around me blurred, but I kept moving. The touch of heavy cloth brought me back to full awareness. I pushed it aside.

Brian lay sprawled at my feet. The wound in his chest was dark and terrible. His eyes stared sightlessly at the ceiling. Still, I fell to my knees beside him. I searched for some sign of life. I searched. And I prayed. Oh, God! how I prayed.

In the end, I could only close his eyes.

Impossible to stand.

I crawled to the front door. It was locked.

I stretched upward, straining to reach the latch. My blood-slick fingers scrabbled uselessly beneath it. I tried again. Tried until the door was sticky with my blood. Until, exhausted, I slumped to the floor.

If I gave up, I would die.

I should want to live.

I couldn't think why.

Best to die here, with Brian.

To hell with Queen and country. To hell with the operation. To hell with the whole bloody organization.

Decision made, I shut my eyes.

Too easy to imagine Brian frowning. He believed in duty.

If I gave up, the red-haired man would go free.

I opened my eyes, reached for the latch again.

2

Near London, England

I thought I heard my grandfather's voice. Strange, because he was dead.

"Janie. Wake up."

Too early, I thought, though the morning light was bright against my eyelids. Let me sleep. I raised my arm to brush the voice away. A stab of searing agony, centered in my right shoulder, stopped the movement almost before it began. The light turned crimson, then black. The voice went away.

"Jane. Open your eyes."

Not my grandfather's voice. Douglas MacDonald's, authoritative, demanding.

Reluctantly, I did as he said.

My right shoulder was swaddled in bandages, a tube ran from my left arm. Mac was standing next to my bed. Beside him, a woman in a white lab coat. A stethoscope dangled from one of her pockets.

I slid my eyes past them to the room beyond. Lacy curtains, barred windows. Floral wallpaper, wall-mounted security camera. Memory provided a flash of burly male nurses, armed with semi-automatic weapons, posted on every corridor. I'd been here before. The organization's private clinic, near London. Someone had tried to make it homey. Hadn't succeeded.

My eyes drifted back to settle on the woman.

"Doctor? My arm?"

The words emerged as a croaky whisper.

"Dr. Bowers," she said. "Your shoulder should heal nicely. No long-term damage."

"Hurts."

"It would. Nature's way of telling you to rest."

Then she turned to Mac.

"She's conscious. And coherent. So you can question her. Briefly."

"I'm as concerned for her welfare as you are."

The doctor snorted in disbelief, then strode from the room.

"Janie."

I dragged my eyes back to him.

"What happened?"

He had the right to ask. He was the director of MI-5's elite counter-terrorism unit. My superior and Brian's. I looked away, not wanting to think about it. Not wanting to remember.

Mac patted my hand.

"Get your bearings. Then we'll talk."

Drop by drop, I watched pale liquid feed into my IV.

Second by second, I listened to the hollow ticking of the clock on the wall.

I watched. I listened. I tried not to count.

Fifteen minutes passed.

I shifted my gaze to Mac.

He was sitting in a chair near the doorway, gnawing the stem of his pipe, shuffling through the contents of a manila folder. He looked as if he had all the time in the world. Undoubtedly, he was being patient because he cared for me.

Mac was an old family friend—my grandfather's crony, my mentor. Five years earlier, he had recruited me into the organization and supervised my training. I had worked hard to meet his expectations, to make him proud of me. Now he was treating me like a wounded child.

I was twenty-six years old. Time to start acting my age.

"Mac . . . I'm ready . . . to report."

He looked up and smiled.

"Good girl."

He reached for the phone on the nearby table, dialed, and murmured into the receiver.

Within minutes, two men came into my room.

Mac stood. He was a head taller and a couple of decades older than either of the strangers. The one with thinning salt-and-pepper hair and a somber suit conversed with Mac in hushed tones. The other—a fellow of about forty, blond, wearing jeans and a yellow sweater—surveyed the room. Finally Mac nodded, settled back into his chair. The men crossed the room to my bedside.

As Yellow Sweater talked, Salt-and-Pepper's eyes moved over the chart hanging at the end of my bed. Those same eyes examined the bandages on my shoulder and followed the IV from its source to where it disappeared under a strip of white adhesive wrapped around my good arm. Then Salt-and-Pepper interrupted his partner's monologue by briefly touching his fingers to my forehead.

Confirming that I have a fever, I thought, amazed at the level of his suspicion.

Then I understood.

I hadn't met this particular team before, but I'd dealt with others like them. Internal investigators. The organization's bulldogs. They were trained to seize upon the details of a disaster, to hold on to them until they'd extracted the last bit of usable information. Never mind that those details might hurt.

My awareness must have shown. Salt-and-Pepper cleared his throat, pulled his shoulders back, abandoned the charade.

"We have questions," he said.

I glanced at Mac, who had not returned to his paperwork. He smiled reassuringly.

Yellow Sweater propped a tape recorder on the bedside table to the left of the bed, asked me to repeat my name several times for the machine's benefit. Then he pulled a chair close to the table, sat down, opened a notebook across his knees.

Salt-and-Pepper sat to my right, on the edge of the bed. He slipped two fingers into his breast pocket, produced a small plastic bag, held it for me to see. It contained a piece of yellow paper. Beneath the heavy spattering of blood was familiar calligraphy and the price of a dinner for two.

"Can you identify this?"

I nodded, tried to speak, found that it wasn't easy.

"A receipt. The Toriko House. In Chicago. I carried it to Rome. With the money. And the plastique. Tony looked at it. And then . . . "

He flicked the bag over. His eyes never left my face.

I read the Italian words printed on the back of the receipt in a heavy, backward-slanting hand.

"It says, 'Kill the stewardess.' "

"Meaning you?"

I nodded.

Salt-and-Pepper extended his arm across me, snapped his fingers. Yellow Sweater pressed a large, brown envelope into his hand. Salt-and-Pepper slid the receipt into the envelope, pulled out a photo. Laid it facedown on his thigh. He tapped the photo's back with his fingers.

"You were the target and here you are, alive. How did you manage it, Miss Nichols? Are you incredibly lucky?" He stopped tapping, narrowed his eyes. "Or did you offer *Brian Hurst's* life in exchange for yours?"

He jerked the photo upwards, held it inches from my face. Morgue photo. Brian as subject.

Detachment fled, replaced by agony. I couldn't move. Couldn't breathe. Suddenly, I understood. He was dead. My Brian was dead.

"No!" I screamed against the pain.

"No!" at the loneliness and fear.

"No!" again and again and again.

Above my screams, I heard Mac's urgent voice. Saw his face. Felt his arms encircle me, hold me down. I heard running footsteps. Felt a needle bite into my arm.

I didn't care.

Nothing mattered.

A terrible ringing in my ears overwhelmed the sounds of my own cries. No possibility of coherent words or thoughts. Intolerable brightness consumed the room. I screwed my eyes shut against it. Abruptly, blessedly, everything was gone.

3

Mac was there when I opened my eyes. He sat on the chair beside the bed, his eyes intent upon my face.

"Back with us, then, Janie?" he said quietly.

I shook my head. Impossible to speak. I was too tired, too empty. I turned away, nestled my cheek into the pillow, stared at the wallpaper. Tiny bouquets of flowers tied with rose-colored ribbons were scattered over a cream-colored background. I picked out lavender and Queen Anne's lace. Bluebells and baby's breath. Black-eyed Susans. Tendrils of English ivy. No tears. I wouldn't allow them. I breathed deeply, exhaled slowly, encouraged the numbness I felt. I drifted.

The touch of cool fingers on my wrist brought the wallpaper back into focus.

"Her pulse is still fast and weak." Dr. Bowers' voice, angry. "She needs rest."

"Unfortunately, Doctor, I need answers. Soon."

"This delay is your doing. Those heavy-handed clods—"

I turned my head, interrupting them. I knew what I had to do, knew what Brian would have wanted.

"Duty," I croaked. Tried again, in a stronger voice. "My duty. To give him information. Please."

Dr. Bowers pursed her lips, turned, walked to the door. She paused, hand on the doorknob, and looked back at Mac.

"No more trauma," she said. Then she left.

The tape recorder was still on the table. I nodded toward it. Mac pressed a switch. He took Salt-and-Pepper's place on the edge of the bed, but looked at me with kindness.

"Janie, lass. Tell me what happened."

I told him. I shielded my face with my good arm and told him how Brian had died. How I had lived. I gave him names, dates, times. Hunches, facts, impressions. Details, details, details.

I told him about the Toriko House in Chicago.

"It's a traditional Japanese restaurant with tiny, private rooms. I'd meet my contact there. Joe Green. A thin, dark-haired hoodlum. I would rent a car, drive into Uptown, park just off Broadway Avenue, near Bryn Mawr. The private dining room had a separate entrance adjoining the alley, but I'd always come in through the front door. Joe and I would have dinner. Then, over tea, he would give me the handbag with the merchandise hidden inside. He'd tell me where to make the drop.

"Joe liked me, and I encouraged him. He wanted to sleep with me. I decided I could use him to work my way further into—"

"But that wasn't your job, Janie," Mac interrupted gently. "You were just to be a courier."

"I know. But we weren't making progress. As Moura McCarthy, all I'd done was ferry parcels. For months. The entire team was frustrated."

"Hurst was team leader. Did you tell him your plan?"

I shook my head.

"He would never have agreed. But he was in danger. He'd been in Rome much too long. Sooner or later, someone was going to recognize him. I had to do something—"

I pressed my fingers against my lips, suddenly understanding my motives. I hadn't been thinking of our team or our operation. I had been thinking about Brian. About bringing him home. To be with me.

And now he was dead.

I looked at Mac. You know, I thought. You have to know. But his eyes were calm, his jaw relaxed. The slight tilt of his head signaled nothing more than professional interest. Somehow that helped.

I took my fingers from my lips, took a deep breath, then another. I schooled my facial muscles so that my expression mirrored Mac's.

"I acted on my own initiative. I told Joe I'd sleep with him if he'd prove how important he was—how important I was to him and the organization. I asked him to introduce me to his boss. I made a mistake. I knew Joe Green had no influence, but I pressured him anyway. He wanted me, so he set his boss up.

"I walked in on Joe and a fellow with red hair. They were packing bundles of hundred-dollar bills into the bottom of the leather handbag. The red-haired man saw me and froze.

"Joe looked up, said, 'Hi! Moura.'

"The other man just stared at him. Joe went pale, started to sweat. The man told him to get out. Joe stumbled up from the table, bolted from the room. I was ready to follow him. But the red-haired man looked at me, grinning. He pushed the money into an open briefcase. He said, 'Moura, me darlin', so good to meet you at last.'

"He had an Irish brogue. He was big, muscular. Six foot three or four, perhaps two hundred forty pounds. Blue eyes.

Lots of freckles. No scars. We had dinner together. He laughed and told funny stories and flirted outrageously. But he never even told me his name.

"While I was in the ladies' room, he finished packing the handbag that I carried to Rome. When he gave it to me, he put his hands on my shoulders and smiled down at me. It was a nice smile, Mac, full of warmth. A smile you could trust—"

My voice cracked. I took a moment to work some moisture back into my mouth, to gather enough strength to go on. I finally managed to continue in a whisper. My lack of volume didn't matter. Mac leaned in closer.

"He said, 'Good fortune to you, Moura. I'll see you next trip.' I left Chicago thinking I'd made progress where no one else had. I was so sure of myself."

Then I stopped speaking. I lay looking at Mac, wondering if I was seeing something beyond professional interest, something near grief, in the lines and shadows of his face. He turned away, switched off the recorder. When he turned back, he simply looked tired.

"I'm going to call in a few favors and have the Chicago police pick up Joe Green. I'll also arrange for a police artist to work with you so that we can fax a sketch and your description of the Irishman to them."

I nodded.

"Good girl." He stood, leaned across the bed to tuck in the edges of my blanket. "Now get some sleep. You've had a terrible time of it and—"

I grabbed his arm.

"*I've* had a terrible time of it? I acted like a bloody amateur. I was so emotionally involved I couldn't think straight. Damn it, Mac, the recorder is off. Say what you've been thinking."

He sighed heavily, shook his head, gently removed my hand from his sleeve.

"Janie, lass, there's little point."
He left the room, left the words unspoken.
But I knew the truth.
It was my fault that Brian had died.

4

4

Mac visited daily as I lay recovering. He brought field reports and newspaper clippings.

Joe Green made headlines in the *Chicago Tribune* and the *Sun-Times*. Police found him floating in Lake Michigan. He had not died quickly.

In Ireland, England, and Italy, tabloids reported on a lovers' triangle that ended with the tragic deaths of an Irish stewardess and two Italian businessmen. Curious readers were treated to fuzzy, after-the-fact photos of the shop's interior. Photos of the victims were unavailable.

Moura McCarthy's obituary notices appeared in newspapers in American cities served by Aer Lingus Airlines. Her closed-casket funeral was held in Dublin. A nondescript male cousin made a point of personally thanking each mourner, and smiled sadly when offered the flight crew's condolences. A camera hidden in his boutonniere photographed everyone who attended.

On the day after the funeral, tabloids screamed new headlines. *Brokenhearted Lover Left in Sex Triangle's Wake?* one asked, reporting on the dozens of pale yellow roses that had been delivered to the church for the funeral. "And not a card among them," the church's organist was quoted as saying.

The words of an elderly florist in Chicago's predominantly Irish Bridgeport neighborhood did not make the newspapers. The yellow roses had been traced back to her shop. When questioned by frustrated investigators, she told them, "He was an Irishman, like any other. And he paid cash."

The red-haired man had disappeared.

5

Near Belfast, Northern Ireland
Seven years later

It was almost over.

I sat in the back of a panel van, shoulder-to-shoulder and knee-to-knee with its other occupants, savoring the thought. It was past midnight, the road was full of potholes, the vehicle's shock absorbers were virtually nonexistent. But the sporadic, bone-rattling jolts drew no response save an occasional grunt. We each held our weapons and our thoughts close.

Tonight would be the gang's most daring raid. If all went well, tonight would also end my assignment. Molly Shanks—with her ill-fitting men's clothing, hostile attitude, and raggedly cropped brown hair—would disappear into a British prison. I could become Jane Nichols again.

I was more than ready.

Three battered and muddied vans were the night's transportation. Sean Harrigan, the gang's leader, drove ours. Six of us crowded into the cargo area. The two vans trailing us had only drivers. Their cargo space was as vital as our weapons were.

I peered through the darkness at my companions. For the most part, they were thugs, their political convictions an excuse for profit. I had lived with them, day and night, for almost a year. I knew them better than I knew any of my fellow agents.

A Belfast tenement was our base of operations. Most members lived nearby with their families and came at night, almost every night, to the dingy basement flat with its windowless rooms and bare bulbs. At any time, there were also at least four of us living in the flat's stinking squalor. Some seemed content with the accommodations. Others, like Molly Shanks, were hiding from the law.

According to the newspapers, I was responsible for a series of violent and profitable robberies. Sean, eager to exploit my ability to bypass electronic security systems, had hidden me from the police. Had he suspected that my technical skill was enhanced by communications with MI-5, my death would have been certain.

The van hit another pothole. Seamus Connolly was sitting on the bench opposite me. The jolt sent him lurching forward. One of his knees slid up along my leg.

He shifted back into the seat.

"Sorry," he said urgently.

One of the others snickered. It was no secret that Seamus was terrified of me. Months earlier, he had tried to rape me. His footsteps, heavier than the nocturnal scuttling of the tenement's rats, had awakened me. I'd opened my eyes as he clamped one filthy hand over my mouth and the other on a breast. Killing him would have jeopardized my position. My knife thrust had been deliberate. He had lived.

Jane Nichols didn't give a damn about Seamus. He was part of the job. But until the operation ended, I had to react as Molly Shanks would. A lapse could be fatal.

"Happens again, I'll slice your balls off," I snarled.

For several more miles, we rode in silence. Then the man on my right belched loudly, polluting the already close atmosphere in the back of the van with the smell of beer and half-digested sausage.

I closed my eyes, sighed. John Wiggins had much to answer for. On assignment in Southampton's dockland area, he had observed a shipment of small arms arriving from South Africa. The shipment changed hands several times, but John had remained with it, eventually identifying Sean Harrigan as the recipient. He had contacted Mac, then the job had become mine.

A memory belonging to Jane Nichols touched the edge of my consciousness. Usually, I would have ignored it, pushed it away. But tension over tonight's operation was creating razoredged agony in my stomach, so I allowed myself the distraction.

Brian and I were walking near his flat early one evening when a man in a torn, oversized pea jacket emerged suddenly from a pub. He stumbled heavily into us.

"Sorry, mates," he mumbled in a broad Cockney, brushing off Brian's coat with his filthy gloves. " 'ad a bit too much to drink." He began saying something else, but was seized by a bout of racking, tubercular-sounding coughing. When the attack ended, he pulled a cigarette from a raggedy pack, lit it, and made his way unsteadily up the street.

Brian laughed.

"That was John," he explained in response to my puzzlement. "Be prepared for company tonight."

I must have looked appalled.

"Don't worry. He cleans up nicely."

Except for his slight build, the man who arrived at Brian's doorstep an hour later bore no resemblance to the street derelict. He was meticulously dressed in a starched white shirt and a black-and-grey herringbone jacket. His tie and slacks were grey, and grey silk gloves covered his hands. John had thinning, sandy-colored hair and a reticent manner that moderated as the night wore on. He proved to be a nonsmoker and a teetotaler.

He didn't seem surprised to see me. In fact, he seemed to know more about me than a stranger should. After one particularly revealing comment, I shot Brian a suspicious look. He smiled apologetically.

"John and I have been friends for a long time. And, well, friends talk about what's on their minds."

After that night, I never saw John again. But shortly after Brian's death, as I was walking in Knightsbridge, an elderly woman with an American accent asked me for directions to Harrods. She clutched her purse under her right arm, as if she was afraid of thieves, and held a small white envelope in her left hand. Though the day was sunny and mild, she wore gloves.

As I pointed the way to Brompton Road, she pressed the envelope into my hand and walked away.

The note inside read, "He was a good man. I regret his passing."

It was signed "John."

My stomach twisted, punishing me for remembering too much. I took a deep breath, controlled the pain. Allowing myself to slip out of character had been a mistake. I couldn't afford such mistakes, especially not tonight.

The man beside me belched again. I cursed and jammed my elbow, hard, into his ribs. He inched away from me, crowding his mates. No one complained. Molly Shanks was not someone to be argued with.

It had taken me almost a year to gather all the names, dates, and contact points Sean and his people could provide.

Tonight, the charade would end. I'd constructed a trap that Sean couldn't resist. The bait was a warehouse full of munitions and a corrupt guard. Money had changed hands, promises had been made. Tonight, all the guards would sleep. The man Sean had paid would drug all the others and then himself.

Sean tapped the window separating us from the driver's compartment. The van slowed to pass through the unlocked gate. Heads went up, faces became alert. Weapons were checked for the last time, duties quickly reviewed, last-minute commands briefly acknowledged. The van stopped.

Michael O'Rourke, armed with his Uzi, pushed the double doors open. He leaped from the van, scrambled onto the loading dock. Our group's most recent recruit, he defied easy analysis. Obviously educated, he spoke easily, laughed readily, and revealed little. Even among those accustomed to risk-taking, he stood out. Suicidal, some speculated. I could offer no better explanation.

For a moment, the rest of us waited. No shots. No guards. I relaxed a little—I wanted no innocents killed in this operation. We moved quickly, past the small, glass-enclosed room where the guards lay slumped at their video consoles, and into the great open bay of the warehouse.

We knew where the crates would be and located them easily. Sean pried up a lid, pulled open the oil-soaked paper wrapping, briefly held up the prize—an M-16, Model B. They were packed six to a crate—eighteen crates total. At twelve hundred pounds each, merchandising death was a profitable undertaking.

I stood watch with Michael as the others loaded the vans. The night sky was clear, the wind howling around the brick warehouse was bitterly cold. I glanced at Michael. His dark stocking cap, like mine, was pulled down over his ears and forehead for warmth. The moonlight created deep shadows along his cheekbones and glinted off his reddish-blond mustache and beard.

He turned his head, flashed me a grin. A pirate, I thought suddenly and for no particular reason, and I wondered if men were still hung from the yardarm. Just as suddenly, I found myself hoping they weren't.

My thoughts didn't surprise me. Jailers and inmates, terrorists and hostages, kidnappers and victims—the pattern of reaching out from isolation to someone, anyone, was well documented.

Too bad I wasn't immune.

"Keep alert," I ordered in a harsh whisper. He gestured obscenely, then resumed the task of looking out into the shadows, alert to movements *I* knew he wouldn't see.

As the other vans left the dock, we abandoned our watch and joined Sean in the relative warmth of the third van's front seat. He drove without lights until the warehouse was out of sight. We traveled away from the city, toward the rendezvous area.

A few miles into the countryside, only two sets of headlights remained to light the narrow road. Six crates were to be kept, so one van was returning to a garage not far from the tenement. The reception I had arranged for them would be a surprise.

Only the sound of the engine broke the silence. Molly Shanks rarely spoke, so I said nothing. Sean's attention was on the rutted, winding road. Michael sat quietly between us, using his penlight to follow our progress on a rough map.

That troubled me. I'd seen Michael under stress before. I felt he should, by now, be talking almost compulsively.

He'd talked nonstop the night Paddy Daley had died. A thin, pale lad in his early twenties with the burning eyes of a fanatic, Paddy's ramblings had been strewn with patriotic utterings. Except for his talent with explosives and timers, Sean would not have tolerated him. But a brutal childhood on the barricaded streets of Belfast had left Paddy with the conviction that "the holy saints" spoke to him of their hatred for the British. It had also left him with a skill that Sean needed. So Paddy had stayed, and we ignored his murmuring as he constructed devices that Sean told him would be used to drive the British out of Ireland. Paddy never noticed that they were most often used to separate Irish merchants from their profits.

But one night, something went wrong. A device triggered prematurely. Shrapnel from an exploding safe was driven deep into Paddy's chest. He was dragged, dying, back to the tenement. Michael had struggled to stop the bleeding. Then, accepting the inevitable, he had held the boy in his arms, wiped the bloody spittle from his lips, and helped him murmur his final prayers. Minutes later, Michael was loudly cursing the dead man for bleeding all over his best shirt. He spent the rest of the night telling us, in great detail, about a miserable tomcat he had drowned.

Grudgingly, I admitted that I had become attached to Michael. But I was not naive. He was a dangerous criminal whose silence on this night was inexplicable. Such inconsistencies could prove deadly. I snuggled my hands deeper into the pockets of my worn leather jacket and wrapped the fingers of my right hand around the smooth steel of the Walther PPK Special I carried. The Special's extra round—seven shots, rather than six—had saved my life on more than one occasion. It was, I had informed Sean, a souvenir taken from the body of a British major I'd killed.

We drove on into the night. The tension grew. Increasingly fearful that its source might affect tonight's operation, I searched for its cause.

My own apprehension I understood. I was also certain it was well concealed. The success of a yearlong operation and my survival were now very much a matter of someone else's timing and a bit of luck. One trigger-happy commando, one ricocheting bullet . . .

I discarded that train of thought as unprofitable, concentrated on Sean.

Sean was a tall, muscular man, constantly enterprising and never lacking for nerve. His lust for money and taste for violence were unrestrained by any spark of conscience. The gang's income came primarily through the sale of explosives and small arms. Sean was its chief negotiator. If tonight's exchange fell apart, his leadership would certainly be challenged.

Michael looked up from the map, pointed.

"Turn right at the next crossroad."

But as we approached the intersection, the van that had been in front of us pulled to the side of the road, cut its lights. Sean passed it, took the left turnoff.

"Sean," I blurted.

"They'll wait. We're making a brief detour. I stashed some ammo out here."

The hairs on the back of my neck prickled. I didn't remember any talk of hidden ammunition. Michael's body tensed next to me. He rearranged his grip on his Uzi. Don't panic! I thought. A burst from an Uzi in the confinement of the cab was a terrifying prospect.

We went on for two miles. Sean pulled the van off the road near some trees.

"Hurry," he said. "I don't want to keep our customers waiting, but this could be worth a few thousand pounds extra."

The three of us scrambled out of the cab. Sean reached behind the seat. The muzzle of Michael's Uzi drifted upward. Sean didn't seem to notice. When he turned back toward us he was holding two compact spades. He passed one to each of us.

"The moon's still bright. We'll be able to find the spot easily."

Then he turned his back on us, walked toward the tree line. Michael seemed reassured, but he kept me between Sean and himself.

We pushed our way through the scrub and into the woods, moving single file along a narrow path. I shivered, not liking the deep shadows beneath the trees, not liking being hemmed in by the two men.

Sean stopped at the base of a gnarled pine and pointed.

"It's there. You two dig, I'll keep watch."

A refusal would raise suspicion where none had existed. Then I would have to kill them both. The operation would fall apart, a year's work would be wasted. Sean was greedy enough that he *might* have stashed some ammo. I decided to dig.

Michael, too, reached a decision. He leaned his Uzi against the tree, pushed his spade deep into the damp earth.

From the corner of my eye, I saw Sean move. He stepped between us, wrapped an arm around Michael's shoulders, dragged a knife across his throat. Michael stiffened, then sagged. The warm, horrible smell of gastric fluids and blood filled my nostrils.

Sean let the body slide to the ground, bent over it, wiped his blade on Michael's jacket.

Every nerve urged me to action, but I stood and watched.

Sean used his free hand to search Michael's clothing. Then he stood, faced me. His knife glinted in the moonlight.

I held my breath, waiting. In my jacket pocket, the barrel of my Walther was aimed squarely at his chest.

He sheathed his knife.

"The Branch. One of our new customers fingered him yesterday."

Oh, God, I thought. A police officer.

Then I did what was necessary. I spat on Michael's body. "Fucking Brit," I said.

I picked up Michael's Uzi and followed Sean back to the van.

6

The exchange took place in an abandoned farmyard.

Sean stopped our van on a wooded rise twenty meters above a dilapidated barn. He flashed the headlights twice, paused, then twice again. A strong light blinked three times in response. Sean grunted with satisfaction, turned off the engine, opened his door.

"Start unloading," he said.

He scrambled down the slope to meet the shadowy figures detaching themselves from the deeper shadows of the barn.

The second van had followed us from the crossroads. I gestured for its occupants to join me. The four of us began shifting the crates to a spot halfway between the barn and the vans. We moved three crates before Sean signaled that the transaction was complete. He and about ten men from the other group came up the hill to help speed the transfer. Most of us were halfway down the hill when a flare exploded overhead. All around us, flares and blinding spotlights illuminated the farmyard. Gunfire riddled the vans, shattering glass, tearing tires, peppering the ground at our feet.

A voice blared over a bullhorn.

"You are surrounded. Drop your weapons."

About bloody time! I thought. I threw myself to the ground and lay spread-eagled, face down, my fingers laced behind my head.

Briefly, the sound of automatic rifle fire came from the courtyard. The shots were returned. Then there was silence.

I moved my head slightly, looked around. Most of my companions had assumed a posture similar to mine. Sean and a few others were standing, weapons raised above their heads. One of our customers lay wounded and groaning near a crate.

Soldiers, each wearing a pale blue beret, emerged from cover. They stood warily around the perimeter of the spot-light-washed farmyard. A group of similarly armed and uniformed men forced several gang members from the barn at gunpoint. From all around me came the sounds of booted feet moving steadily through the brush—British commandos methodically gathering up their prisoners.

The next few minutes were not pleasant. I hadn't expected them to be. Unlikely that a security-conscious commander would announce to an entire British Army unit that among those terrorists was someone who was on their side. An ambivalent, "If there's a woman, we want her alive," was the only warning that might have been offered on my behalf.

So when I heard heavy footsteps behind me and felt a gun's cold muzzle touch my neck at a spot under my right ear, I was carefully noncombative. My arms were pulled roughly behind me, my wrists were cuffed with nylon wires, and a cursory search was made for weapons. My Walther was taken from me. My captors grabbed the back of my jacket, wrenched me to my feet, shoved me in the direction of the group gathering under the harsh lights in the yard.

I stood in a ragged line with my former comrades and waited.

A baby-faced soldier was assigned to frisk me more carefully. Breasts proved to be the giveaway.

"Hey, this one's a girl!"

He stopped his search.

I decided that what I did next would establish me as one who deserved to be singled out for special treatment. It might also someday save the young fool's life. I moaned to get his attention, rolled my eyes back behind their lids, swayed as if I were going to faint.

Predictably, he moved forward to catch me.

I met him halfway, jammed my knee into his crotch, took off at a dead run.

For my trouble, I was knocked to the ground by a sweeping kick delivered by a more seasoned soldier. The eyes of a very pale young commando widened as a thorough search revealed a knife and a tiny .25 caliber Beretta. I was dragged to my feet. For effect, I shouted an obscenity and kicked the shin of the nearest man.

He reacted more violently than I expected. He slammed the metal barrel of his MP5 into my ribs. No need for acting after that. I gasped, collapsed to the ground.

Enough, I thought. Enough.

They were loading the prisoners into various official vehicles when a grey-haired sergeant detached himself from a group of officers. As he approached, I looked past him to a nearby procession of prisoners. Sean was among them.

The sergeant rolled me over with the toe of a well-polished boot. The movement sent pain tearing across my chest.

"We've a place just for ones like you, bitch."

"Sodding bastard."

The words emerged more like a sob than the snarl I'd intended. But they were loud enough to carry clearly to the prisoners.

The sergeant didn't like what he had heard. When our eyes met, he was frowning.

I turned my head, spat on his boot.

I saw the kick coming, twisted to avoid its impact.

The sergeant's boot landed between my waist and the ground, catching my jacket but only skimming the area below my ribs.

I screamed anyway.

The sergeant uttered a satisfied grunt and walked away.

I looked back at the other prisoners. Sean was watching and acknowledged me with a nod. Then, shrugging off assistance from a soldier at the rear of the truck, he clambered aboard. Burn in hell, you bastard, I thought as the truck pulled away. I was left lying on the cold loam.

When the last of the prison-bound vehicles had rolled out of sight, the sergeant with the well-polished boots returned. He stood looking down at me, his expression unreadable.

"Mac," I said softly.

He squatted down beside me, freed my hands.

"Sorry, lass," he murmured. He helped me into a sitting position, began massaging the circulation back into my wrists. "You took more abuse than I had anticipated."

"Part of the job."

Because he looked so terribly concerned, I dredged up a smile. Unfortunately, it was impossible to keep smiling as he helped me to my feet.

"Can you walk?"

I unclenched my teeth to mutter, "Of course."

I ruined the effect by sagging against him.

Mac held on to me, shouted. A uniformed aide came running. He scooped me up in his arms, carried me to a waiting car. Mac slid into the backseat first. I was placed gently beside him. The aide settled into the driver's seat.

"Hospital, sir?"

"Yes, Captain. Our Miss Nichols is in need of some medical attention."

"But, Mac—"

He raised a hand, interrupting me.

"Was it absolutely necessary for you to knee that soldier in the balls?"

"I had to be convincing."

"You were that. Your report can wait. First, we'll find out what that touch of realism cost you."

Doesn't matter, I thought. It's over.

I leaned back, closed my eyes.

The car lurched slightly as it pulled onto the road.

"Jane?"

It took me a moment to realize he was talking to me. I had been Molly Shanks for so long. Now, in a matter of minutes, I was Jane Nichols. And I was going home.

I opened my eyes, smiled.

"You're interrupting thoughts of hot showers and clean sheets."

"Sorry." Mac pulled a photo from his breast pocket. "But we need to sort this fellow out. Tonight, if possible. Thought you might know where he is."

He handed me the photo, continued speaking as he switched on the dome light.

"Calls himself O'Rourke. Scotland Yard. Anti-Terrorist Branch. Damned lucky he didn't foul up the operation."

The face in the photo brought me painfully upright.

"You knew about Michael? You knew and you didn't tell me?"

"We agreed it would be best if you weren't told about each other. How did you find out?"

I kept my emotions to myself.

"Sean told me tonight. Just after he cut Michael's throat."

Then I turned away. I pressed my forehead against the cool window, looked out at the breaking dawn.

Welcome back, Jane, I thought.

7

The debriefing was held in a meeting room on the third floor of a well-fortified building in the center of Belfast. Because of the special circumstances, the interview team included Michael's superior from the Branch. He began the session. Coincidence, he told me, that his people had targeted a group MI-5 had already infiltrated. Unfortunate that communication between the two organizations wasn't better. Tragic that Michael had died. His family would be provided for.

"And how are you holding up, Miss Nichols?"

The strapping around my cracked ribs made breathing difficult. I'd lived on cigarettes for the past eighteen hours. I couldn't remember when I'd last slept. And I knew that no one at that table gave a damn.

"I'm doing very well, thank you," I said.

We moved to the business at hand. Their job to gather information. My duty to provide it. Manners were irrelevant.

I drank endless cups of weak tea, choked down a procession of rubbery beef sandwiches, related my experiences.

They challenged my information, made hostile accusations, badgered me for details. They questioned me through the day and into the night.

I answered until their faces blurred before my eyes, until their words held no meaning. Then I told them to piss off. I left the conference table, staggered to the battered leather sofa at the far end of the room. I lay down, draped my arm across my face, and slept.

I awoke to discover that someone had covered me with a soft blanket.

A young corporal sat in the chair I'd abandoned. His feet were propped up on the table, the chair tipped back on two legs. The other chairs were empty.

I half-turned my wrist, peered at my watch. Six hours had passed. The room was cold, my muscles had stiffened as I slept. I lay, quietly flexing my muscles, until the young man looked up from his magazine.

"Good morning," I said.

Chair legs and booted feet slammed to the floor.

"You're awake!"

He bolted from the chair, rushed out the door.

I wasted a moment envying his youth, then sighed. I was thirty-three. This morning, as I creaked into a sitting position, that felt very old.

I was running my hand through my hair, trying to force the grimy spikes into some sort of order, when the corporal returned. Behind him was Jack Edwards, a bureaucrat from MI-6's London office. I wondered how he had managed to bully his way into the operation. MI-5 was responsible for Britain's internal security, MI-6 took care of external problems. Usually the only thing our organizations shared was loyalty to the Crown.

The corporal and Edwards were followed by Mac. He paused in the doorway, looked at me appraisingly.

I looked back. He had changed into a bulky grey sweater and dark trousers, and was freshly shaven. I still wore Molly Shanks' filthy clothing and hadn't had a proper bath for months. Trying not to be resentful, I sat up a bit straighter.

It was then that the damp cold of the room struck me. I shivered involuntarily, glanced around for the blanket. It had slipped off the couch and lay in an impossibly distant heap at my feet. Damn, I thought.

Mac shook his head, gave me a slow smile.

"You look like hell," he said by way of greeting. He crossed the room, retrieved the blanket, tucked it around my shoulders. "I didn't think you'd want to be disturbed even to sleep somewhere more comfortable."

"Thanks," I said, meaning it. "It was the best sleep I've had in months."

That, too, was the truth.

The corporal pointed at a thermos in the center of the table.

"I've tea, Miss Nichols. Would you like some?"

Un-British of me to want coffee. But time spent undercover in Toronto had taught me to appreciate it. I wanted coffee. A good, strong cup. No, a mug. And a *real* breakfast, with eggs and sausage and fried potatoes and buttered toast.

The tea was available.

I smiled at the corporal and nodded. He poured a steaming mugful, started across the room with it.

Edwards was standing next to the table, tapping his fingers impatiently on its surface.

"Never mind that," he said. He snatched the mug from the corporal's hand, slammed it down on the tabletop, jerked his head in the direction of the door. "Leave."

The corporal flushed red up to the roots of his very blond hair and looked at Mac.

Mac nodded.

"Get yourself some breakfast, lad."

With an apologetic shrug in my direction, the young man beat a hasty retreat.

"Actually, *I'd* like some breakfast," I said mildly.

"For Christ's sake, Douglas," Edwards said, "I don't have time for this."

Mac retrieved the abandoned mug.

"Behave," he murmured as he handed it to me. Then he walked to the far end of the conference table and took a seat.

I took as large a sip as the hot liquid allowed, watching Edwards over the top of the mug. What questions could he possibly ask that I hadn't already answered at least twice?

Edwards met my gaze. Then his eyes shifted to the chair that the corporal had occupied. He ran his fingers along its back, slid his foot behind one of its legs. With a quick jerk, he sent the chair skidding across the floor.

I wrenched my legs out of its path. Hot tea slopped on my hands. The chair bounced harmlessly against the front of the sofa.

Edwards crossed the room in several quick steps, stood scowling down at me.

"I'm a busy man. Your little nap has delayed me by two hours. So let's just try to remember what we're here for, shall we?"

"Jack—"

I heard the warning in Mac's voice.

Edwards cut him off.

"Do all your agents need mollycoddling or just the girls?"

He didn't wait for a reply. He took hold of the offending chair, straddled it, tipped it forward until his face jutted uncomfortably close to mine. He lifted his hand, palm open, and brought it down swiftly—

I reacted to the threat. Reacted as I had to so many threats during the past year. I dashed my teacup to the floor between his legs, cuffed his hand aside, grabbed him by his lapels. With a fistful of his expensive suit clutched in each hand, I wrenched his weight forward and sprang from the couch.

He was overbalanced, but he left the chair before it toppled.

I didn't give him time to recover. I reestablished my grip on his lapels, glared into his face. I hated him with all of Molly Shanks' uninhibited rage. Hated him for threatening me. Hated him for nights of terror and scuttling rats. I hated him for attempted rape. For greed. And brutality. And murder.

I wanted to kill him.

Mac stepped between us. He grabbed my hands, twisted them away from the jacket.

Edwards stumbled aside.

Mac hung on to my wrists.

I struggled to free myself.

Mac's grip was unyielding, his voice firm. He kept calling me Jane.

"Jane. Stop it, Jane. You're safe, Jane. Jack is not your enemy. Jane."

He shifted so that I had a clear view of Edwards. He was leaning against the table, trembling and pale. No threat to anyone.

Not my enemy.

He had little to do with my anger.

Abruptly, I relaxed.

Mac released my wrists.

Edwards watched warily as I approached. I paused a few feet from him, arched an eyebrow, lifted my chin in the direction of the nearest chair, waited until he pulled it out. I murmured "thank you," took the seat, nodded toward the chair opposite me. He sat down. I lit a cigarette, exhaled slowly.

Molly Shanks was incapable of the disdain that colored my voice.

"Now what exactly did you want to know?"

chair opposite me. He ran down—I lit a cigarette, exhaled
slowly.

Molly Shanks was incapable of the dreams that enjoyed no
words.

"Now what exactly did you want to know?"

8

London, England

After Belfast, I took six weeks of leave. London was home.
Its familiarity made it easier to discard my alter egos. Over
the years, I had developed a routine. Each morning I awakened in my airy flat, in the comfort of my own bed, and forced
myself to walk naked and unafraid to the bathroom. I stepped
into the yellow and white tiled shower, savored the luxury of
warm water and expensive shampoo, and dried myself with a
soft white towel. Each morning, I looked at the reflection in
the bathroom mirror and reminded myself who I was.

Molly Shanks was finished. Like the other identities I had
adopted and abandoned over the years, she was no longer useful. Everything she was, everything she had endured—all the
horrors, large and small—had to be stuffed into a well-
guarded corner of my mind.

Her experiences refused to be put aside. And other experiences, ones that I'd kept carefully confined for years, joined
my memories of the Belfast operation. They invaded my
sleep.

I expected nightmares, had dealt with them before. But the

images that now tortured me were unendurable. Michael lay before me, his head half-severed from his body. His blood, spurting ceaselessly from his gaping neck, drenched my clothing, dripped from my hands. Finally released from invisible bonds, I ran wildly through the dark, malevolent woods. I twisted and turned along the narrow paths, but always returned to the same moonlit clearing. There, I spat into a face that was no longer Michael's. It was Brian's.

Night after night, I fought for sleep. But each time my eyes drifted shut, the nightmare returned. I woke screaming and covered with sweat. Finally, I abandoned my bed for my typewriter, and my fourth novel was born. Through the days that followed, when dreams made sleep unwelcome and memories haunted my waking hours, Andrew Jax, private eye, offered me moments of escape.

The woman was tall, blonde, and wore a tight red dress.

Her footsteps along the wooden floor of the hallway had given Jax just enough warning. He had stashed the bourbon bottle and pulled his feet off the desk as she walked through the open door, into his office.

The heels on her red patent pumps were three inches high.

Fuck-me heels, Jax thought. The thought was appealing.

"You Andrew Jax?"

"I'm Jax. What can I do for you?"

He gestured to the folding chair nearest his desk, hoped she was a client. The rent was due.

She sat down, crossed her magnificent legs. She had the biggest blue eyes Jax had ever seen, the most straightforward eyes he'd seen in a long time.

"I've come about the job." Her voice was low and

sweet. "Your phone was disconnected. The agency suggested I just drop by."

Jax looked startled.

"Where the hell is it?"

He dug frantically among the papers, cups, and empty carry-out containers littering his desk.

"You mean the phone?"

"Of course, I mean the phone. Where the hell did I put it?"

The woman sighed, stood up, walked around to examine the wall behind his desk. She spied the jack on the baseboard, picked up the wire, and followed it.

"Here."

She bent to open the bottom drawer. Her tight skirt stretched tighter. Without comment, she pulled out the phone, handed it to Jax.

As she returned to her chair, his attention was torn between the wayward instrument and the gentle sway of the woman's hips. It wasn't until she was seated that Jax raised the receiver to his ear, listened for a moment, slammed it back into its cradle.

"Dead."

He looked over at the woman, rubbed his hand across the dark stubble on his jaw, settled back into his chair.

"What's your name?"

"Millicent Jones."

"Can you make coffee?"

Her smooth blonde hair bounced as she nodded.

"And type?"

"Sure."

"Think you can clean up this mess?"

Millicent's eyes widened as she looked around the room.

Jax held his breath.

"Yeah. Why not?"
Jax gave Millicent a slow, lopsided smile.

On some days, I abandoned my typewriter and tried to pick up life's tempo. I took brisk walks through the park, visited shops and museums, chatted with my neighbors. But I couldn't match the easy laughter and unguarded conversation I heard all around me.

A couple of times, I called up an old school chum. He was a good companion, willing to spend a night or two dancing in the moonlight and making love on satin sheets. He didn't want entanglements any more than I did. So when dreams destroyed the sex-satiated sleep I found in his arms, no explanations were expected or offered. I simply left him in the middle of the night.

Most of the time I wrote. Andrew Jax and his adventures obsessed me, drove me, kept me sane. I wrote at a frenzied pace, moving my feelings to paper. My discarded memories and experiences had made earlier novels popular while keeping me intact. It had worked before. It would work now. I drove myself to write, to put it all down, get it all out.

Physically, I changed. My ribs healed, my bruises faded. Regular meals, which I ate without appetite, transformed my face to a more familiar softness. Curves appeared where, for months, only angles had existed. I had my hair dyed back to its original honey brown. It grew longer, framing my face with curls. The lines around my eyes and mouth faded. Within weeks, the face and body that greeted my critical early-morning inspection were distinctly Jane Nichols. But the hazel eyes that stared back from the bathroom mirror were haunted as they had never been before.

Burnout, I thought as I gazed at the mirror. It's finally happened.

From my first days at the organization, I had heard about

burnouts. They were spoken of in hushed, reverent tones, as if they had died. To us, for all practical purposes, they *were* dead. Like bereft relatives at an accident victim's wake, we analyzed our departed colleague's weaknesses, reassuring ourselves that it could never happen to us. But the reality of our business was that, if we survived, sooner or later our minds or our bodies would betray us. We would be forced to seek a different life.

Some of us didn't leave soon enough.

Jerry, for instance.

I'd been with the organization for a couple of years when he befriended me. Jerry was experienced, perpetually calm, and had a well-deserved reputation for nerves of steel. His weapon of choice was the knife. He cheerfully agreed to help me refine my technique.

One morning, while we sparred with switchblades in the gym, Brian interrupted his workout to watch. I successfully parried an unexpected thrust.

"Good girl, Janie," Brian called.

His praise distracted me.

Jerry slipped his knife through my defenses, pressed its point to my breastbone.

I looked down with horror at his blade.

"Attempting to put a knife through someone's heart in this manner is an extremely risky way to kill an opponent." He drifted his blade upward until it rested under my chin and exerted just the slightest pressure. "I'd choose this spot, or the gut." Then he took his blade from my throat, pointed its tip toward Brian. "However, my dear Janie, the greatest risk you can take is falling in love with one of us."

I'd admired Jerry's perceptions, but ignored his advice.

Not long after that, he returned from a routine assignment and locked himself in his office. His screams of rage were punctuated with the sounds of smashing furniture and breaking glass. We forced his door, reached him within minutes. In that time his shouts had turned to whimpers. We found him on the floor in a corner, curled in a fetal position. He had slashed his wrists, professionally and thoroughly.

I wrenched my gaze away from the mirror, wrenched my thoughts from the past. I am not like Jerry, I told myself. I am strong enough to work this through.

Day by day, the time vanished. The nightmares and emotional upheaval remained.

A call from Mac's secretary marked the end of my leave. She cheerfully reminded me of the meeting I had scheduled with Mac early the next morning. I hung up the phone, sat at the kitchen table, stared morosely at my hands. Idly, I began rubbing the callus on my right index finger with my thumb.

I'm not ready, I thought. Not nearly ready. Wooded areas still evoked near-panic. Reactions developed over months of living as Molly Shanks had become more acute. And I was tired. Terribly tired.

With death would come peace. I could sleep forever.

I stopped rubbing my trigger finger, looked at my wrist. It would be so easy . . .

I curled my hand into a fist, slammed it against the table.

No. I would *not* end up like Jerry.

9

Mac rose from his chair as his secretary, Arlene, showed me into his office. The room was familiar territory. Elegant, well-worn furnishings; shelves filled with handsomely bound books and small art objects; and the mingling smells of pipe tobacco, leather, and wood polish created an atmosphere of peaceful introspection. The impression was for the uninitiated. I had worked for Mac for twelve years. I knew better.

"Come in, Jane, come in," Mac said.

He walked across the expanse of burgundy and brown Turkish carpet, smiled, clasped my hand. He asked Arlene to bring tea, indicated a comfortable chair, and waited until I had settled into it. Then he took his seat behind the massive mahogany desk.

Arlene came in, put a steaming mug near Mac's right hand, then winked owlishly from behind her horn-rimmed glasses as she handed me mine. My mug was filled with coffee, not tea. Tea, fixed the way Mac liked it, could peel the paint from a battleship. I smiled my gratitude. Arlene left, pulling the heavy door closed behind her.

Mac reached for his mug.

"Relax for a few minutes, Jane, while I review these reports. Then I'll be able to bring you fully up-to-date."

I sipped my coffee—incredible how Arlene always remembered how I liked it—and studied the man who had directed most of my adult life. I had once seen a photo of him, taken early in his naval career. In it, a solemn young man saluted proudly from a battleship's bridge on VJ Day. Over the years, his close-cropped hair had greyed and his skin had acquired an indoor pallor. But the chiseled, no-nonsense profile I'd seen in that picture had never softened.

After a few minutes, he lifted his head, pushed the papers aside, and cleared his throat.

"To date, your little charade has put twenty men, including Sean Harrigan, behind bars. The local terrorist network is in an uproar. We left them with no one to blame, so they are turning on each other. I fully expect the ripples to be felt for months to come. GHQ and the Yard are delighted. I've added their commendations to your file. I've also gathered some interesting information. I'd like to go over it with you so we can begin planning our next operation."

I shook my head.

"No, Mac. No more." I handed him the envelope I'd brought with me. "My resignation."

There was no surprise in the long, hard look he gave me. Without a word, he looked away from me, reached for his pipe, and began filling it methodically.

I'd seen the ritual before. He wouldn't be hurried. It gave him thinking time and, I suspected, was intended to be thoroughly unnerving. But I had been one of his star pupils. I settled back into my chair, crossed my legs, took my cigarettes from my purse, and lit one.

At the sound of the match being struck, Mac glanced up. Amusement touched his features and was gone. He went back to his pipe. I concentrated on making the cigarette last. It wouldn't do to appear to be chain-smoking. Finally, the first wisps of smoke curled up around his face and he looked at me. He was ready. I put out my cigarette.

"Explain," he said.

"I've decided to settle down. To write full-time. I've started another Andrew Jax novel, and royalties from the other three are coming in quite steadily. And, of course, there's the income from Grandfather's estate. So—"

"So you're pulling out."

"Yes."

He clamped his teeth hard on the stem of the pipe, puffed vigorously for a few moments. Then he took the pipe from his lips, shook it in my direction.

"For years I've maintained that it is a mistake to recruit young women. You've just confirmed that belief." Mac watched me closely as he continued. "Too emotional, inevitably unreliable. Hormones and all that, I suppose. Loyalty to country is too abstract a concept for most women to understand."

He was trying to provoke me. A skilled interrogator like Mac would find a spate of ill-considered words revealing. Too revealing. I refused to take the bait. I stood, walked to the window, looked out at the dismal weather. Brian's funeral had been on a cold, drizzly December morning, too. On that day, lying in my hospital bed, I had stared out at the rain, remembering his touch and the sound of his gentle laughter in the dark.

Mac came and stood quietly beside me. Tamped his pipe, dragged at it experimentally, grunted with satisfaction at the result. Somehow, as in times past, he managed to read my thoughts.

"You buried Brian seven years ago. You didn't quit then, though I thought perhaps you would." He stopped speaking, as if a thought had suddenly occurred to him, then looked at me speculatively. "You and Michael weren't . . . ?"

I shook my head.

"I liked him. Nothing more."

"Then why, Janie? Why now?"

I wandered back to my chair, lit a cigarette, stared into its smoke as I framed a careful answer. Mac leaned back against the windowsill, crossed his arms, waited.

"Maybe I felt I owed it to Brian—and to you—to carry on, to serve Her Majesty's government without reservation. And I have. I've been with this organization for twelve years. I've given as much as anyone should be asked to give. So now *I'm* asking, Mac. Please, let me go."

Mac's raised eyebrows told me that I hadn't imagined the note of entreaty I heard in my own voice. It seemed to linger and echo back at me from the corners of the office.

For a long time, he studied me with his pale blue eyes.

"This is a hard business, Jane, but I've never asked you for anything you couldn't do. You're talented, you've been well trained, and you're good, perhaps the best I've got. I need you. The organization needs you. I don't intend to let you walk away so easily."

He returned to his desk, picked up my resignation, tore it in two.

I pressed my eyes shut for a moment, set my jaw, raised my chin. Ground my cigarette out slowly and stood.

"I quit, and you bloody well can't stop me."

I turned, walked toward the door.

"Jane!"

I stopped, but didn't face him. I couldn't trust what he'd see in my expression.

"Your request for leave is approved. Get away. Write your book. When it's finished, we'll discuss this again."

I took a breath, forced myself to relax, half-twisted to say over my shoulder, "I won't change my mind."

He waved his hand in dismissal. But as I put my hand on the doorknob, he called me again. "You'll send me an advance copy of your next novel, won't you? I'm quite taken with Andrew Jax."

10

Over the next two weeks, I sent my literary agent five chapters and an outline. I established a schedule that included writing, shopping, and regular meals. And I nearly—but didn't actually—attacked a neighbor who came up too quietly behind me as I returned from a late evening walk. So when I awoke after dawn on Monday, and the clock's luminous digits revealed that I had slept for five solid hours, I had reason to believe that leaving the organization was the best possible decision I could have made.

The phone rang while I was in the shower.

"Damn!"

I snatched a towel, ran to pick up the phone in the bedroom.

"Hello," I said breathlessly.

"Jane, darling, this is Dora. Did I wake you?"

I glanced at the clock a second time. Fifteen minutes had passed. It was seven A.M.

"No. Had you intended to?"

She chuckled.

"I had intended to catch you in bed with some devastatingly handsome male, then invite myself over to have breakfast and a good look at him. I don't suppose you were awake because you were . . ."

I laughed.

"Forget it, Dora. Better luck next time."

"Too bad. But I'd still like breakfast. If I pick up some croissants and bring a contract from our favorite publisher, may I join you, say, within the hour?"

"A contract?"

"Yes, dear. And a healthy advance."

"I'll put on some coffee."

I hung up the phone and stood grinning stupidly to myself until the growing puddle at my feet reminded me to get dressed.

Dora Hollingsworth was one of the most successful author's representatives in the U.K., a status she'd achieved through equal measures of talent, intuition, and nervous energy. Six years earlier, she had represented me on the sale of my first novel, *Jax Wild*. I'd found her warm, practical attitudes much to my liking. Over my next two books, *Pair o' Jax* and *Jax and Diamonds*, our relationship moved easily from business to friendship.

Dora had come up with my pen name, Max Murdock. We had been having lunch at Dora's club.

"How *can* I put you on the back cover of a detective novel?" she'd said suddenly between bites of salmon mayonnaise. "No one would ever believe . . ."

My bewilderment must have shown.

"You see, dear, many male readers still think that only tough men can write hard-boiled detective novels. They'll never believe that someone who looks like you . . ."

By the time dessert arrived, Dora and I had invented Max Murdock, drawn his cigar-chomping profile on a piece of note-paper, and composed his personal history. He'd really been around, Max had—ex-cop, mercenary, private eye. He was, Dora observed with satisfaction, the perfect thug.

So when Dora arrived in a whirl of expensive perfume and tweedy clothes, I was delighted to see her. She was a stocky woman whose reserve disappeared in the company of friends. Her hug, accomplished with both hands full of parcels, was an extreme test of my newly mended ribs.

She took a step back, looked me over.

"Just as I expected. Too skinny." She held up her parcels and smiled. "This breakfast will help take care of that."

Dora's threatening expression was made less so by the glop of marmalade hanging from the knife she wagged in my direction.

"You disappeared for a year."

I had just taken my second grateful gulp of coffee. I half-choked on it.

"I told you—"

"Yes, I remember. 'I'll be gone for a bit,' you said. You handed me your power of attorney, said 'Make whatever decisions you have to,' and vanished. For months, I worried about you, wondered if something terrible had happened. Then, out of the blue, a couple of chapters arrive in the mail."

"And a note," I said defensively.

"Oh, yes, and a note. 'Hi, I'm back.' Where did you go? To the moon?"

I looked away from her glare, stared down at the coffee in my mug, wondered if the confrontation I had always dreaded had finally come. Even away from his employ, I owed Mac silence. Casual words, innocently spoken, too often cost my fellow agents their lives. Perhaps it was unfair, but my relationship with Dora—with anyone—had to be on my terms. And if those terms lost me a valued friend? I shrugged unhappily at the thought, but so be it.

I raised my eyes to Dora's.

"Do you really want me to tell you the carefully constructed and absolutely verifiable lie that was prepared for my acquaintances? It's a marvelous work of fiction."

We sat, eyes locked, for what seemed a long time.

"All right," she said finally, "I'll keep my questions to myself. Now eat your breakfast."

I obediently took a bite of croissant.

"By the way, we made quite a bit of profit in your absence." My mouth was full. I raised an eyebrow.

"Seems they like you in the colonies."

"Good," I mumbled.

I poured more coffee, and we finished the croissants in silence. Dora watched me quizzically as I ate.

"The past year must have been ghastly," she said suddenly.

"I'm all right."

"I know you better than you think. You were away longer this time, but you've reappeared as before—silent as a clam and writing obsessively. Not that I'm complaining, mind you. But I am curious. How long did it take you to write the chapters you sent me?"

I shrugged.

"Six, eight weeks."

"And now," she said briskly, "you'll drive yourself unmercifully, brutalize your characters as you take them with you through your own private hell, and produce a bestseller in record time. I must tell you, dear, that as your friend, I disapprove. Of course, as your agent, I applaud your methods." She raised her coffee cup. "To Andrew Jax. And to the Americans, who want to do a movie."

I stared at her, stunned.

"Movie?"

"Yes, dear. Based on *Jax Wild*. They *love* Andrew Jax. They *love* the Chicago locale. If you don't already have them, plan on tax problems next year."

I laughed, lifted my cup, touched it to Dora's.

"Thank you," I said.

And I thought, Screw you, Mac. I am not coming back.

II

11

Bleak January weather gave way to a cold, damp February, and I remained extraordinarily productive. I scrawled notes on the notebook next to my plate as I ate my solitary meals. I constructed dialogue as I shopped, revised plot as I walked. Twenty hours of intense daily activity, from dawn until past midnight, were broken only by occasional catnaps. I kept Andrew Jax as a buffer between me and everything else.

Until February, I believed that I had succeeded in distancing myself from my past.

February fifth. Paradise lost.

At dawn, an anonymous phone call to the Metropolitan police prompted the evacuation of the Savoy. Reporters, arriving in a dead heat with the bomb squad, covered the drama for the early-morning audience. I stood in the kitchen, dressed in jeans and a comfortable old sweater, and listened to the radio as on-the-spot commentary documented the removal of the three reported incendiaries from the hotel's basement maintenance area.

A reporter was wrapping up her coverage of the event with

a tribute to the skills and courage of the local bomb disposal
unit when a roaring explosion interrupted her. Her voice
broke only once as she described the scene unfolding around
her—dust and debris spewing from the building, shards of
glass slicing into the crowd behind the police barricades,
medical personnel rushing into the building and hurrying to
tend the wounded onlookers. Minutes later, victims of the unexpected fourth bomb were loaded into ambulances. As sirens
wailed in the background, the reporter delivered the unofficial
tally. Seven injured. Two dead. One dying.

Too bad, I thought. I switched off the radio. Not my problem.

I retreated to my typewriter.

*Millicent volunteered to make the drop and Jax knew that
what she proposed—*

Not my problem.

*—what she proposed made perfect sense. She was no threat
to anyone and—*

Anyone could study the videotapes, look at the photos that
were routinely taken of the crowds during incidents such as
these.

*—they would certainly have no problem spotting her in a
crowd. It was logical. Jax knew that, handled properly—*

Others could handle it. Surely others were just as familiar
with the terrorist community as I was. Besides, there were always informants.

—but he was still reluctant to risk . . . reluctant to risk . . .

No! I won't go back.

I pushed my chair away from my desk, went to the living
room, flopped down on my sofa. Beside it, on a small, spindly
table, was the telephone. I stared at it for a long time, trying
to balance what I owed Mac and my country with what I owed
myself. Twenty minutes later, and I wasn't sure I'd answer the
phone if it rang, much less make the call if it didn't.

Once when I was quite young, I'd sought out my grandfather in his garden and asked his advice about some childhood problem. I didn't remember what my question was, but in my memory the smell of warm earth and roses and the roughness of his old tweed jacket remained as vivid as his words.

"Never fear, Janie," he had said, giving me a hug. "You have good instincts. You'll always know what to do when the time comes."

Good instincts, I suppose, prompted me to pick up the telephone on the second ring.

"You've heard the news?" asked Arlene.

I said I had.

"Mac asks that you please come in. We need you."

I had known all along what my answer had to be.

"On my way," I said and broke the connection.

I sat up, pulled on my boots. Went to the closet, took my worn leather jacket from its peg and slipped into it. Walked to the dresser and opened the top drawer. Picked up the Walther, checked its load, tucked its familiar weight deep into my jacket pocket.

I wasn't the only one called to headquarters that morning, but my presence proved to be necessary. In the fourth-floor conference room, agents from MI-5, MI-6, and Scotland Yard ignored interagency rivalries and shared information. I was the link to my counterparts in the Branch. They knew me, they said, by reputation. I wasn't some bureaucrat. I was one of them. No one mentioned that my last mission had cost one of their men his life.

We spent most of the day going through videotapes frame by frame and looking carefully through stacks of photos, studying each person caught by hidden cameras. We looked for a certain position of the head, an oddly shaped ear, a peculiarity of dress or stance, a familiar face or profile hidden in the crowds. No database could substitute for the subtleties of human memory.

After we'd exhausted all the visual clues, our team cross-referenced the names of people we thought we recognized with photographs and activity reports drawn from different field operations. The result, at the end of the day, was a list of three possibles, including last known addresses, aliases, habits, and alliances. It was sent by messenger to those in charge of the investigation.

At seven o'clock, I returned to sit alone in the shadows of the darkened room. Mac found me there. He had the good grace not to switch on the light. He merely reached for the intercom in the center of the table.

"Arlene, Jane and I are in the conference room. Would you please send someone in with tea and a couple of sandwiches?"

Then, with a sigh, he sat down. He dug his pipe out of his jacket pocket and a match flared bright in the darkness. Briefly, it illuminated the papers, used Styrofoam coffee cups, and overflowing ashtrays littering the table.

"Just like old times, eh, Janie?"

I grunted and reached for the pack of cigarettes that lay open on the table. Shook out the last one and did a quick inventory of the number I had consumed in the past six hours. I shrugged, crushed the wrapper, lit up. Then I leaned back in my chair, shut my eyes, exhaled.

"Rotten habit, that," Mac said.

"Your concern for my health is touching."

Over the past two months, I'd worked myself down to two cigarettes a day. This morning's return to old times had brought my pack-a-day habit back with a vengeance. But Mac couldn't know that.

I made my tone deliberately martyred.

"If it would make you happy, I could start smoking a pipe."

He chuckled. Springs creaked as he shifted deeper into his chair. For a few minutes we sat in silent accord. The room filled with the sweet smoke from his tobacco. Black aromatic Cavendish. I liked the smell. It reminded me of home.

Arlene came in with the tray. She used an elbow to switch on the lights, then stood in the doorway, shaking her head.

"Just look at the two of you. Sitting here in the dark. Imagine what people might say."

"Oh, yes," said Mac. "Rumors. Have to watch out for those, Janie."

"Uh-huh," I agreed. I cleared a space on the table for the tray. "Our reputations could be ruined." I grinned at Arlene. "But at least we've proven we're not afraid of the dark."

Arlene snorted, set the tray down, laughed.

"Well, your reputations are probably already ruined." She pointed at the teapot. "There's whisky in your tea. Enjoy dinner."

We thanked her sincerely as she left.

"One of your people managed to get his picture taken this morning," I said after we'd both taken a few bites of sandwich. "The camera caught him bareheaded, full profile, standing at the edge of the crowd."

"Damn. Did anyone else recognize him?"

"They weren't given the opportunity."

Our eyes met briefly. I caught the flickering edge of Mac's smile—a "thank you" where none was required.

"He's careless. You might consider pulling him in."

"No. His cover's sound. Next time he might do us more good."

I raised an eyebrow.

"He didn't know the bombs had been planted until after the fact." Mac frowned, took a swig of his tea. "Three good men murdered. And the bloodthirsty bastards talk about sending a 'message' to those who would stop revolutionary progress."

"Rotten intelligence work," I said under my breath.

Mac heard me.

"Judgment, Jane?"

I sighed, shook my head.

"Sorry. I'm tired and irritable."

It was Mac's turn to shake his head.

"No, you're right. It was rotten intelligence, and I'm sick about it. We trained him well, Jane. But he's young and inexperienced. As you were once."

"He'll improve. If he survives."

"He'll improve." Mac leaned toward me, emphasized each separate syllable. "But he won't be as good as you are, Janie. That's why I'm asking you to come back."

I had an answer ready.

"No. Today was an emergency. My information is still current, and duty demanded that I help. But I'm not coming back. Not ever. It's been two months, and I'm just beginning to listen to conversations without searching for hidden motives, to look at a rolled-up newspaper without imagining a hidden weapon."

"That's not why you left, Jane. You can run as far and as fast as you will, but you can't run away from who you are."

Suddenly, I was angry.

"And who exactly *am* I? I've lost track. Am I a stewardess? A terrorist? A prison inmate? British? Irish? American? Canadian? Moura McCarthy? Molly Shanks? Gina Miller? Mary Pearson?"

"Are you Max Murdock, perhaps?" he replied softly. "That seems to be the role you're playing now."

12

With the urgency of a junkie craving a fix, I hurried back to my flat and rolled a piece of paper into my typewriter. Damn you, Mac, I thought as I skimmed my chapter outline, I know who I am. Max Murdock, indeed! He's my creation, a character like any other conceived by Jane Nichols, author of three successful novels. Just because you'd rather I remained one of *your* creations.

Next chapter, a new client for Andrew Jax. Someone Millicent doesn't trust. I poised my fingers over the keys, willing the words to come.

No inspiration. I backtracked and reread the last few paragraphs of the previous chapter. Suitably primed, I went back to my typewriter and tried to find a single sentence, a single word, to put on the blank page. I couldn't.

I went into the kitchen and fixed myself a cup of tea. Listened to the radio as I washed the few dishes that were in the sink. Went back to the typewriter to try again.

I sat up all night trying to write something, anything. But Andrew Jax had gone into hiding. I couldn't seem to bring him back. At dawn I folded my arms across the top of the typewriter, rested my head against them, closed my eyes.

I dreamt of spurting blood and endless forested paths. And awakened with a headache.

I wrote nothing more that day. Or the next.

Writer's block had struck with a vengeance. And I was afraid, perhaps more afraid than I ever had been. Because the memories my writing held at bay rushed in to fill the void.

Brian hurled himself from the dark hallway.

"Wrong!"

He knocked me to the floor.

"Wrong!" he repeated as I lay pinned beneath him. "I was the enemy. You let me live. Now you've paid for it with your life."

I resisted the urge to struggle, convinced that it would have little effect. He was heavier—and faster—than he looked. Undoubtedly he was also stronger.

Brian shifted his weight, wrenched the manila envelope from my outflung right hand, discharged his weapon's dye pellet against my vest.

"Reaching the objective," he murmured next to my ear, "doesn't count if you're dead."

He sprang lightly to his feet and blew two ear-piercing blasts on the whistle hanging from his neck.

The overhead lights went on. From the rooms all around us, I heard the nervous laughter of my fellow combatants as they moved from where they'd fallen. Everyone drifted toward the classroom where our performance would be evaluated by our new instructor, Brian Hurst.

Damn! I thought, rolling onto my back. How I hated to lose! And I had been so close.

Brian stood over me, anger showing in every tense line of his body. He offered me his hand.

Well, I wasn't happy either. I ignored him, got up unassisted with far less grace than he had managed, and concentrated on dusting off the front of my jeans.

"Look at me."

Not eager for the rebuke I knew I deserved, I slowly drifted my gaze up toward his face, lingering on his faded jeans and black turtleneck, postponing looking at the spot of red dye on the shoulder of his padded vest.

Earlier, I'd had an opportunity for a clear shot at him. I'd taken it, and he'd fallen. But even in the dim light, it was clear that the wound wasn't fatal. Contrary to his counsel during the first lecture of the morning and now much to my regret, I hadn't finished him off.

Our eyes met.

He made a deep bow, swept an imaginary hat from his head. "If you haven't the stomach for killing, M'lady, I can recommend a number of situations more appropriate for a woman."

I recoiled as if I'd been slapped. Here, unlike anywhere else, I expected to be judged by performance rather than gender. And now, this bloody man . . . Though he was a bit taller than I was, I did my damnedest to look down my nose at him.

"I didn't ask you for alternatives. I'll do whatever it takes to be effective. But I'll leave assassination to the likes of you."

As I said the words, I knew I'd made another mistake.

Brian went very pale. His eyes narrowed, the muscles along his jaw tensed. He raised his hand swiftly.

I flinched back, convinced that he would strike me.

No blow landed. His leg lashed out, and he swept my feet from under me.

I landed hard. For a moment, my vision blurred with tears. I dashed them away with the back of my hand, glared at him.

His expression was glacial. He leaned over, grabbed the

front of my vest with one hand, twisted its padded fabric in his fist.

"Effectiveness requires survival. *That* requires learning from the likes of me. So I will teach. You, M'lady, will learn. And you will practice until you can't recall a time when you *didn't* kill instinctively. The amateur practices until he gets it right. The professional practices until he *can't* get it wrong. Do you understand?"

He waited until I nodded before releasing me and stalking off toward the classroom.

The nights passed slowly. Exhausting runs in the park at dawn and long walks late into the evening did nothing to shorten them. I watched television, filled in crossword puzzles, reread favorite books to occupy my mind and fend off sleep. But eventually I'd have to rest, to relax my vigil, to sleep, to remember.

"Ah, my lovely Lady Jane," Brian whispered, "you are the most marvelous woman . . ."

I was laying naked beneath him. I couldn't help myself—I giggled.

"Not two hours ago you told me, in front of a witness, that I was the most aggravating woman ever to set foot on British soil."

He nuzzled my right breast.

"You are the most marvelously aggravating woman . . ."

I ran my hands up his back, began kneading the tense muscles along his spine.

"You told Mac that I was headstrong, overly independent, and impossible to predict."

He sighed melodramatically.

"My dearest lady, you are by far the most difficult woman I have ever known. That's why I love you."

"Oh," I said, suddenly at a loss for words. He'd never said he loved me before.

"Just 'oh'? That's all the most argumentative agent in MI-5 has to say?"

I laughed, turned my head, nipped gently at his arms.

"Jane."

Something about his voice caught my attention. I looked closely at him, saw uncertainty and, perhaps, a little fear. So I kept my eyes locked on his as I smoothed my hands lingeringly over his chest.

"There are some things I find absolutely agreeable."

He smiled as I'd never seen him smile before.

I touched that wonderful smile with my fingertips, caressed the angles of his cheekbones and chin with my lips, smothered his soft moans with my mouth, moved urgently against him.

Much later, I lay on the pillow opposite, watching him sleep. Long, dark lashes fringed his eyes, almost touched his cheeks. The remnants of a smile lingered at the corners of his full mouth. His face, too often brooding and intense, was relaxed and sweetly vulnerable. Dark, unruly curls tumbled onto his forehead.

I ran my fingers through his curls, watched them spring back as I released them. Then, with a sigh that was a weak echo of the contentment I felt, I nestled in close to him.

Brian's muttering awakened me. He was talking in his sleep.

I murmured his name, wrapped my arms around him.

His muttering stopped.

My arms relaxed.

Suddenly he was thrashing, struggling wildly against me.

"No!" he cried, sitting bolt upright in bed.

"Brian!"

At the sound of his name, his eyes flickered open. He

turned toward me, half-sobbed, and sank back into our bed. He buried himself in my outstretched arms.

"Go back to sleep," I whispered. "I'll keep you safe."

I awoke with a start at dawn. Once again, I'd fallen asleep in a chair in the living room. I'd been crying in my sleep. The dream that had brought the tears fled with my awakening, but left behind a lingering ache in my body and soul.

Days went by and the pages remained blank. Mac called twice. Afraid of his perceptions, I stopped answering the phone. For a few days, I cooked meals that I couldn't bring myself to eat. After that, unless it could be eaten directly from a tin, I simply didn't bother.

Memories, like hidden bombs, lay everywhere.

My meandering through the streets of Rome brought me to a little shop that sold and repaired leather goods. I stepped up to the counter.

"*Buon giorno,*" I said.

I stifled an attack of the giggles as the shop assistant turned his full charm in my direction.

"*Buon giorno, signorina!*"

His dark eyes sparkled mischievously as he seized my hand and pressed it briefly to his lips.

Then he added in slow, careful English: "It has been so long since we have seen you."

I smiled shyly at him and laid the broken purse on the counter in front of him. In deliberately awkward schoolgirl Italian, I told him a tale of misfortune that ended with damage to my favorite purse.

He patted my hand as I spoke. When I finished, he flashed me an endearing smile that revealed slightly crooked teeth. And then—very slowly and distinctly so that I could understand—he explained to everyone within earshot how greatly honored he was to be asked to do this small thing by one of such beauty and how his poor clumsy hands and, indeed, his entire being, were the *signorina*'s to command.

Though my heart urged me to make some other response, I chose to insult him.

"This bag was a special gift from my sister in Chicago. I prefer that the *maestro* do the repair."

He shook his head mournfully.

"As you desire. *Momento*. I will fetch him."

I thanked him and began to turn away. But he trapped my hand beneath his, stopping me. Surprised, I looked up at him. Our eyes met. He curled his warm fingertips deep into my palm, mouthed my name. Then he freed my hand and left me standing by the counter.

A few long strides took him past the racks hung with merchandise, to the back of the shop. He disappeared through a curtained doorway. When he reemerged, he nodded in my direction. Then he returned to the front of the shop.

The shop owner didn't appear until the last customer had been shown out. He made his way ponderously to the cash register.

"Ah, my lovely friend, I am so glad to see you again."

He motioned me to follow him to the workroom at the back of the shop.

The shop assistant said: "I'll lock the front door. Then I'll join you."

"No!"

I threw myself from the corner of the sofa, flung aside the glossy magazine I was reading. It was full of pretty people, pretty words, pretty pictures. Nothing more. Except a travel ad. Page thirty-three. "Visit Beautiful Rome."

I knew what I had to do. I reached for the telephone,

punched in a familiar number. I would return to the organization, request another assignment, bury myself in another alter ego. A hostile environment would allow me to live absolutely in the present, the immediate. And a fictitious past had no barbs.

The phone rang on the other end.

I would work for Mac. Jane Nichols' memories would disappear. At least until the assignment ended. Then I could take another assignment. And another. Mac would be pleased. I would be back under his control.

I didn't *want* to be under his control.

The phone rang a second time.

I hit the switch hook with my thumb, cut off the familiar voice mid-greeting.

I sat for a few minutes, staring at the phone, considering my options.

I called my friend, Dora.

13

Ambivalence arrived long before Dora did. By the time the doorbell rang, I was wondering how little I could tell her before sending her away.

"I wasn't sure what the problem was," she announced without preamble when I opened the door, "so I brought you a cure-all."

She shoved a foil-wrapped box of Godiva chocolates into my hands.

"Thanks."

I moved back from the threshold, motioned her to one end of the rose-colored settee just inside the foyer, opened the box on the cushion between us. "Ah, truffles, my favorites. Have one?"

Dora shook her head, but looked at me expectantly.

I selected one, nibbled its edge. My stomach lurched. I took another tiny bite, put the chocolate back in the box.

"Delicious. But I have to confess to taking this under false pretenses. When I called, I'd been up half the night trying to solve a problem with the plot. Of course, the solution was obvious the moment I hung up."

Very deliberately, Dora removed her floppy black felt hat, put it down next to the chocolates.

"How dense do you think I am, Jane Nichols? Plotting problems, indeed! You've got dark circles under your eyes. You've obviously lost weight. Don't you ever eat or sleep?"

"All the time," I muttered.

"Oh, I'm sure. Have you eaten today?"

I didn't answer. I doubted she'd consider cigarettes and aspirins as nourishment.

"Just as I thought. And how long since you've slept?"

I didn't answer that question either. Whatever had possessed me to call her? I pressed my eyes shut and wished wearily that she'd just go away. Not surprisingly, when I reopened them, Dora hadn't disappeared. She had, in fact, gotten up to walk determinedly down the hall. I followed in her wake as she marched across the kitchen and pulled open the refrigerator door.

"A stick of butter. Tinned milk. Two slices of cheese. A dehydrated lime and half a tomato. Nice."

"Dora!"

She'd already started toward the pantry. She stopped midstride, turned to look at me.

"All right, so you don't want bullying," she said quietly. "How about candor? Until today, you've never called me for help—not once in all the years we've known each other. So whatever prompted you to call was serious. Jane, you must have trusted me enough to make that call . . ."

Her voice trailed off. I answered the question it implied.

"I do trust you."

"Then suppose you accept my help?"

"I can't." I shook my head, started again. "So much of what I do can't be discussed."

"I'm not asking that you give me the details of your secret life. Just tell me what's wrong."

I nodded. Then I spent the next few minutes deciding what, exactly, I wanted Dora to know. She dropped into a kitchen chair and waited.

"What you called my secret life," I began tentatively, "the job I really can't tell you about . . ."

She nodded.

"I resigned."

Dora smiled.

"That, my dear, is a good start."

So, in the vaguest possible terms, I explained how just as I decided to abandon my old life all my writing ability had evaporated.

Dora looked relieved.

"You're trying too hard, my dear. Step away from your work. You can afford to ignore Andrew Jax for a bit. You need to spend a little time just eating, sleeping, and relaxing."

I sighed, pursed my lips, shook my head.

"Easy for you to say."

"Actually, I have just the solution, something I'd intended to call you about anyway. Why don't you join me for dinner at my club at seven? You can set a precedent by eating a meal—and don't lie, you haven't eaten properly for weeks—and I'll tell you about it."

"You need to get away from your flat," Dora said later as we sipped dry sherry in her club's dining room. "Away from England. It's far too bleak this time of year. You need sunshine, new scenery, a little fun."

She suggested I accompany her to a convention in the United States at the beginning of March. Atlanta, Georgia, she said. A lovely, historic city with a number of excellent restaurants.

"We live in a lovely, historic city with excellent restaurants," I said as the waiter slid a plateful of broiled Mediterranean prawns in front of each of us.

"But this is a lovely, historic *American* city. Full of American book buyers eager to hear about a writer's life from a suddenly popular British mystery writer."

"Me?"

"Yes, dear, you. Your publisher will be launching a new line of paperback mysteries, which includes all of your novels. He wants you to help publicize them."

Maybe it wouldn't be so bad, I thought. At least I wouldn't have to write.

14

Atlanta, Georgia, U.S.A.

The only source of tension in a week marked by sunshine and good meals was a full day behind me. In the ornate banquet hall of the Westin Peachtree Plaza, at a luncheon for publishers, agents, and book buyers, I had spun credible and entertaining fictions about living with an alter ego like Max Murdock. After that, I'd talked shop, shaken hands, and signed autographs until evening.

I had awakened early, attended a formal breakfast, then done more talking, shaking, and signing. By mid-afternoon, I retreated gratefully to my room, determined to do nothing worthwhile for the rest of the day. I sprawled in the center of the neatly made king-sized bed, aimed the remote at the television, scanned the channels, and found mostly cartoons, comedies with loud laugh tracks, and talk shows. I hit the Off button.

Perhaps, I thought, this would be a good day to go beyond the first few pages of the local newspaper. I fetched the *Atlanta Journal & Constitution* from the desk, dropped back onto the bed. I skimmed the local news, read through the features, smiled over the comics. I almost put the business news aside, but an article about ostrich farming caught my attention. I turned the pages, following the story to C-7.

His photograph was at the top of the page.

He stood in front of a hospital in Sarajevo. A tiny girl rode in his arms, looked up at him with huge, half-frightened eyes. He was smiling at her. That man—that benevolent, comforting smile—inspired hatred so intense that the newspaper shook in my hands.

I'd found him. The murderous, red-haired bastard I'd met in Chicago finally had a name. Jim O'Neil had ordered my death in Rome. Jim O'Neil was responsible for the bullet that killed Brian. Jim O'Neil. Georgia's businessman of the year. Recognized for his commitment to the welfare of children throughout the world.

I almost laughed.

Dora's alarmed voice broke through my reverie.

"Jane, what's wrong?"

I looked up, quickly replaying the unconsciously registered sounds of the last few minutes. She'd very properly tapped at the unlocked connecting door before walking in on me. She'd come, I was sure, to invite me to dinner. Too late to school my face into an expression that I wouldn't have to explain. I twisted my face into a grimace and stood. The newspaper slid to the floor.

"Stomachache. Feel lousy." I groaned, tightened my stomach muscles and bent slightly at the waist, muttered "Sorry. Be back." I made a beeline for the bathroom, slammed the door between us.

When I reemerged, Dora was standing beside the bed, talking to room service. The business section was in an untidy heap next to her feet.

She replaced the receiver.

"Poor dear. No wonder you looked so ghastly. I've ordered you some tea and toast. Shall I pop down to the chemist and get you some tablets?"

"No need." I tried to look convincingly green as I dropped down onto the bed. "I've already taken some. Actually, tea sounds just the thing. That, and just lying here for the rest of the evening."

I convinced Dora to go to dinner without me. When the sounds coming from the connecting room ended and I heard the solid thud of an outer door closing, I called room service, canceled the tea, substituted coffee and a sandwich.

I thought about delivering some justice.

15

Lies and deception were the tools of my trade. I used them with considerable skill. But I was intolerant of those traits in my personal relationships. From those few I called friend, I expected absolute honesty and unconditional loyalty. In return, I gave them as much of myself as I could. Usually, that was pathetically little.

I continued to lie to Dora. Or, more kindly, I offered her selective truths.

I told her I'd decided to stay in the United States.

That was true.

"This novel will take Andrew Jax away from Chicago," I said enthusiastically. "Put him in a completely unfamiliar environment. I've been talking to people at the convention, and the city of Savannah is ideal. It's an old port town on the coast, very historic, not too far from Atlanta. It has a river, and I'll bet it has a seamy riverfront district where he can get into a brawl. And swamps! I've never seen a swamp, but I can imagine Jax wading through the murky, foul-smelling water, terrified of snakes. I've already thought of some terrific dialogue."

That, too, was true. I had decided that afternoon that as Jane Nichols I had the ideal cover. A writer could poke around asking all manner of odd questions without raising anyone's suspicions. As if in response to a summons, Andrew Jax had appeared readily in the corners of my mind, volunteering lines of dialogue. Welcome back, I had murmured before calling the newspaper office to get the name and location of O'Neil's company. Coastal Limb and Orthopedics. Savannah, Georgia.

Dora laughed with pleasure.

"That's fantastic, Jane. I knew if you just gave it a bit of time, you'd get that spark back."

"Thanks to you, Dora." Oh, so very true. "I have a favor to ask, though. I really don't want to spend weeks in a hotel. Could you ask your American publisher friends if they know of a bed-and-breakfast or a rooming house around that area? Somewhere I could set up my typewriter for a month or two, come and go as I pleased, and not have to worry about maids straightening out my room and shuffling my notes?"

Dora was enthusiastic, as I knew she would be.

"This," she said with a grin, "is a job for super-agent. I'll find you a place before the end of the conference."

The conference had two more days to run.

I spent those days extending my plot outline and gathering information on Jim O'Neil and Coastal Limb and Orthopedics. I visited the library, the newspaper morgue, and made a phone call to an old friend who was connected with the American side of our business. From Dun & Bradstreet, I learned that Coastal Limb and Orthopedics was a financially sound corporation that O'Neil had owned for fifteen years. Over the past five years, the Savannah *News Press* had run half a dozen stories about Jim O'Neil and his philanthropic work. My friend with the FBI assured me that O'Neil had done nothing, ever, to raise alarms on his side of the Atlantic.

Obviously, O'Neil was confident that his reputation was above reproach, that nothing would ever connect him with the deadly smuggling operation in Rome. But I couldn't believe he'd abandoned the trade completely. He'd killed too readily to protect it. I wondered about his new contacts, about the methods he'd adopted since he'd ordered me killed. At the same time, I knew it really didn't matter. I didn't care about O'Neil's operation. I wanted O'Neil. I intended to trap him in his own country, in his own town. And kill him.

Late afternoon on the last day of the conference, Dora tapped on the connecting door and let herself into my room. I had one of my suitcases open on the bed and was busily reorganizing its contents, anticipating an early checkout the next day. A smaller case had only been opened briefly during my stay in Atlanta. In London, I'd packed it with the notes and manuscript I'd been working on, hoping—but not really believing—that Dora's remedy for writer's block would work. That unfinished novel would help establish my legitimacy once I arrived in Savannah.

Dora plopped herself down on the bed.

"Abandoning ship so soon?"

I dropped a pair of slacks into my suitcase.

"Tomorrow morning."

I'd arranged for a rental car and reserved a room at the posh Savannah Marriott Riverfront. Its 400 rooms would make it easy to remain anonymous until I found other accommodations.

"Can't stand the company any longer, huh?"

I sighed.

"All these publishers. And a literary agent who snores living right next door. This environment has driven me to seek refuge in the swamps."

She laughed.

I thought, with a surge of affection, how lucky I was to have Dora as a friend.

"But where in the swamp could a writer of your reputation stay?" she asked melodramatically. "Who would put up with you?"

"You've found a place?"

"Ah, I see you had some doubts." She produced a piece of paper from her pocket and waved it under my nose. "But your agent has found you the perfect place to stay in that swamp. An old family home on an estate just outside Savannah. Lots of atmosphere, very peaceful, with a suite of rooms that is occasionally rented to writers and journalistic types. You're expected tomorrow, late afternoon. I have already wired them six weeks' board, in advance."

I laughed out loud as I gave her a hug that knocked her floppy felt hat askew.

"You are a marvel. This calls for a celebration. Let's grab a cab. I'll treat you to the best meal in town. Your choice of restaurant."

She grinned.

"Sounds lovely. But business first. Can you wait long enough for me to make several phone calls?"

"Actually, I want some new jeans. There's a shop down the street. Suppose I meet you in the lobby in, say, thirty minutes?"

"Make it an hour and you have yourself a deal."

"An hour, then."

Dora retreated to her room, adjusting her hat as she went. I dropped the lid on my suitcase, ran a brush through my hair, grabbed my bag, and called a cheery goodbye. Dora was sitting on the edge of her bed, phone already in hand. I got as far as the hotel's front desk, went to look at my watch, and realized I'd taken it off to shower. It was on the bathroom counter.

I disliked being without a watch, so I took the elevator back upstairs. I opened the door to my room, noticed that the connecting door to Dora's room was still ajar. I entered quietly, trying not to disturb her.

"She's going to Savannah, Mac."

I stopped mid-stride.

No. Not Dora. Not my friend.

"I don't know what's happened." Dora's voice again. "But suddenly she's as determined and self-directed as ever."

Damn them! Damn them both! Two steps sideways brought me to the connecting door.

"I can't believe that the change of scenery was enough. But whatever happened, I think we should leave her alone for now. Of course, I'll monitor—"

I'd heard enough. I stepped into her room, went directly to the dresser.

Dora turned at the sound, gasped.

I ignored her to rifle methodically through her bag. I found her passport, slipped it into my skirt pocket. Dora sat mutely, watching me. Genuine surprise, I thought, believing it only because of the circumstances. She was apparently a far better actress than I. Before she had time to recover, I crossed the room and took the phone from her unresisting fingers.

"Hello, Mac."

There was silence on the other end of the line. I thought, for a moment, that he would break the connection. But he didn't.

"How are you, Janie?"

"As determined and self-directed as ever," I said, mimicking Dora. For the first time, I understood the insight and sensitivity she'd demonstrated over the years. "How long has Dora been working for you?"

More silence. Then an answer.

"Since before your time."

"Well, she could do with a bit of retraining. A remarkable performance in a sustained role, but careless where connecting doors are concerned."

"We've only had your best interests . . ."

I couldn't keep the bitterness from my voice.

"Of course. Why else would you have me under surveillance for six years? Or have there been others, before Dora?"

This time, no answer. At least he wasn't lying to me. Or maybe he knew I wouldn't believe any answer he gave. The silence lengthened. I considered how I could use the situation to my advantage.

"I've found the man who ordered my death in Rome," I said finally.

"Ah, that explains it," he murmured. His voice became brisk and businesslike. "Congratulations! I've wanted that bastard for a long time. Tell me who he is. I'll verify your information and contact the Americans."

Though I knew he couldn't see me, I shook my head.

"I'm going solo on this."

"You work for me. You're not authorized to operate in America. I won't allow you to ignore their laws."

Dora was still sitting on the bed. I tilted my head, idly watching her. I thought about leverage, smiled as a wisp of an idea took on substance. The smile mustn't have been a very nice one. Dora didn't seem comforted by it.

I kept my tone conversational.

"I do work for you, don't I? And so does Dora. What an awkward situation. Two MI-5 agents operating on American soil and no one from your office bothering to contact the appropriate American agencies. I don't know about Dora, but I'm sure that among our colleagues in this country I have a reputation for being involved in, um, disruptive activities. If they heard that I was *ordered* to target a particularly prominent American politician for the purpose of blackmail, and if that politician just happened to come from an influential family that traces its ancestry back to Ireland . . ." Then I added, as if it were a sudden afterthought, "Oh, by the by, I have Dora's passport. I rather doubt she's capable of taking it from me. If I thought that you were going to interfere, I would feel compelled to call the nearest FBI office and turn myself—and Dora—in."

A career at sea had equipped Mac with a considerable vocabulary. I held the phone away from my ear, waiting for him to finish his methodical and heartfelt recitation, and smiled at Dora again. My smile was more kindly this time. She was proving useful.

Mac sputtered to a halt.

"I don't want to embarrass you or Her Majesty's government," I said. "If I were to get caught, I would much rather be able to explain how I'd left the organization months ago—stress, you know. MI-5 would be above reproach because, you see, you'd have proof. My resignation, appropriately dated, would already be in your hands. Personally delivered by Dora. No one would ever have to know that you tore the original in half. Otherwise . . ."

For a time, the sound of my threat hung between us.

"That wouldn't get you what you want and we both know it," Mac said into the silence. "You could embarrass the organization. And me. But in the end, the Americans would simply ship you home. You'd never get near the man you're after."

"Understand me, Mac. I want him. I'd find a way."

Dora started in response to the savagery in my voice.

This was a Jane Nichols she'd never seen. Your spy isn't very good, Mac, I thought. Six years and she hardly knows me.

Just as well.

"Come home, Jane. Report back. We can work something out."

"Not negotiable."

"Very well, then. Give Dora her passport and write out your resignation."

He'd agreed too easily. Then I realized that he hadn't, in fact, agreed to anything.

"I want your word that you won't try to stop me."

More silence. Then Mac sighed heavily.

"You have it."

I almost believed him.

"I'll put Dora—"

"Jane!"

"Yes?"

"Do you intend to kill him?"

I gave him an answer I knew he'd understand.

"I've given you and the organization an opportunity to distance yourselves from me. I'd suggest you do just that."

"Janie, listen to me."

Because I'd seen him do it on so many occasions, I imagined Mac leaning forward, fixing his intense blue eyes on me, concentrating all his persuasive powers into one final argument.

This time, he wouldn't change my mind.

"I watched you grow up. Sat at the club and listened to your grandfather brag about you. Later, I listened as you told me about your teachers and your friends, about your dreams and ambitions. You were a thoughtful, creative child with an adventurous spirit—a winning combination in our profession. Even then, you were willing to put personal considerations aside to work for a common good. I was convinced that with maturity and training you'd be an asset to the organization. So I would remind you that what you're now proposing is contrary to everything you've ever believed in. Besides being morally indefensible, this quest for revenge—and, I suspect, some sort of personal absolution—is dangerous. Seven years ago you misjudged a situation—*misjudged*, Jane—with disastrous results. But you returned intact. This time, I doubt you'll be lucky enough to survive."

If I believed he had my best interests at heart, I might have listened. But as with Dora, I was seeing *this* old friend from a very different perspective. I wondered how young I was when he began thinking of me as an asset.

"My survival these past several years was hardly a matter of luck," I said coldly. "You underrate my training."

"I underrate nothing, particularly you. It's my job to know my people. After you've had your revenge, your guilt will destroy you. I've seen it happen before. So have you. Will you spend the rest of *your* life searching for an excuse to die?" A harsh tone crept into his cool, reasonable voice. "Think about it, Jane. You were there. Could Brian have *avoided* that bullet?"

I didn't respond. Couldn't. Too many questions long unanswered. Too many feelings long suppressed. Sensing my turmoil, Mac went on.

"Have you thought this assassination through, Jane? Planned the details? You're a professional. You've located your target. Exactly how are you going to kill him? Do you want him to die like Brian, with his chest torn away by a bullet? Or would you prefer to drag a knife across his throat?"

Stop it! I thought. Why are you doing this? I thought you cared about me.

Mac kept talking.

"Will you spit on *his* body, too, Jane? Will that make the pain go away?"

"No!"

The word escaped as a strangled shout. I couldn't stop it. But the sound shocked me from my emotional muddle. I resisted the urge to wrench the phone from my ear, to fling it far away from me. Mac continued speaking, but I ignored him. He knew my vulnerabilities, I reminded myself. He had used them before to get what he wanted. But not this time.

"You're a bastard, Douglas MacDonald."

Though quietly spoken, my words silenced him.

With greater volume and more deliberation, I repeated, "A *bastard*."

Then I dropped the receiver onto the bed next to Dora, pointed at it.

"Tell your employer that the price of my resignation and your passport has gone up. I'm going to draw up a list of items I want delivered by diplomatic pouch. You and I will remain at the hotel until they arrive."

Obediently, Dora picked up the phone, but hesitated before putting it to her ear. She worried her lower lip between her teeth, searched my face with anxious eyes. Apparently, she didn't find whatever it was she was looking for.

"Please, Jane. You must understand. You were never under any suspicion. After Brian died, Mac asked that I approach you. He thought you needed a friend. We had common interests and needs. You showed promise as a writer. I'm a good literary agent. We might easily have met and become friends quite by accident."

I ignored her. I walked back to my room, closed the connecting door, bolted it so I wouldn't have to protect my back. I retrieved my watch from the bathroom, strapped it on, walked over to the desk, pulled open the drawer. I took out a piece of hotel stationery and a plastic pen with the Westin logo on it.

Lies and deception, I thought as I made my Walther the first item on the list. They were the tools of our trade. Selective truths were the best any of us could manage. I'd never trust Dora or Mac again.

16

Savannah, Georgia, U.S.A.

Planning makes sense. Planning without information is an exercise in futility. Jim O'Neil was my target, but what lay ahead of me was unknown and, at the moment, unknowable. I focused my thoughts in a more profitable direction. With a tank full of petrol and the leased car's air conditioner humming, I imagined that Interstate 16 was an endless road to nowhere. No duty, no obligation, no past, no future. Just Andrew Jax and a half-finished novel in need of refinement. I sped along, dictating the next scene into my tape recorder, savoring the illusion that nothing else really mattered.

Still west of Savannah, I turned right on Dean Forest Road, then right again onto Highway 17. From there, the route I followed was traced in bright yellow marker on a local map and supplemented by directions written in Dora's loopy hand. The turnoff from Highway 17 took me past a grove of pecan trees. Minutes later, I turned left onto a narrow road bordered by marshland. The Callaghan property was just past a stretch of old plantation rice fields.

The entrance was marked by double stone pillars supporting open wrought-iron gates. A private lane swept across a well-tended lawn spotted by towering, wide-branched oaks, flowering dogwoods, and clusters of low-growing azaleas. My trip ended in a circular driveway in front of an 1820s plantation home.

The house was huge, white, and imposing. Six Doric columns, two stories tall, supported the first-floor porch and second-floor balcony. Porch and balcony ran to the far corners of the house. Between the center columns, wide steps led up to the porch.

I stood beside the car for a moment, looking the place over carefully. Fresh paint covered old wood. Screens were much-mended but intact. The ancient gutters were clean. Not disrepair, I diagnosed. Just constant repair.

No one seemed to be home.

When I'd called the evening before to confirm my arrival, a very young-sounding female voice had answered, "Callaghan Realtors," and invited me to leave a message after the tone. Now I wondered whether anyone had heard that message. No one had appeared to investigate the noisy crunch of my car's tires on the lane's crushed oyster-shell surface. No one seemed to have heard the car door slam.

The mid-afternoon sun was bright and hot on my back. I walked up onto the shady porch. There was a small envelope stuck in the crack between the front door and its frame. "Max Murdock" was printed in black ink on the front of the envelope.

"Dear Max," the note inside read, "Sorry I can't be here to meet you, but duty calls. The door is unlocked. Come in. Make yourself at home. As you stand in the foyer, your bedroom is to the left, through the library. The library is your work area for the duration. Liquor and food are in the kitchen, straight back beyond the staircase. Cigars are on the desk in the den (to the right of the foyer, through the living room). Help yourself. I should be back by early evening. Plan to join me for dinner."

The note was signed "Alex Callaghan."

Someone had a sense of humor, though I suspected that the butt of the joke wasn't me. But the smile that curled my lips was more gratitude than laughter. Callaghan's absence provided an irresistible opportunity.

A long canvas case and a multipocketed photographer's bag were the only items I left, securely locked, in the boot of the car. The night before, they had been delivered by courier from the British Embassy. Each contained items I'd demanded Mac send from London.

I quickly unloaded the rest of my luggage and carried it into the bedroom. A walnut wardrobe, with doors left invitingly open, stood against the far wall. I put my large suitcase and portable typewriter beside it, hung my garment bag inside, then opened the smallest suitcase in the center of the four-poster bed.

I took out a folder full of blue-penciled, dog-eared manuscript pages and carried them back into the library where a cleared oak table seemed the obvious place to work. I turned on the brass desk lamp, spread the pages under its light, and pulled one of the leather chairs slightly askew. I stepped back, surveyed the scene I had created, made a few minor adjustments, mentally added the props I would bring back from the kitchen, and was content. Still-life with manuscript.

That done, I set out to rifle systematically through Alex Callaghan's possessions. As a child, I had been taught manners. Along with using the proper utensils, saying please and thank you, and covering my mouth when I coughed, I had learned that reading private papers, eavesdropping, and other forms of prying were unacceptable behaviors. While I could still manage a formal social function without embarrassment, I had long since discarded childhood's more restrictive inhibitions.

Using the central foyer as a starting point, I toured the first floor, opening drawers, checking shelves, and looking into closets. I found very little of interest beyond the home's architecture and decor.

The vast rooms were comfortable and attractive. Strategically located ceiling fans, hung from the twelve-foot ceilings, kept the interior cool. Light rugs on the polished dark wood floors and light oak furniture offset the dark tones of the cherry tongue-and-groove paneling. Lacquered screens painted with stylized birds and flowers covered the gaping mouths of the fireplaces in each room, and a collection of intricate blown-glass sculpture graced the mantelpieces.

But I'd grown far too wary to appreciate the house's main architectural feature. Each room in the front of the house— my room, the library, the living room, and the den—had a pair of French doors that could be flung wide to catch the breeze from the porch. The locks were flimsy, easily opened with a pocket knife or credit card.

The quaint kitchen at the back of the house was equally insecure. A back door with a glass pane at the top opened onto a small cottage garden that was a riotous mix of colors and fragrances. It was surrounded at waist height by a white picket fence. A flagstone path led across the garden, through a gate, and down toward the tree line. Along the path, clusters of magnolias, oleanders, and dogwoods provided an attractive shelter for anything that wanted to remain hidden.

The inevitable French doors opened from the kitchen into a bright solarium with white wicker furniture, large potted plants, and wide open windows. Another door, tucked beneath the main staircase, led down to a shelf-lined cellar with a trapdoor that opened up into the yard. Finally, I discovered that the unobtrusive door at the back of the kitchen was a servants' access to the second floor. I climbed the steps to confirm that the door on the second-floor landing was unlocked. It was.

Before leaving the kitchen, I spent a few minutes locating the good Scotch, a heavy tumbler, a bag of pretzels, and a bowl. I broke a few pretzels into the bottom of the bowl, poured myself a stiff drink, and sipped it as I walked through the swinging kitchen door into the dining room. There, big windows overlooked the backyard. I turned right through an open set of pocket doors into the living room. Another right turn and, with the den at my back, I completed the circle by walking through the living room and into the foyer.

I detoured quickly to abandon my drink and the pretzel bowl next to the manuscript in the library, then returned to the foyer. I stood at the foot of the staircase, took a last long look around me, fixed the location of the various doors and windows in my memory. On the positive side, I thought with a grim smile, I would never be trapped in this house. Crept up upon, perhaps. Trapped, never.

I went upstairs to search the bedrooms.

The staircase from the foyer swept up to the open second-floor landing. From there, twin wings branched east and west. The rooms in both wings opened onto the wide hallway. I spent very little time in the east wing. The four bedrooms there were above the living room, den, and dining room. Dust covers protected the few pieces of furniture in them and, although the rooms were sunny and clean, they smelled unoccupied. A search yielded nothing to contradict that impression.

The rooms on the left of the landing were more interesting. The two overlooking the backyard seemed to be for visiting friends and family members, though neither appeared to have current occupants. Quilts covered the beds, a couple of dolls and some bedraggled stuffed animals nestled against the pillows, and a wooden hobby horse trotted in one corner. Framed collections of demitasse spoons and thimbles decorated the walls.

I stood at a window in the back corner bedroom and let my eyes follow the flagstone path to where it disappeared among the trees. From my map, I knew that the Ogeechee River was hidden by the dense foliage. I wondered if the path went that far.

I glanced at my watch. It was almost five o'clock. I didn't know how Callaghan defined early evening. With a growing sense of urgency, I crossed the corridor to his room. The spacious suite ran the length of the east wing and overlooked the expanse of front lawn. From the balcony, I could see the front gate, the narrow access road, and glimpses of the main road. Callaghan's sleeping area was above my bedroom. A pair of massive, built-in bookcases and a large cubbyhole desk were on the opposite wall, above the library.

I learned a lot about Alex Callaghan by going through his room. He was apparently unmarried and indulged in no obvious vices. Beyond the money spent on maintaining the house and yard, he had no expensive hobbies. I found no records of alimony or child-support payments among the canceled checks that he kept, along with a very ordinary assortment of bills, in his desk.

Back issues of *Playboy*, *Popular Mechanics*, and *Architectural Digest* were in the bathroom adjoining the suite. An assortment of paperbacks, mostly mysteries and science fiction, were in the bedroom. A battered book of Tennyson shared the space under his unmade bed with a pair of sneakers and one sock. A hardcover copy of *Jax and Diamonds*—complete with a sketch of the cigar-chomping Max Murdock on the back cover—was open, facedown on the nightstand. I looked for, but couldn't find, evidence of alcohol or drug abuse or unusual sexual practices.

I wouldn't have wanted to be assigned to blackmail Callaghan.

I finished my search, stood in the center of the room, wondered where Callaghan kept his important papers. They weren't in his files. A bank deposit box, perhaps. Or a safe. I hadn't seen any evidence of one on the first floor, but in the master bedroom . . .

I turned slowly on my heel, considering possibilities.

Too many windows and doors on the south wall. And, unless it were a very modern safe, not enough depth in the wall adjoining the hallway. An oil painting of a fox hunt hung above Callaghan's bed. I walked to that end of the room, lifted the edge of the heavy frame, found bare wall.

That left the east wall, with its massive oak bookcases and Callaghan's desk. I returned to the center of the room, surveyed the bookcases with unfocused eyes, looking for pattern rather than detail. There was something odd about one of the shelves in the bookcase on the right. The books were similar in size and not as haphazardly arranged as the books on the adjacent shelves. I moved closer, found nothing in the titles to justify the grouping. So I took the books from that shelf, bounced my fingers against each corner of the varnished back panel. When I hit the bottom left corner, the panel swung smoothly open.

The safe hidden behind the panel had been decades old when Lincoln gave the Gettysburg Address. I took a quick look from the balcony, then trotted quickly downstairs, went outside, and unlocked the boot of my car. One of the small pockets in the photographer's bag yielded the device I needed. It looked like a tiny stethoscope—two pea-sized earpieces were connected by thin wire strands to a disk, which was the same diameter and about three times the thickness of an American penny. But with this technology, the sound of a human heart would be deafening.

Back upstairs, I spent a moment back out on the balcony, then concentrated on the safe. I held the disk against the safe, slipped the earpieces into my ears. I closed my eyes, visualized the interior of the thick iron door, and "listened" for the tumblers with ears and fingertips as I manipulated the dial. Minutes later, the safe was open.

I tucked the device into the pocket of my slacks, spent a moment memorizing the arrangement of the safe's contents, then systematically removed and examined them. I found the documents I had expected, plus discharge papers, two commendations, and a Purple Heart. And I discovered Callaghan's one area of vulnerability.

Although unmarried, he was apparently a devoted family man. His papers included expired guardianship papers for Josephine Callaghan, twenty-five years old. A ledger, marked simply "Joey," carefully recorded twelve years' worth of landmark events and unusual expenses. At nineteen, medical bills marked "broken leg" were recorded just after notations for "skis" and "Aspen/hotel/airfare." "Next year, push Florida," was scrawled in that margin. Alex Callaghan's will and insurance policies (moderate coverage) named Joey Callaghan, sister, as sole beneficiary.

I closed the safe, looked more closely at a photograph on the cubbyhole desk. Old and expensively framed, it showed a family posing at the base of the staircase. The banister was decorated with red bows, lights, and evergreen wreaths. Two smiling, middle-aged adults stood on either side of a young man in a U.S. Marine Corps uniform. Off to Vietnam, I thought. A little girl of about five sat on the young man's shoulders. Though she was blonde and he was dark, the family resemblance was strong. The children had inherited their mother's straightforward dark eyes and their father's high cheekbones and narrow nose.

A crayon-scrawled note was tucked between the back of the photo and its frame. "Dear Daddy + Mommy + Alex," it read, "Mary Christmas. I love you." The note was signed "Joey."

I had just finished checking to be sure that everything looked undisturbed when I heard the sounds of an approaching car. I was back at the table in the library before it cut its engine. As the front door opened and heavy footsteps crossed the foyer, I took a sip of Scotch. I let the fiery liquid trickle down my throat as I thought about the unexpected things I had discovered upstairs. Newspaper clippings jammed haphazardly into a file. Uniforms hanging neatly in the bedroom closet. Boxes of bullets in a locked drawer.

A man appeared in the doorway, an indigo uniform covering his tall, muscular frame. At the top of each sleeve was a shield-shaped insignia embroidered in violet, purple, and white. A fine gold chain was anchored to the uniform's right shoulder and looped under his right arm. A silver tie bar anchored an indigo tie. Silver letters—SPD—rode on each collar point. CALLAGHAN was printed in block letters on the nameplate over the right pocket. A badge was pinned over the left.

The unexpected discoveries made sense now.

Dora had unwittingly provided me with the ultimate alibi.

I dredged up my most sincere smile.

"Hello."

Alex Callaghan's brown eyes widened.

"Who the hell are you?" said Savannah's chief of police.

17

Alex Callaghan's dark good looks were classic Black Irish. The fine white scar that marred his otherwise perfect features angled rakishly above his right eyebrow. Except for his accent, which was distinctively American and slightly Southern, a filmmaker would have unhesitatingly cast him as a heroic IRA freedom fighter. If I hadn't experienced the unembellished reality, I might have gone to see the movie.

His aggressive stance relaxed as I quickly explained who I was. I added that I was sure my agent had been very clear about my name and identity when she'd made the arrangements.

"Jeez, I'm sorry," he said. His voice matched his looks.

He crossed the library. I stood, briefly grasped his outstretched hand.

"That was a lousy way to greet you, Miss Nichols. I'm Alex Callaghan, and I'm usually not so rude."

"Hello, Alex. Please, call me Jane. And I'm not offended. I can understand your reaction if you thought I'd look like Max Murdock."

I brought an invisible cigar to my mouth, twitched my lips, and raised my eyebrows in a Groucho Marx imitation.

Alex grinned. The effect was extraordinary. His eyes crinkled at the corners, the laugh lines that framed his mouth deepened, he gave his lips a self-deprecating twist that simultaneously acknowledged and dismissed his appearance. I found myself liking the man.

"What I don't understand is how the mistake was made."

His smile faded to a scowl.

"I think *I* understand. My sister Joey prefers living in town, but this is our family home. We have an agreement. She takes care of the reservations and the finances. I play host and innkeeper. This situation is Joey's idea of a practical joke."

"No harm done."

"Unfortunately, that's not really true. I'm sorry, but you can't stay here."

I didn't give a bloody damn about the circumstances that had given me an alibi as credible as the one Alex Callaghan would provide, but I sure as hell wasn't going to abandon it easily.

"What? Because I turned out to be a woman, you won't let me stay?"

"Well, no, not exactly. It's just that . . . well, it was stupid of Joey to book you here right now. She wasn't thinking. And I'm sure she didn't know you'd be so damned pretty."

"What?" I repeated. This time, I allowed my mounting confusion to show on my face. "You won't let me stay because I'm a *pretty* woman?"

He looked at his feet.

"Yeah. So I'll carry your bags out to your car. You can follow me into town. One of the hotel managers owes me a favor. He can give you a nice room. Then, if you like, I'll take you out to dinner. Tomorrow, Joey can find you somewhere else to stay."

"Screw you," I said clearly.

His startled eyes shifted to meet my glare.

"I have too much to do to waste time looking for other accommodations. Your sister confirmed my reservation and accepted my money. If you're worried about controlling your sexual urges, never fear. I have enough control for both of us."

"Oh, hell," Alex muttered.

He shook his head, looked back down at his feet, ran his hand through his straight brown hair, sighed. Finally, he looked at me again.

"Believe me, I'm not doing this to make you angry. The fact is that this house is impossible to secure . . ."

No kidding, I thought.

". . . and it's terribly remote . . ."

I couldn't argue that, either.

". . . and I've got a killer wandering loose who likes to strangle pretty women."

"The key to this game," Mac told me when I'd first joined the organization, "is to understand your adversaries. Jealousy, greed, anger. Duty, love, loyalty. A motivation is also a weakness. You have to recognize and exploit another's weaknesses while minimizing your own."

I had learned.

The earliest lessons had been like playing a children's game. Mac would sit at his desk, smoking his pipe or sipping tea, and describe characters, settings, and circumstances. Sometimes he'd clear his desktop and, using paperclips and office supplies for props, create miniature landscapes of violence and death. He varied his plots wildly, but always asked that I analyze the characters, predict what they might do next, and respond accordingly. Good decisions brought a nod and, occasionally, a smile. Mistakes or inattention invited abuse. Mac would point his pipe at me as if it were a weapon.

"You're dead, Janie. You're dead. And you've taken others with you."

I remember thinking that he was being melodramatic.

Later, the game became harsher. I was sent to Peterborough, to a remote compound secured by fifteen-foot-tall electric fences topped with razor wire. The Elizabethan estate served as a playing board upon which people like me were the pieces. Within the stone walls of the manor house and outside, in a maze of sunken gardens and topiary, the scenes from Mac's desktop came to life. Reality was distorted by isolation, drugs, and lack of sleep. The cost of misjudgment was humiliation and deprivation. In that amoral, friendless environment I learned that my own emotions and natural responses could turn, like savage snakes, to attack me. I was taught techniques to control them.

Not long after that, I was sent into the field. At first, my forays were balanced by lengthy debriefing and analysis sessions in the security of Mac's office. As I became more confident—and more competent—my assignments grew complex. The sessions became, for the most part, opportunities to exchange information. Experience added depth and nuance to my skills.

Perhaps I was naive, perhaps just lucky. I played the game for five years before learning its real lessons. Morality is subjective. Survival is its own reward. And the price of failure is not death, but memories.

Alex Callaghan, I suspected, was a typical male cop—overprotective, chauvinistic, and convinced of his own righteousness. I manipulated him accordingly.

I stood looking at him with my face reflecting my very genuine dismay. My eyes filled with tears. One trickled down my cheek, and I blotted it against my shoulder. Then, carefully underplaying my obvious distress, I bravely lifted my chin and accused him of sexism.

Of course he denied it.

"Damn it, I'm just trying to keep you safe!"

"I know you are." Another tear flowed, unchecked, down my cheek. I gazed up into his big brown eyes, opened my hazel ones wide for emphasis. "But I won't be very safe if I have to live in some remote, fleabag motel."

Alex burst out laughing—a reaction I hadn't anticipated.

"Spare me! You? In a *fleabag* motel?"

I pouted.

"Well, even if I'm in a regular hotel, it seems to me that I'd be safer here than elsewhere. Besides, you've informed me of the risks, I've accepted them, and we *do* have a verbal agreement . . ."

Alex sighed heavily.

"You win. Welcome to my home, Max Murdock, a.k.a. Jane."

Good, I thought. I carefully kept the triumph from my smile as I grasped Alex's extended hand.

He smiled in return, and kept my hand firmly within his grasp.

"I want your promise, Jane. No solitary walks beyond the tree line. Not for any reason. And when you're alone, you'll stay inside and lock the doors."

The slight tightening of his grip forestalled any objections I might have. I wondered who, in fact, had manipulated whom.

"This is not negotiable." His tone and the set of his mouth combined stern big brother, platoon leader, and police chief. "And it's not being done to reassure you, okay? It's to reassure me, the male chauvinist cop. I've broken enough bad news in the past six months. I don't want to be talking with *your* next of kin."

"I understand, Alex," I said with appropriate meekness. "And I promise I'll be careful."

"Good."

He released my hand, then invited me out to dinner.

After suggesting that I add a sweater or light jacket to the slacks and tailored blouse I wore, Alex went upstairs to shower and change into civvies. By the time he reemerged, dressed in jeans and a knit shirt, I had finished my Scotch, smoked a cigarette, and pushed away my growing fatigue for a bit longer. Then, because I insisted, I drove. Alex cheerfully agreed to navigate.

We turned from the private lane onto the road.

"The stuff that hangs in clumps from all the branches is Spanish moss," Alex said. "It's infested with lots of little bugs, and if you shove a handful of it down someone's shirt, they get real itchy."

"So glad you told me that."

"Hey, you can never tell when some absolutely useless piece of information might make it into a book. Admit it. If you had known about this when you were writing *Pair o' Jax*, Andrew wouldn't have had to walk back to that pay phone to lure the crook away from his bedroom. He could simply have dropped Spanish moss through an open window, onto the guy's bed, and waited until the itching drove the guy into the shower. Then he wouldn't have been mugged as he stood in the phone booth."

"You're right, Alex," I said dryly. "If I had known about the bugs in Spanish moss, and if Andrew Jax had just happened to have some sealed in a plastic bag in his pocket there in Chicago in the middle of a snowstorm and then been able to climb up to the twentieth floor to drop it through the bedroom window, it would have been the perfect solution."

"Hot damn," he said. He drawled the words out slowly, scratching his head in perfect imitation of a backward country boy. "That's what I love about you mystery writers. So analytical." He paused. "Did you learn analysis at the same place you learned to make one tear trickle down your cheek?"

I glanced at him, startled. You couldn't know, I thought. Not unless Mac had betrayed me. But how else? Tense moments passed. I focused on the road. Alex remained relaxed on the seat next to me.

"You knew I was faking?"

Undoubtedly he heard the embarrassment in my voice. But it was more for the strung-out state of my nerves than for being found out.

Alex laughed softly.

"Yeah. I knew. But don't feel bad. My sister, Joey, could never use tears to get past me either. Too much time spent in interrogation rooms, I guess."

Bloody cop, I thought. You scared the hell out of me.

"May I still stay?"

"Of course. But seriously, Jane, be careful. Four women died horribly just because they were pretty and went for a walk by themselves."

"I won't do anything foolish, Alex. And I'm sorry."

"Forget it. I just wanted to let you know. Now, if you'll slow down as we go around the next corner, I'll show you the pecan tree I fell out of when I was ten. Landed on my bike and broke my arm in two places. Bike was never the same after that."

Too late, country boy, I thought. I won't forget again that you didn't get where you are by being dense.

Ten minutes later, Highway 17 merged with Martin Luther King, Jr. Boulevard, the west boundary of old Savannah. We drove northward.

"Are you going to do much shopping while you're here?" Alex asked.

"As little as possible."

"How do you feel about carriage rides and bus tours?"

I glanced at him, wondering why he was asking. A hint of a smile curved one corner of his mouth. Playing, I decided, but with a purpose.

"Generally, I prefer driving myself."

"What about boat tours?"

I kept my eyes on the traffic, offered him some history.

"The last time I took a boat tour, I saw the Thames by moonlight. I was seventeen and thought I was in love. Charles had brown hair, big ears, and, as it turned out, very fast hands. I slapped him, hard, somewhere along Victoria Embankment. Our romance ended there. He eventually married a young woman named Diana, had two lovely sons. But he was a complete cad, couldn't stay away from his mistress."

I turned my head briefly. Alex was staring at me.

"Never mind." I grinned. "Now just where is this line of questioning going, officer?"

Alex laughed.

"Just trying to be a good host. Based on your answers, I doubt you'd appreciate the usual drive around the historic squares."

"Too right."

"You know, when Joey told me Max Murdock was coming, I planned on giving him—you—the cop's nickel tour of historic Savannah and letting the tourist guides fill in the rest. I've read your books. In a funny sort of way, I feel like I know you. I figured you would want to get a feel for the whole city."

"That's *exactly* what I want," I said. "Thank you, Alex."

Following his directions, I slid into the right lane, then turned right onto Oglethorpe.

"Oglethorpe cuts east-west through the center of the historic district." Alex pointed past me to the left. "That's the Chatham County Courthouse. It's a good landmark. Did you know that Savannah was the first planned city in North America?"

I shook my head.

"It was founded in 1733 by General James Edward Oglethorpe. If he's ever reincarnated, I hope he comes back as a traffic cop."

I couldn't tell from his tone if he was wishing Oglethorpe karmic reward or punishment. I decided not to ask.

"He laid Savannah out on a grid of intersecting north-south and east-west streets, built around twenty-four public squares. Today, most of the east-west streets are one way, alternating direction from block to block. Traffic moves around the squares counterclockwise."

We stopped for a light at Bull Street.

"This is the center line of the historic district. Turn right, and you'll run into Forsyth Park, the district's south boundary. Go left, and you'll end up at the *restored* riverfront. That's definitely worth a visit. You can walk along the cobblestones, watch the ships, get a feel for Savannah and its history. You'll see cotton warehouses, museums, little shops, restaurants. And tourists. Lots of tourists."

The light turned green. I waited for a group of grey-haired women to clear the intersection before stepping on the accelerator.

"You sound disapproving."

"Actually, I *like* tourists. They're good folks, mostly. And good for the economy. They spent more than six hundred million dollars here last year. But when some of them pack their bags, they leave their common sense behind. Sometimes we— cops, I mean—get tired of saving them from their own stupidity."

Like tourists everywhere, I thought. Like cops everywhere.

We continued along Oglethorpe.

"We're passing Colonial Park Cemetery. It dates back to 1750. Because of the marshy soil, the dead were buried in above-ground vaults—like in New Orleans. It's interesting to walk between the vaults, look at the plaques. But *don't* wander through after dark."

"Ghosties and ghoulies and long-legged beasties?"

"I wish."

He sounded angry.

I glanced sharply at him.

"Historic or not, Savannah is a *city* of a hundred and fifty thousand. Half a million people live in the Metro Savannah area. I've been chief for five years, and I've got good people working for me. We've been pushing citizen involvement. Neighborhood watches, tips on keeping your family and property secure, beat cops, cops visiting schools. By the way, that's the police station."

He pointed to the right, but I wouldn't have had any problem picking out the building. It was surrounded by a small fleet of white squad cars with red-and-blue pinstripes running the length of their side panels and POLICE spelled out in blue block letters.

"Anyway, we must be doing something right," Alex continued. "Auto theft is down by thirty percent. Aggravated assaults and burglaries are down. But robberies, rapes, and—lately—homicides are up. Way up."

Alex muttered the last words almost under his breath, fell into a gloomy silence.

I filled the time thinking about personally boosting Savannah's homicide statistics by one. Less risk, certainly, in making Jim O'Neil's death look accidental, but the satisfaction of delivering a violent death—

"Sorry. Sometimes I let things get too personal."

I raised an eyebrow in Alex's direction, my thoughts still on O'Neil.

"Sometimes things *are* personal."

"Yeah, but that's no excuse for behaving badly." He smiled. "I'll try to do better. After we cross Broad Street, you'll want to turn left. This is the Savannah that doesn't interest the tourists."

The change in scenery was abrupt. The landscape changed from historic preservation to urban decay. The heavy pedestrian traffic disappeared. We drove past a stretch of boarded-up shops, cracked sidewalks, and crumbling buildings. The smell of the city—a peculiar mix of damp bricks, river, and paper mill—was particularly strong.

We crossed some railroad tracks, passed a big brick building with a line of people at its door.

"The homeless shelter," Alex explained. "Sleeps a hundred, give or take, and provides meals for a lot more. Last Sunday at lunchtime, we fed maybe two hundred."

Another turn took us back into a more populated residential neighborhood. It was predominantly black and obviously poor. Small frame houses and blocky frame duplexes with sagging wooden balconies stood on the narrow lots. A "Callaghan Real Estate" sign was posted in one yard. I slowed to get a better look at the house. Its front porch was trimmed with particularly ornate gingerbread.

"A Victorian cottage," Alex said. "Joey says that if it were a couple of miles south, in the Victorian District, it'd sell for around ninety thousand dollars. That area's being restored, mostly by middle- and upper-class black families. Here, the owners will be lucky to get thirty thousand."

We made several more turns. The area became more industrial. Single-family homes with tiny front yards were replaced by warehouses, tenement buildings, and weed-choked empty lots. It was getting dark when we stopped to park along a street of dilapidated row houses. Scantily clad prostitutes lounged on the cement steps, leaned against the wrought-iron railings, stood under the few unbroken street lamps.

"Nice," I said, switching off the engine.

"Yeah, well, that's why I don't wear my uniform when I come down here. Might cause a panic."

I laughed, stepped from the car before he did. I had just slammed the door when a couple of scrawny black teenagers swaggered out from a nearby alley. One tossed a jagged piece of brick from hand to hand. The other waved a can of aerosol paint in the direction of the car.

"Hey, mama," the one with the aerosol can said, "watch your car? Five bucks."

I stood quietly, loath to react to so minor a threat, and watched their faces as Alex unfolded his six-foot-plus frame from the passenger's side of the car. He walked around the car, laid a possessive hand on my arm, nodded at the boys.

"Joe, Marv."

The one with the brick spoke quickly.

"Just a bit of free enterprise, Chief. No charge for you."

"Considering the parking rates downtown, guys, five bucks is a bit steep. Three would be more reasonable." He took several dollars from his wallet, hesitated. He wagged the bills at the boys. "That is, if people didn't think they were being threatened. Now, if they were being in-ti-mi-dated, that would be against the law. Know what I mean?"

Both kids smiled sheepishly. The brick bounced onto the pavement. The aerosol can was tucked into a pocket.

Alex handed them the money.

"We'll be in Harrys. You come get me if anyone gets possessive about the car."

"Don't worry, Chief," Marv said. "We'll handle it. You just focus on the lady."

"Come on, Jane," Alex said. "It's this way."

He pointed down the block, past the prostitutes, toward a noisy corner. Before we encountered the first group of "working girls," he leaned down and murmured in my ear.

"When I was told I'd be hosting Max Murdock, I decided that this was just the sort of place he'd like. Good local color, lots of authentic dialogue. Please note, I did *not* change my plans because you turned out to be female."

A woman called to Alex as we passed the stoop where she was sitting.

"Hey, sugar, that piece of skinny white meat won't do you no good. Come on back later. I'll show you a really good time."

Before he could answer, a woman standing on the next porch laughed.

"You're gonna get your ass busted propositioning the police chief. Ain't I right, Alex, honey?"

"Oh, he's not bustin' anyone when he's got hisself a date," the first woman replied. "We miss your pretty face down here, Chief. But why you bringin' that poor white girl into this neighborhood? She a social worker?"

Alex laughed.

"Naw, Lilia. Jane writes detective stories, full of tough men and gorgeous women. Thought I'd give her a look at you beautiful ladies and then take her to Harrys."

"Don't you give me any of your sweet talk, Alex Callaghan. Beautiful ladies, indeed!" But Lilia was beaming. "Well, you watch out, girl. Alex is a heartbreaker. And the mixed drinks at Harrys are weak as piss."

"Thanks for the warning," I said.

Alex sketched a farewell salute in Lilia's direction.

We'd almost reached the corner when a woman dressed in a silver-studded leather miniskirt and matching halter top stepped away from a lamppost. She stroked red lacquered fingernails down Alex's free arm.

"I heard the ladies back there, mister policeman." Her gaze wandered down over Alex's body and back to his face. "I'm not talking money. I'd be happy to fuck you for free."

She pursed glossy red lips at him, then walked back under the street light.

I tried not to laugh.

"You were right. Great dialogue. Though I'm not sure how to describe that funny little choking noise you just made."

Alex blushed, made another little choking noise. We rounded the corner, and he guided me through the doorway of a crowded tavern.

The bartender waved as we sat down in one of the broken-down booths. He was a short, powerfully built white man with a crooked nose and tattoos on the bulging biceps of both arms. From the opposite end of the smoke-filled room, a burly black man with a stained white apron around his waist hollered, "Be there in a minute, Chief." Either man would have made an excellent stand-in for my alter ego, Max.

A single battered menu was propped between the sugar dispenser and a pair of mismatched salt and pepper shakers. Alex offered it to me. I scanned the short list of offerings, lifted my eyes and surveyed the grease-streaked walls, wondered what was safe to eat. I looked across the table at Alex.

"What would you recommend?"

He read the handwritten menu upside down, pointing to each item as he mentioned it.

"The smoked oyster po'boy is a specialty."

I wrinkled my nose.

"No, huh? Well, the crabcake sandwich is very good. So is the catfish and the steak sandwich. I'd stay away from the chipped barbecue. Talk is that its popularity is endangering the local gator population."

I looked horrified.

Alex laughed.

"Just kidding. The barbecue's fine, too."

The black man with the white apron came to our table.

"Hey, Chief," he said. Then he looked at me, nodded, and briefly touched two fingers to his forehead. "Ma'am."

Alex responded to the curiosity in his voice.

"Harry, meet Max Murdock, a.k.a. Jane Nichols."

Harry laughed uproariously, obviously appreciating the joke.

"This sweet little thing is Max Murdock? The tough PI you told me you'd be bringing around? Your baby sister playing practical jokes again, Chief?" Harry reached out, engulfed my hand in his. "Welcome to Harrys, Miss Nichols. Would you autograph your book for me the next time you come by?"

I said I'd be delighted.

Harry produced a beaten-up order pad from one of his apron pockets, took our order, then walked off toward the kitchen.

Alex pointed at the bartender.

"They're partners. Both ex-military police."

"What's the bartender's name?"

"Harry."

Just then, the argument that had been going on in the booth next to ours escalated from drunken shouts to swinging fists. Within moments, two men were rolling around on the floor near our feet.

Alex looked down at them, sighed, shook his head. He looked toward the back of the tavern. I followed the direction of his gaze in time to see the black Harry erupt from the kitchen. He bent over the nearest combatant, closed his fists around the man's shirt collar and belt, and lifted him off the floor. The white Harry came from behind the bar and dealt with the second fellow in a similar fashion. Both combatants were carried through the tavern and flung out the front door.

Harrys was the kind of place that law-abiding citizens go out of their way to avoid. It was dirty, noisy, and dangerous. I felt right at home. So, I noticed, did Alex.

The crabcake sandwich was delicious.

18

I awakened before dawn feeling remarkably well rested. I slipped into my oldest, most comfortable pair of jeans and a loose, sloppy sweatshirt, picked up my shoes, and walked barefooted through the dark, peaceful house to the kitchen. My night vision was good, so I easily located the coffeemaker in the shadowy recesses of the kitchen counter, and slid the switch to Brew.

Alex had pointed out the coffeemaker the evening before.

"This household runs on strong coffee. I never know when I'll be called away, so I always try to have a pot ready to go. If you're up first, just turn it on."

Nice system, I thought, filling a large mug under the running stream before putting the carafe in place. I went out onto the back porch, dropped my shoes beside me. I leaned back against the railing, sipped my coffee, and watched the brightening eastern horizon.

With the entire bird population cheering it on, the sun rose, blazing its way through the foliage and trees beyond the yard, mounting the treetops, gradually illuminating the flagstone path that wound through the garden. The scenery was magical, irresistible. I decided to take a walk.

I stood. Holding my half-empty mug, I attempted to gauge the distance to a particularly attractive cluster of magnolias while locating my shoes with my toes. I slipped the right shoe on easily enough, but nudged the left one too hard. It tumbled down the steps.

Rattlesnakes, I discovered, are not happy creatures when rudely awakened. I heard a quick, rustling movement and glanced down in time to see a snake strike at my shoe. Then, rather tardily to my way of thinking, the creature began rattling.

I threw myself back against the screened door. That put the snake out of sight. But the sheer volume of its nonstop rattling left no doubt as to its state of mind. Enough noise to wake the dead. Or to scare the hell out of a cop who had just come into the kitchen. I heard an exclamation from the house's interior and a rush of footsteps.

"If you fling that door open, Callaghan, you'll knock me off this porch," I said hastily over my shoulder, "and that bloody snake will have me for breakfast."

I moved cautiously aside and let him slip past me. He looked over the edge of the porch, in the direction of the rattling.

"My God!"

He looked quickly at my feet.

I wiggled my bare left toes, managed a weak smile.

"Dropped my shoe on him."

"Oh, I see."

Alex took my elbow, steered me back through the kitchen door to a seat at the kitchen table. He walked over to the cupboard, took out a second mug, carried it and the coffeepot to the table.

I was still clutching my mug with white-knuckled fingers.

I put it down. Alex's hand shook slightly as he poured the coffee, warming up what was left in my mug, filling his own.

"What should we do?" I said.

"About the snake or the sneaker?"

He returned the pot to the warmer, took a pint of half-and-half from the refrigerator.

"The snake."

"Well, I could shoot it or club it. But that'd get blood on your sneaker."

"Perhaps something less violent?"

He paused in the center of the kitchen, checked to be sure that I was looking at him.

I was. The view was spectacular. Red running shorts revealed the long, muscular legs that last evening's blue jeans had only suggested. A dark blue T-shirt with SAVANNAH P.D. emblazoned across its front stretched across broad shoulders and hugged a flat stomach.

"Well, I guess I could arrest him and take him downtown," Alex said. "Charge him with . . ."

With growing amusement, I watched him tilt his head, chew his lip, and look extremely puzzled. Then he brightened, stepped nearer the table, regarded me very seriously.

". . . possession."

My giggle was rewarded with a lopsided grin.

"Any chance he'll surrender my property voluntarily, Officer?"

Alex dropped into the chair opposite me.

"Yeah. He's not the criminal type. My guess is he'll leave it behind when he crawls home to tell his wife and all the little snakes about you."

"What's he going to tell them?"

"He'll make up a fable about a man who forgot to tell his

guest that she should watch out for snakes. Of course, the man didn't know the guest would be up at dawn."

"Early riser," I said, grimacing.

"Apparently."

He picked up his mug, blew across the top of the liquid for a minute, took a sip, then settled back with a contented sigh. He was apparently recovered from the aftermath of his adrenaline rush. I felt steadier, too. Silliness had been as good a cure as any, perhaps better than most.

A few minutes later, Alex got up to refill our cups.

"So. How about some breakfast, Jane? Bacon and eggs? Maybe some toast? I've got homemade peach preserves."

"Toast sounds wonderful."

I sat back in my chair, sipped my coffee, watched him putter around the kitchen. I found myself wondering what he'd be like in bed.

Tut, tut, I thought, dismissing the possibility. We are feeling better, aren't we? All it had taken was a bit of undisturbed sleep, the prospect of killing a man I hated, and the giddy aftermath of an encounter with a poisonous snake.

It wasn't until he'd put a plateful of toast in the center of the table that Alex paused to look at *me* speculatively. But sex wasn't on his mind.

"You must have nerves of steel. Most women would have screamed. You didn't even spill your coffee."

"Male chauvinist cop," I retorted lightly. And I reminded myself of who—and what—he was.

Equipped with a map and a phone book, I spent the balance of the day in my car learning firsthand about Savannah and its people, and exploring the city with an eye for access, concealment, and escape.

I looked up Coastal Limb and Orthopedics in the phone book, then drove past. The narrow, two-story frame ware-

house was on the riverfront, east of the historic district. I
drove systematically through the area, looking for information not on the map. Detours and alleyways. Bridges and
ditches. Rooftops and fire escapes. I discovered that Coastal
Limb and Orthopedics was separated from Harrys by half a
mile of brick-paved alleyway and a desolate corner of railyard.

Finding O'Neil's home was more difficult. Several J.
O'Neils were listed in the residential section of the phone
book. I went back to Oglethorpe, parked near the cemetery,
walked over to the Chamber of Commerce offices. I introduced myself, told them how excited I was to be doing a book
with a Savannah locale, and left with a city map, a copy of *Savannah Real Estate Today*, and several restaurant recommen-
dations. Harrys wasn't among them.

I drove south to the Johnny Harris Restaurant on Victory
Drive, ordered crusty French bread and a bowl of creamed
crab soup. As I ate, I read the real estate guide, compared the
listings with my map, and got a better feel for Savannah's
neighborhoods and suburbs. Then I looked back over the addresses I'd found in the phone book, eliminating possibilities. I settled on an address in the historic district and drove
there.

The house was on Whitaker Street, overlooking Forsyth
Park. It was a three-story stucco rowhouse trimmed with dark
shutters. Stone steps, bordered by an ornate ironwork
handrail, led up to a high front stoop trimmed with Victorian
gingerbread. A vine, heavy with clusters of pale lavender
flowers, grew up and over the doorway.

A few hours of surveillance would confirm it, but I was certain the house belonged to O'Neil.

I parked, walked through the streets surrounding the park
and then the park itself, trying to get a feel for the neighborhood. Most of the residences were similar to O'Neil's—

obviously well kept, obviously affluent. Two historic inns within half a block created a steady stream of pedestrians wandering up and down the streets and through Forsyth Park.

As I crossed the street to the park, a busload of Japanese tourists were following a tour guide into the Fragrant Garden for the Blind. At the park's center, dozens of tourists tossed coins into an extravagant fountain. In another area, a young black woman moved smoothly from southern-accented English to impeccable German as she translated a plaque on a Confederate statue for about twenty people. Only the playgrounds—the domain of young mothers and uniformed black nannies with small children in tow—escaped the curious attention of the tourists.

Too many potential witnesses, I thought as I sat on a bench, soaked up a little sun, and considered the information I'd gathered that afternoon. I suspected that I would kill O'Neil near his warehouse. But I didn't seek him out. I wasn't ready.

When I returned to the house in the late afternoon, Alex greeted me at the door. He'd had an alarm system installed in my absence.

I kept a straight face as I thought of foxes and henhouses, barn doors and horses.

"That's probably something Andrew Jax should know about," I said. "Would you mind telling me how it works? I mean, if it's not too technical."

Not surprisingly, he was delighted to accommodate me.

"Well, the brains of this alarm system is its CPU—"

I wrinkled my forehead.

He caught himself, smiled, kept his tone informational rather than condescending. He probably did well speaking to the public, I thought. And with those looks . . . I imagined that the female citizenry of Savannah was enthusiastic about law enforcement.

"—central processing unit. The sensors and the sounding device are wired into it."

The sensors, Alex told me, were essentially pairs of magnets placed on each of the doors and all the windows. Open the doors or raise the windows above a certain height, and the circuit would be broken. The alarm would sound, alerting the creeper, the resident, and the police dispatch.

"When you're here by yourself, especially at night, be sure that all the doors are locked and the windows are down."

The remote arming station was mounted on the foyer wall, near the front door. It had a keypad and a couple of simple displays. Alex pointed to each one as he described its purpose.

"This tells you that everything is properly closed. Then you can activate the system." He gave me a slip of paper with a series of four numbers written on it. "You'll have to memorize this. You enter it here. And this is the On/Off switch. The alarm is wired into the household current. There's a battery backup in case the power fails."

"But what if *you* need to get into the house, and I've turned the alarm on?"

He was amazingly patient.

"I'll use my key to open the front door. Then I'll have two minutes to punch in the security code. Otherwise the alarm sounds. There's a siren mounted on the outside of the house. And the system uses the phone lines to automatically contact police dispatch."

I thanked Alex for his explanation, told him I was sure I would be able to work it into my book. A little later, I spent a few private moments looking closely at the system.

As he and I chatted over a dinner of ham, peas, and baked

sweet potatoes, we didn't talk about the two serious flaws I'd identified in the alarm system. The exterior siren had no interior backup, and the RJ31X jack—the modular interface between the alarm system and the telephone line—was unprotected. Using the electronic devices in the boot of my car to disable the alarm would have been overkill. If I had wanted to, I could have done it with a screwdriver and needle-nosed pliers.

At dusk, Alex and I took a walk. Once again, the evening was cool enough for a light jacket, and the breeze was brisk.

Alex held the back door open for me as I stepped onto the porch.

"Stone holds the heat long after the sun goes down," he said conversationally. "Reptiles seek out warm places, preferably sheltered from the wind."

I didn't bother suppressing a shudder as I stepped past the spot where the snake had been.

"Such as where a flagstone path meets the back steps?"

He laughed.

"Yeah, just like that. They also enjoy curling up by foundations and along paved roads and tucking in next to rocks and fallen logs. The trick is to watch where you put your feet and avoid stepping blindly over obstacles."

Words to live by, I thought. And not just where reptiles were concerned.

The flagstones ended at the tree line.

"The path gets progressively swampier beyond this point and the mosquitoes are horrible. It goes through the woods for a couple of miles. There's a long wooden dock at the end of the path. It extends out over the marsh to the river's deeper water. My dad and I built it, kept a boat tied up there when I was a kid. We'd go fishing, catch mostly catfish . . ."

As Alex spoke I peered into the darkness beneath the

canopy of trees, trying to concentrate on the echoes of childhood happiness I heard in his voice.

". . . lost a lot of bait to crabs and turtles. Sometimes we'd
see gators sunning themselves. I remember one time . . ."

When I picked up my car in Atlanta, the young woman at
the rental counter remarked that I would be traveling along
some of the state's oldest roads. Generations earlier, slaves
had toiled on the roads until starving, exhausted, and delirious
with fever, they had collapsed and died. Others escaped, but
vindictive gang bosses and the relentless swamp ensured that
few survived the journey to freedom. Some locals, the young
woman had added cheeringly, still avoided the swamps at
night. They believed that the slaves, so cruelly treated in life,
walked unhappily even in death.

I stared down the gloomy path, trying to see beyond the
mist that rose from the ground between the massive, moss-
hung trees. In Atlanta, the tale had been nothing more than a
bit of local color. Now, it seemed to be a portent of violence
and lonely death. Unbidden, memories of Belfast came drifting back. My stomach lurched. The bitter taste of bile rose in
my throat. Once again, I saw Michael standing in the darkness
beneath the trees, saw the knife blade flash in the moonlight,
saw—

Someone grabbed my arm.

Instinctively, I repelled the attack. I freed my arm with a
sweep of my wrist, stepped back quickly, assumed a defen-
sive posture with feet firmly planted, legs slightly bent, arms
and hands poised.

Abruptly, intellect caught up with instinct.

Alex, looking more surprised than fearful, had stepped
back, too. But he was holding his hands open, palms toward
me, in a universal gesture of nonaggression.

"Sorry," I muttered. How was I ever going to explain?

"I didn't mean to startle you. I'd just asked if you wanted

to head back. You didn't seem to hear me, so I touched your arm." He paused awkwardly, then added, "Where did you learn that style?"

Selective truths. "In a small gymnasium in London."

"The way you moved . . . Your form is excellent." His voice carried equal shares of tension and confusion.

I laughed softly, moved deliberately forward, closed the distance between us. I touched his chest lightly with my right hand, tilted my head back to look up at him. I'm no threat, I let my body language say. Look how fragile I am next to you. I need protecting.

"Actually, that's the only movement I know," I said. "It's intended to scare the bloody hell out of mashers. I was thinking about your strangler. Then someone grabbed my arm."

Alex stood very still as I spoke. His head was bent forward, his eyes focused on mine. The yard was lost in shadows, creating an atmosphere of isolation, intensifying the intimacy between us. I felt the throb of his heart through the thin fabric beneath my fingertips, saw the muscles along his jaw tense. Slowly, he moved to touch, once again, the bare skin of my upper arms.

This time my body flushed in response.

Congratulations, Nichols, I thought with quick irritation. Now he sees you as small and vulnerable. Was the desire your idea or his? A more detached interior voice observed that a bit of desire on his part might prove useful. But not tonight.

I spoiled the mood.

"Can snakes see in the dark?" I asked nervously. I half-turned to look over my shoulder at the lighted house. "They won't creep up on us while we're standing here, will they?"

Eye contact was broken, tension fled. Alex stepped away from me with a self-conscious grin.

"City girl," he said softly. "Come on. I'll take you back to your typewriter."

19

The plan made sense, Jax told himself. Nothing could go wrong.

Still, he was worried.

The photos and information in the oversized purse Millicent carried were worth a fortune. Some very influential people had made the mistake of becoming addicted to some very illegal substances. Jax's client had made himself rich by threatening to expose their little weaknesses. Now he was trading the evidence that had made him rich for the life of his son.

Jax didn't trust the blackmailer. Or the kidnapper. But he and Millicent had agreed. They couldn't let the boy die.

As he followed her north up Michigan Avenue, Jax kept the hordes of shoppers between himself and Millicent. Tailing her was easy. Even in a crowd, she stood out. The kidnapper—and Jax—had counted on that. She was a big girl. In her snappy red pumps, she looked straight into Jax's eyes, and he was six feet tall. Dressed

*in a tight red dress and wearing a big, floppy white hat
tied with a bright red scarf...*

*Well, thought Jax, a man would have to be dead not to
notice her. She was the perfect person to make the drop.
He knew that.*

Still, he worried.

*The kidnapper had agreed that Millicent should make
the drop. An envelope was delivered to the office that
same day, carried by a wino who'd barely managed to
make it up the stairs. Inside the envelope were a photograph, a map, and a note.*

*Jax already had a picture of the kid, taken at his sixth
birthday party. He wasn't anyone's idea of cute, thought
Jax, but at least in that picture he'd been happy. In the
picture that fell from the envelope, the kid's thin face was
bruised, his eyes terrified. A clear warning not to screw
up.*

*The route Millicent was following had been drawn in
yellow marker. The note was printed in heavy black letters: Tell the broad to walk north up Michigan Avenue at
noon. Follow the map. Carry the goods in a big red
purse. Tell her to wear that red dress she looks so sexy
in. Tell her to walk slow, to window-shop, to take her
time.*

*Between noon and two o'clock someone would ap-
proach Millicent, show her something that proved the
boy was still alive. She'd hand over the purse. If all went
well, the kid would be home for dinner.*

*Jax watched the top of Millicent's hat bobbing in the
crowd. He kept it in sight as she lingered in front of one
chic window display after another. Lost it for a moment
as a turning bus blocked his view. He dodged around
the bus, ignoring the burning, twisting jab in the pit of
his stomach. The pain quit when he spotted her hat*

again. He was more careful after that. He followed her, his eyes constantly on her hat, as the crowds washed around her.

The kidnapper had selected Jax as the go-between. He had given Jax's name to the kid's blackmailing father. The father had agreed. Why not? he said. He knew Jax by reputation. Certainly Jax was more trustworthy than the cops.

The blackmailing son of a bitch should know, thought Jax, seeing as how he was a cop himself.

For two hours Jax followed Millicent up Michigan Avenue. It was mid-July, it was hot, and he'd worn a jacket to conceal his shoulder holster. He envied Millicent her skimpy red dress and the hat that protected her from the sun.

He glanced at his watch. Two-thirty.

Enough. Something had gone wrong. Too much time had passed.

He watched the white hat bob its way across Chicago Avenue.

Enough. It was time to go back to the office, to wait for new instructions.

He quickened his pace, crossed the street as the Don't Walk sign flashed its warning, called her name as he elbowed his way through the crowd of shoppers.

She kept walking, detouring suddenly to the right, toward the doorway of an exclusive women's shop.

He reached her, grabbed her arm before she went into the store.

With a gasp, she swung around. The blonde with the tight red dress and the white hat with a red scarf swung around. She glared at him, jerked her arm free.

"Back off, creep, or I'll scream."

She turned away. With her back held defiantly straight, she walked into the shop.

No!

Pain lanced through Jax's stomach. A pounding agony exploded behind his eyes.

No! It couldn't happen twice.

Frantically, he ran back through the crowd, back south down Michigan Avenue. This time, he didn't watch for a white hat. Or a red dress. He looked for a face. Millicent's face.

He searched for a long time before admitting that he had lost her.

At nine, Alex poked his head into the library to say goodnight. He was back in uniform, neatly combed, freshly shaven.

"I'm leaving for the station. I'll set the alarm on my way out. Emergency numbers are posted by all the phones. There's one in the kitchen, one in the upstairs hallway, and one on the night stand in my bedroom. The bedroom door locks. It's left at the top of the stairs, then left again. I'd feel better if, the next time you take a break, you'd go upstairs, take a look at the lock, and locate the phone. If anything scares you, lock yourself in and call me. I can be here in ten minutes. Okay?"

I smiled sweetly, said I would. I thanked him for his concern, assured him that I wouldn't hesitate to call if I needed help.

"Good." He retreated from the doorway, then stopped. "Oh, I almost forgot." He pulled a small book from his back pocket, tossed it to me. "This is for you."

I looked at the title and laughed.

"I'll be back at dawn," he said, "to share coffee with you and your snake."

I watched as he drove away. Instead of walking upstairs to

a bedroom I'd already seen, I went to my room, pulled out my map, and memorized its details as I planned my evening. The streets are different after dark. I had some neighborhoods to revisit.

Unlikely that Alex would check on me, and I doubted that he'd risk scaring me by calling or coming in after midnight. Even so, I could justify my absence if, by some chance, he came home and found me gone. That time of the month arrived a bit unexpectedly, I'd explain. I had to make a trip to a convenience store—sanitary supplies already in the car to prove it—and got lost. Ended up driving around until I got my bearings. So sorry and all that.

By midnight, I'd had a light snack and was sitting with my feet up on the kitchen table, sipping Scotch. To occupy my time, I was reading the book Alex had given me. I'd skipped the "Snakes as Pets" and "Snakes as Useful Creatures" chapters and gone straight to the one entitled "Venomous."

I'd leave for town, I thought, at one A.M.

The best laid plans . . .

At twelve-fifteen, a car pulled up to the house.

Alex, I thought immediately, cursing the man's unpredictability. But the fumbling at the lock on the front door changed my mind about the identity of my visitor. I watched the door open from the shadow of the stairs.

A large black man, wearing an SPD uniform with sergeant's stripes on its sleeves, half-carried Alex into the foyer.

Alex's face was pale beneath the bandage that encircled his forehead and anchored a thick rectangle of gauze above his left ear. His ear and neck were brown with dried blood, his shirt was soaked in it, and the right leg of his blood-soaked trousers had been cut completely away. More gauze, reinforced by adhesive tape, circled his right thigh.

The police sergeant paused as Alex punched in the alarm code, then helped him limp through the open doorway to the right. He deposited Alex carefully into a corner of the sofa in the living room.

I stepped into the room, gasped most convincingly.

Alex greeted me with a sick-looking smile.

"It's not as bad as it looks. Just a bump on the head and a few stitches. No big deal."

He began struggling to his feet.

His attempt was stopped promptly by his companion. He was a big man, close to six four, with broad shoulders, a thick chest, and biceps that bulged beneath a short-sleeved uniform shirt. He put his hand in the center of Alex's chest and held him, without visible effort, against the cushions.

"He's a liar," the police sergeant said. "Keep it up, Callaghan, and I'll pick you up and take you back to the hospital. Doc Reinhart says that if you had any sense, you'd be there right now."

"You know how I feel about hospitals. Besides, I've got company to take care of."

The large hand didn't move.

"Let's take care of you first," I said.

I squatted down so that my face was level with his and looked closely at him. That he hurt, I had no doubt. Pain was etched in every tense line of his face. Even small movements seemed to amplify it. Gently, I touched his chin so that he'd look directly at me, then looked questioningly at the man who'd brought him home.

"Concussion?" I asked, straightening.

The man nodded.

"Sit," he said ominously to Alex. Then he removed his hand from Alex's chest, extended it to me. "Tommy Grayson, Miss Nichols. I'm Chief Callaghan's second in command and, on good days, his friend."

"My nursemaid," Alex muttered darkly.

"Not a good day." Tommy smiled briefly. But he looked worried. His eyes constantly returned to Alex as he spoke. "Concussion, stitches in his scalp, and a couple dozen stitches, give or take, along the back of his thigh."

"How—?"

"Not a word, Tommy," Alex interrupted. "I don't need this showing up in Jane's next book."

"Unlikely. It would be out of character for Andrew Jax to be so concerned about a bag lady. But our Alex . . ."

Tommy shook his head, frowning. But I'd heard resignation in his voice. This probably wasn't the first time Alex had been too concerned for his own good.

"Ah, hell, go ahead," said Alex. "The story'll be all over town by tomorrow, anyway."

"Well," said Tommy with obvious relish, "our hero is out prowling the streets alone and sees this old gal sprawled between a couple of dumpsters. So he figures he better check on her. Turns out, she's only sleeping. She wakes up, sees this shadowy figure leaning over her, and smashes him in the head with a pipe."

"She was afraid of being strangled," Alex said flatly.

"Oh, yeah. An old wino like that gotta protect herself these days. So he's knocked on his ass—"

"Not ass, Tommy. Thigh. If this does get in her book, I want it told properly."

"—lands on a broken bottle and it slices his *thigh* open. Too embarrassed to call for backup, he drives himself, concussed and bleeding, to Candler Hospital. He parks the squad roll—legally, mind you—in the parking lot and walks to the emergency room. According to the nurses, they had the usual roomful of patients and Alex wanted to sit and wait his turn. So they told him that the amount of blood he was dripping on the floor was upsetting the other patients and hustled him in to Doc Reinhart. And *he* calls me 'cause Alex here is too damn stubborn to spend the night in the hospital."

"This town," Alex said bitterly, "is full of people who can't keep their mouths shut."

Over Alex's objections, he slept in my bed. Practical considerations, I said. He was hardly fit to negotiate the stairs, and the only downstairs bathroom adjoined my bedroom.

I waited in the library as Tommy helped Alex into the bedroom. There—judging from the growling and cajoling I could hear through the half-open door—the unwilling patient was escorted to the bathroom, washed up, helped into clean clothes, and put to bed.

Tommy and his bullying tactics reminded me so much of Dora that, for the briefest moment, I smiled at the memory. A lurch of regret twisted the smile into a grimace. Damn her.

"Damn him." Tommy echoed. He came back into the library carrying a bundle of torn, blood-stained clothing. "He's a stubborn bastard."

"From what I overheard, you two are well matched."

"Maybe so. We've been friends a long time. I know all his moves. Would you stay with him while I dump this?"

"Sure."

I slipped into the bedroom. Alex lay pale and exhausted against the pillows. He didn't open his eyes until he heard me by his bedside.

"I came to say goodnight."

"Good night, Jane. I'm so sorry . . ."

His voice trailed off. His eyes drifted shut.

"Good night, Alex," I murmured.

Rest and time, I knew from my own experience, were the best remedies for his present miseries. I went to intercept Tommy.

*   *   *

Despite his objections, I sent Tommy home to his wife and twin boys. As long as Alex was home, I was resigned to delaying my plans. I wasn't resigned, however, to having a second observant cop hanging around the house.

In the kitchen, over chocolate sandwich cookies and milk, our relationship moved easily from "Sergeant Grayson" and "Miss Nichols" to "Tommy" and "Jane." But, while the beginnings of friendship were established, trust—at least where the welfare of his friend, Alex, was concerned—was extended reluctantly.

"The twins are sleeping through the night, now. And I called Ginnie from the hospital so she wouldn't worry about Alex. Told her not to expect me till tomorrow."

"Surprise her." I softened the words by adding, "I imagine that your schedule keeps you two apart too much as it is. Leave me your phone number and the hospital's. I won't hesitate to call if there's any problem."

Tommy twisted the top off another cookie, dipped the naked half into his milk, looked at me consideringly.

"The doctor said someone should watch him closely tonight. And Alex's not exactly steady on his feet. What if he needs to go to the john?"

"I'll sleep in the big chair in the library and listen for him. You left his cane next to the bed. If he needs help getting to the bathroom, I'll help him."

"He won't like it, you being a woman and his guest and all."

I smiled.

"No, he won't, will he?"

The grin that I received in return was pure, gleeful anticipation.

*   *   *

Fucking hell, I thought as I snuggled deep into the oversized chair. If Tommy had his way—and I saw no possibility that he wouldn't—Alex wouldn't be back on duty for at least a week. Bloody, fucking hell. I shifted slightly to find the most comfortable position, shut my eyes, drifted back to another time.

"Jane?" Brian called softly from the bed.

I was sitting in a nearby chair, rereading a report Mac had given me that afternoon.

"Thought you were asleep," I said, my eyes still fixed on the report.

"No, not for a while."

Earlier, we'd argued and apologized. Made love and fallen asleep in each other's arms. But I'd awakened with our conflict very much on my mind. Its roots were in the pages I held.

"I've been lying here just thinking," Brian said.

"About what?"

"Jane, let's have a baby."

I dropped the report into my lap and looked up slowly, letting my eyes adjust to the darkness beyond the pool of light under the reading lamp. Brian was lying on his stomach, chin propped on his hands, looking at me intently.

"Are you serious?"

"Yes."

I glanced down at the report.

"What about Rome?"

He didn't answer. Even in the dim light, I could read his expression clearly. Tears welled up in my eyes. I looked away.

He slipped from the bed, padded across the room, knelt next to my chair. He took my hands in his, pressed them to his lips.

"I have to go to Rome. I owe it to Mac. But then, my love, I'll retire."

Alex whimpered in his sleep, and I jolted awake. It took me a long time to fall asleep again.

20

Just after six, I heard Alex stir. I waited, giving him time to adjust in privacy to the discomfort of awakening with injuries. Then I tapped at the door and entered the bedroom. He was sitting on the edge of the bed, hunched over, cradling his head in both hands.

"Christ! Tommy," he said without looking up, "I feel like shit. It's like having the world's worst fucking hangover. The room won't stop spinning. My leg hurts like blazes, and I've got to piss—"

"Tommy went home."

At the sound of my voice, Alex sat up with a jerk—a movement that I was sure did nothing to improve his headache. I caught a flash of Technicolor bruising and acute embarrassment before he returned his head to his hands.

I walked over, sat gingerly on the bed beside him.

"Sorry you heard that," he murmured. More carefully this time, he raised his head. The scrapes had darkened, bruises had bloomed overnight along his left cheek, and dark stubble shadowed his jaw.

"You do look ghastly. Come on, put your arm around my shoulders. I'll help you to the bathroom."

He looked appalled. I sighed.

"Pretend I'm Max Murdock."

"Pass me my cane. I'll make it on my own."

"The devil you will. If you fall, you're too big for me to pick up. Beyond that, I promised Tommy I'd take care of you. *He's* too big to argue with."

Alex still looked mutinous.

"Damn it, Callaghan, I swear I'll turn away while you take a leak."

A wash and a shave—accomplished without my assistance, while he sat on the closed lid of the stool and hung on to the basin—improved Alex's looks considerably. It did little for his general disposition. His injuries frustrated him. He was not, I quickly discovered, a man who dealt well with frustration. By the time I'd fixed us some breakfast and carried it into the bedroom on a large silver tray, my respect for Florence Nightingale had grown dramatically.

"Stop growling, Callaghan," I finally said in exasperation as I passed him a piece of buttered toast. "Focus on the word 'patient.' As in you are a . . . Or, alternatively, you must be . . . Did you ever wonder what joker began using that word when referring to a bedridden individual?"

He failed to see any wit in that. The next few minutes were spent in silent discord. Alex sullenly munched his toast in bed, his back and injured leg bolstered by pillows. I sat in a nearby chair wondering if the rattlesnake wouldn't be a more congenial early-morning companion.

"Jane?"

Reluctantly, I looked up from the coffee in my mug, bracing for the next volley of ill humor. I was surprised to see that he looked apologetic.

"Thanks for, well, everything. I'm sorry for being such a pain in the ass."

"I thought you said it was your thigh."

Breakfast was a fairly pleasant affair after that.

I'd cleared our dishes and returned to the bedroom with a couple of aspirins for Alex when we heard a car coming up the drive.

"Got to be Joey," he said. "I'd know that muffler anywhere. I didn't get around to giving her a key to the alarm system, Jane. Please, would you spare my poor aching head and, quick, switch it off before she unlocks the door?"

I rushed to the door, flipped the switch to the Off position, and opened the door as an elderly green MGB skidded to a stop near the front steps. Joey Callaghan hurried from the car. She was dressed in a pale pink linen suit and her golden blonde hair was pulled into a French twist. She took the steps two at a time—no mean trick in high heels. Worry lines creased her forehead, and she'd chewed all the lipstick from her bottom lip.

She rushed past me toward the stairs.

"How bad is he?" she blurted.

Alex's voice rerouted her before I could.

"I'm in here, Joey!"

I followed her as she ran through the library to Alex. He flinched as she hugged him tight. Then he wrapped his arms around her.

"Hey, Pumpkin, don't cry. I'm okay."

She pressed her face against his shoulder.

"One of the waitresses at the diner said you'd been hurt. Said her husband saw you come into the hospital last night and that you were bleeding real bad. Stabbed, he thought. That's what he told her. So I used their phone to call the hospital. When you weren't there, I called the house. But the line was busy. So I was certain you were here with Tommy taking care of you, and that he was having to call an ambulance, just like last time . . ."

Her rush of words ended in a small, hiccuping sob.

"No, nothing like that." Alex's voice was low and soothing. "I was just calling the station to let them know I was taking the day off. And last night was an accident. I bumped my head, lost my balance, and cut my leg on a piece of glass when I fell."

He shot me a look over Joey's head that dared me to contradict him. I didn't say a word, just shook my head in admiration. The man had a talent for understatement.

Joey sniffed once, then sat up, still within the circle of Alex's arms. She looked at him closely.

"But your head . . . It's all bandaged. And your poor face . . . Are you sure you're all right?"

"Of course." He gave her a reassuring smile. "I'm a little sore, that's all. Scrapes and bruises. Nothing to get upset about."

"I'm not upset." She stood and pulled herself up to her full height, which, even in high heels, was well under five and a half feet. "I'm not upset," she repeated. "I'm furious. You knew I'd be scared half to death. But you didn't bother calling me. You are the most irresponsible, self-centered . . ."

A bewildered look crossed Alex's face. He looked helplessly in my direction.

"She's right," I said, choking back laughter. "As fit as you were last night, you probably should have called her."

Alex scowled. Joey, with a startled gasp, turned toward me.

"Oh, jeez, I was so worried about Alex, I forgot you were here."

She was, I suspected, really seeing me for the first time. I was a less than elegant sight. The oversized cotton shirt and grey warm-up pants I wore looked as if I'd slept in them—

which, in fact, I had. And I'd been too busy playing Florence Nightingale to do more than pull a comb through my hair.

Not surprisingly, Joey wasn't particularly thrilled with what she saw. For a moment, her feelings showed clearly. Then she caught herself. I watched her consciously change from possessive younger sister to sophisticated woman of the world. She took a deep breath, composed her face, lifted her chin, then stepped forward and gracefully extended her hand.

"Welcome to our home," she said in a cool, cultivated voice that bespoke generations of breeding. "I'm Josephine Callaghan. You must be a friend of Alex's."

She really doesn't know who I am, I thought with amusement. But she suspects—and rightly so—that I've spent the night with her brother. She obviously hadn't even considered the possibility that I might be Jane Nichols, which made me wonder what she imagined Jane Nichols looked like. Not much, I decided.

I stepped forward, grasped her hand.

"Actually, Miss Callaghan, I'm Max Murdock. But you can call me Jane."

The sophisticate disappeared into the warmth of a woman's giggle.

"Hi! I'm Joey." She grinned at her brother. "That was a better joke than I thought. She wasn't at all what you expected, was she?"

Once over her initial shock, Joey turned out to be surprisingly businesslike. She confirmed that Alex had eaten, landed a kiss on an unbruised bit of his face, switched off the bedroom light, and told him to shut up and get some sleep.

I suggested she join me for coffee.

She faced me as we entered the kitchen.

"Jane, you could save me several phone calls if you'd tell me, straight out, exactly what his injuries are. I don't buy what he said for a minute. I've seen him injured often enough."

I told her. She looked appalled. Tried to hide her distress by walking to the solarium and squatting down to poke a carefully sculpted, pink-lacquered fingernail into the soil around a large split-leaf philodendron.

"Needs water," she said to no one in particular. Then she sighed, straightened, muttered, "Dumb, lying cop," and turned back toward me. She didn't quite meet my eyes.

"Well, this certainly spoils your stay. Give me an afternoon. I'll refund the money your agent wired, make a few phone calls, and find you other accommodations."

Holding on to Chief Callaghan as an alibi was becoming a never-ending challenge, I thought dryly.

"You and your brother are terribly eager to get rid of me considering that I really don't want to go."

Joey's brown eyes, so much like her brother's, shifted to meet mine. The quietly appraising look was also much like his, but she hadn't his instincts. I wondered how much reality he'd sheltered her from.

"There'd be no one here to take care of you," she said doubtfully, "and I simply can't take time off to play hostess."

I laughed.

"Actually, your brother is the only one who needs taking care of. I think I can handle that. If I'd wanted service, I'd have booked into a hotel. But I wanted atmosphere and a relatively private place to work. Besides, Alex is a marvelous source of information for my novel. He's got an insider's view of police procedures and attitudes. Frankly, this is an opportunity I won't give up easily."

Joey looked relieved. It occurred to me that the upkeep on the family home was a tremendous drain on their resources. The loss of that extra income . . . I wondered if part of the reason Joey had played her little joke on Alex was to ensure that he'd open his house to a paying customer, even if she was female.

"Do you often have women staying here?" I asked between sips of coffee.

"No. Alex generally prefers men. Says they're less bother. And of course lately . . ."

Her voice trailed away. She looked at me guiltily. Joey Callaghan was not one for hiding her feelings. Let it all hang out, I thought, imagining how much easier my job would be if everyone did.

"He told me about the strangler."

"I didn't think you'd be so young and pretty."

"Max Murdock with breasts?"

She nodded.

"And smoking a cigar?"

She laughed.

Joey left. Alex slept. I washed dishes and reminded myself that I was building my credibility. By lunchtime—tinned soup and ham sandwiches—I had arranged chairs strategically between bed and bathroom and pronounced Alex steady enough to take a leak on his own. We were both grateful.

The dreaded Doc Reinhart dropped in at three.

"I do not make house calls," the grey-haired doctor announced after he'd introduced himself, and I'd asked if he wanted to see Alex.

He was, I guessed, in his late sixties. He looked tough enough to spend long hours in an emergency room and still have energy to spare. His handshake was bone-crushing.

"This is strictly a social call. Last night that stiff-necked young cop told me that he had a famous author visiting. I decided to drop by for an autograph."

I smiled, showed him into the library, invited him to sit in one of the leather chairs. He didn't stay seated long—too much nervous energy. He paced the room as I signed the prescription pad he'd offered me, then stopped to collect my signature and peer at it through his bifocals.

"Max Murdock, is it?"

He said my name like he'd never heard it before and wanted to be sure.

"Do you ever read detective novels?"

"Nah." He shoved the pad back into his jacket pocket. "Don't have time for that kind of silliness. You have a real name, missy?"

"Jane. Jane Nichols."

He nodded sharply, apparently approving.

"Well, Jane, as long as I'm here, might as well look in on that scalawag. First baby I ever delivered, you know. Watched him grow up. Was the one who had to tell him his parents died in that car wreck. Saved his sister though."

My stomach twisted. His words lost meaning as I remembered huddling under an olive tree, staring up through its branches. Thick, black smoke darkened the sky. The smell of gasoline hung on the air.

I forced the memory aside, not wanting this piece of my childhood. I had stopped trying to remember long ago. Parents died, children lived. It happened all the time. What mattered now was killing Jim O'Neil.

I concentrated on Doc Reinhart.

"Pretty young thing," he was saying. "Ought to be married. Both of them." He picked up the leather medical bag he'd come in with, focused his bright blue eyes on me again. "Well, what are you standing there for? Be a good girl and take me to him."

"Yes, sir," I murmured.

I wondered how Alex had managed to escape the hospital when Doc Reinhart had wanted him to stay.

*   *   *

I was standing in the drive with Doc Reinhart, saying good-bye, when Tommy pulled up in a squad car. He rushed from it, automatically adjusting billy club and holster as he stood.

"Don't look so worried, Grayson," the doctor said. "Callaghan's got a hard head. And that thigh will heal. Be a nice addition to his scar collection. Only thing to do is keep him quiet for a few days. Rough job, but I'm sure you two can handle it. Call me if you need reinforcements."

With another sharp nod, Doc Reinhart climbed into his dented white station wagon and drove off.

Tommy brought lunch, compliments of his wife, Ginny.

"She thought you'd like to try some old-fashioned Southern cooking, Jane. And she also sends her thanks—the twins decided *not* to sleep through the night."

He opened containers, releasing a series of delicious smells.

"Shrimp pie. Benne seed—that's the same as sesame seed—biscuits. A tossed green salad. And for dessert—"

As Tommy pulled the lid off the last dish, Alex sighed long and loud.

"Ginnie's praline cookies. I do believe I've died and gone to heaven."

The three of us sat—rather, two of us sat and one of us lay—in Alex's bedroom. We balanced TV trays on our laps and ate as Tommy reported on the day's criminal activities. The most significant was a holdup at the All Cash Pawn Shop on Eisenhower and White Bluff.

"Three guys in a stolen van in broad daylight. They got seventy-six handguns."

Alex stopped eating, shook his head.

"Just what we need. More guns out on the streets."

"Yeah. Add to that the rumor of the day. Fort Stewart is experiencing a 'shrinkage' problem."

"Oh, fuck." Alex looked at me, grimaced. "Sorry."

I shrugged.

"I've heard worse. Is Fort Stewart a military base?"

Alex nodded.

"The largest Army installation this side of the Mississippi—three hundred thousand acres, give or take. About forty miles southwest of here. Home of the Third Infantry Division, Mechanized. That means warehouses full of field artillery, small arms, and munitions for tanks and helicopters. Any idea what's being stolen, Tommy?"

Tommy shook his head.

"No. I made some phone calls, but nobody's talking specifics. They sound real worried, though. I got the impression that the problem's ongoing."

"Shit. When was the last time we reminded our people to wear their vests?"

"Been a while."

"Might be a good time to tell them again. Especially the rookies. Especially the women. And tell them I don't give a damn if they don't like the way the things fit."

Tommy nodded. The rest of the meal was finished in silence. Tommy was still looking grim when he reached over to take Alex's empty plate. Suddenly, he snickered.

"Almost forgot. You had a visitor this morning. A very pissed-off tourist. He stormed in, thumped the front desk, demanded to see the chief of police. Ended up, he wanted to report his wallet stolen. He lost his driver's license, all his credit cards, and about seven hundred dollars in cash. Funny thing, seems his wallet disappeared while he was taking a little nap *all by himself* at the Azalea Motel over on Bonaventure 'Course, he's registered at the Mulberry."

Late that evening, I got ready for bed and settled more or less comfortably into the big chair in the library. One more night,

I had decided, just to be sure. The lamp was on, and I was scratching notes onto a lined pad, working over Andrew Jax's next scene, waiting for sleep.

A soft moan and the sound of movement in the bedroom broke my concentration. I raised my head, alert for trouble. When I heard nothing more, I went back to writing. The mantel clock chimed the hour, then the quarter hour, then the half hour. One-thirty.

"Jane?" Alex called.

"I'm here."

I walked across the darkened bedroom, switched on the bedside lamp. He was sitting up against the pillows, dark circles under his eyes, face pale and strained.

"Can't sleep. Saw the light under the door and figured you might still be working."

Earlier that afternoon, Alex had noticed that I was gathering up my typewriter and notes to move them upstairs.

"I put you out of your bed," he had said when I explained what I was doing. "I will not be accused of evicting you from your work area. Please."

I'd agreed. He didn't know I'd spent the previous night in the library. I didn't intend to let him know I was sleeping there again.

"I'm working on a scene, a bridge between a couple of chapters I've already written."

He looked interested—or perhaps just eager for distraction.

"I could read it to you," I said tentatively.

"Yeah, I'd like that." The lopsided smile beneath the drooping bandages on his forehead made him look very young. "It's been a long time since anyone read me a bedtime story."

I retrieved my notebook and glasses from the library. After arranging Alex's pillows more comfortably, I sat on the bed beside him and began reading in a low, soothing voice.

Jax glanced at his raw, rapidly swelling knuckles, then glared down at Karl Vickers. As a result of a well-timed uppercut, Vickers lay sprawled unconscious in the center of the office.

The place was a shambles. The job of methodical destruction Vickers had started as he searched the office had been finished when he and Jax slammed into the furniture as they fought.

Millicent, thought Jax, would be furious.

Pure luck that he had discovered Vickers. An irresistible yen for bourbon, no cash, and the memory of the half-empty fifth stashed in his center desk drawer had prompted Jax to drive into the Loop at dawn.

Vickers had dispatched the bourbon as he dismantled the office.

Jax kicked him once, hard, in the ribs.

"Stupid fucker."

He dragged Vickers across the floor, shoved him close to the front of the heavy metal desk. He tied his wrists together around one of the desk's stubby legs and his ankles together around another.

"That should hold you 'til I get back."

The petty cash was hidden in a sugar cube box next to the coffee pot. Jax took it, set out on a quest for an all-night liquor store.

I quit reading when I noticed that Alex was snoring gently on the pillow beside me. Another reader carried away by my gripping prose, I thought. I slipped quietly from the room, shut my own eyes a few minutes later.

The next day was much like the one before. At Alex's request, I cooked grits for breakfast. He taught me to pronounce "grits" with two syllables. Once we got past that bit of excitement, the temptation to put the man out of his misery grew with each passing hour. Headachy and bored, he spent the morning walking unsteadily around the house.

Around eleven, Joey arrived with lunch for three. The combined effect of food from the diner and Joey's relentless good humor improved Alex's disposition briefly. Then she left. I fought the urge to call her back. Instead, I cornered her brother—whom I'd caught trying to hobble up the stairs—and read him the riot act.

"You have a choice, Callaghan. Either you sit down and rest that bloody leg of yours or I will pick up the phone and call Doc Reinhart."

That brought us quickly to a mutual understanding. I retreated to the library to work on my book. Alex fled—actually, he limped—to the solarium and napped on one of the lounge chairs until dinnertime.

21

I thought I heard my grandfather's voice. Strange, because he was dead.

"Janie. Wake up."

Too early, I thought, though the morning light was bright against my eyelids. Let me sleep.

I raised my arm to brush the voice away. A stab of searing agony, centered in my right shoulder, stopped the movement almost before it began.

"Jane. Wake up."

Not my grandfather's voice. Douglas MacDonald's, authoritative, demanding.

Reluctantly, I opened my eyes.

My bed was in the center of an operating theater. Mac stood at my bedside, dressed in a white lab coat. His blue eyes were intense above the surgical mask covering his nose and mouth. Brilliant overhead lights glinted off the scissors he held in his right hand.

Carefully, methodically, he cut through the bandages that swaddled my shoulder.

He pushed the dressing aside.

"It's healing," he said.

He plunged the scissors point downward into the wound.

The phone rang. I flung myself from the bed in the guest room, snatched the receiver from the extension in the hallway.

"Jane, it's Tommy. Sorry to bother you, but I need Alex."

"I'll get him. Are you somewhere he can call you back?"

"Yeah." Tommy gave me the number. "I'll wait by the phone."

I disconnected. Dressed in my warm-up pants and a T-shirt, I hurried downstairs, slipped into the library, and paused at the doorway of the darkened bedroom. Alex's breathing was deep and regular. The only phone on the first floor was in the kitchen. Its ringing had apparently not disturbed him.

Too bad.

I wasn't particularly keen on waking anyone from a sound sleep. And not because I was kindhearted. Some people were dangerously unpredictable in those few seconds between sleeping and waking. In my opinion, a cop who'd soldiered in Vietnam fell into the high-risk category.

I'd once incautiously awakened a Scotland Yard inspector. He, too, had received an urgent phone call. After spending almost twenty-four hours working with us during an emergency, he had pillowed his head on his arms at an unoccupied table in the wardroom and fallen asleep. Feeling a bit sorry for the fellow, I walked up quietly behind his chair and gently touched his shoulder. A split second later, I was pinned flat against the table, staring up at a man whose forearm was pressed hard against my throat. The incident embarrassed the inspector, who apologized while emphasizing that I should never, *ever*, sneak up on someone like that. It also convulsed Brian and Jerry, who happened to be standing nearby, with laughter. I'd redefined the term "rude awakening."

So I was in no hurry to go dashing to Alex's bedside. Instead, I tapped on the open bedroom door.

"Alex, wake up. You have a call."

No response. Damn, I thought, my sympathy well under control. The deeper, the more exhausted his sleep, the more potentially dangerous his awakening. The bedroom had no overhead light. With a sigh, I crossed to Alex's bedside and turned on the lamp.

He lay unmoving, blankets in a tangled heap on the floor, head and injured leg nestled deeply into a clutter of pillows. I saw blue shorts, a grey sleeveless sweatshirt, acres of white gauze and adhesive tape, and a face lined with fatigue. Alex's eyelids twitched, his lips moved in silent speech. I wondered what dreams haunted *his* sleep.

Prepared for a violent response, I put my hand firmly on his shoulder and shook him while I called him again, more urgently this time. He opened his eyes, propped himself up on an elbow.

No aggression, just immediate wakefulness.

"What's wrong, Jane?"

"Tommy wants you to call. He left a number."

He glanced at the clock.

"Damn it! It's three in the morning."

But Alex's tone was more anxious than angry. He slid his bandaged leg carefully over the side of the bed and reached for his cane. I waited until he was steady on his feet, then went ahead to the kitchen to switch on the coffee.

By the time I pushed a steaming mug into Alex's hand, he was leaning against the kitchen counter with his head down, his eyes fixed on the floor, and the phone to his ear. He raised the coffee to his lips and sipped automatically, his attention absorbed by what Tommy was saying.

The past few days had been invaluable in establishing my cover with Alex. Dora had taught me that a little good-natured bullying went a long way toward building a relationship of trust. There was little need to involve myself further in his affairs. Logic, in fact, dictated that I avoid entangling myself with his professional life, leave him to his phone call, and go back to bed. But nothing short of a disaster would have prompted Tommy's call. Instinct, though I was hard pressed to say whether it was good or bad, demanded that I stay. So I poured myself some coffee and parked my hip on the edge of the kitchen table.

For a few minutes, Alex's side of the conversation was limited to monosyllables. Then he asked in an even voice, "Who found her?"

As Tommy answered, Alex lifted his head. His expression was absolutely bleak, unexpectedly reminding me that I'd wondered about his dreams. I thought, perhaps, that now I'd never need to ask.

"Call the coroner, but don't let anyone touch the body until I've seen it," Alex said finally. "I'll be there in thirty minutes—"

He stopped speaking abruptly. Tommy's deeper tones carried across the kitchen.

"Damn it, Grayson," Alex cut in, "back off. If I'd wanted a fucking nursemaid, I'd have asked for one."

He slammed the receiver into its cradle, glared at it for a moment, then sighed. "Shouldn't have done that," he muttered as he moved his shoulders and neck, working the tension from them.

His face was completely composed when he looked over at me.

"Thanks for the coffee, Jane. Before you go back to bed, would you do me one last favor? I can't face those stairs. Would you get me a clean uniform from my bedroom closet?"

I went on the errand, knowing bloody well I couldn't simply go back to bed and furious because I gave a damn about Alex's welfare.

Minutes later, I handed Alex his uniform, and the grim set of his jaw relaxed briefly into a smile. I returned it and reminded myself of the bitter consequences of emotional involvement. I wouldn't let it happen again.

I went upstairs, pulled on jeans and a white cotton shirt, ran a brush through my hair. What I intended was reasonable, I told myself. My safety and the success of my mission depended on strengthening my relationship with my host.

Within minutes, I returned to the kitchen by way of the servants' staircase. I poured myself another mug of coffee, slipped out the back door, used the illumination of a small penlight to pick my way carefully around to the front drive. As I checked carefully for wayward reptiles before each step, I convinced myself that Alex was nothing more than a pawn in a game I controlled.

By the time Alex emerged from the house, I was in my car, smoking a cigarette. There was no doubt in my mind that I was an absolute fool.

I waited until he'd made his way carefully down the steps before turning on the engine, putting the car into drive, and pulling up so the passenger side door was nearest him. I leaned over and pushed it open.

"Get in."

Alex bent to look into the car and shook his head.

"Thanks, but no. I'll drive myself."

"You're having enough trouble just walking. Why don't you save your energy for the crime scene?"

"I appreciate the gesture, but another girl's been killed. I don't want a civilian around."

I bit out my response, cursing myself for caring.

"I'm not asking to interfere with your investigation. I'm

simply offering to drive your stubborn ass into town. I swear I won't even step out of the bloody car."

Alex still hesitated.

"You've already antagonized one friend tonight. Are you trying for two?"

Alex grimaced, then smiled.

"Thanks, Jane. I'd love a ride."

He hung his cane over the back of the seat, slid in next to me. I had a moment, just before he extinguished the dome light by pulling the door shut, to admire his transformation from convalescent to tough cop. He'd removed the bandages from his head and combed his hair so that the only visible hint of injury was the bruising on his cheek. No bulky bandages showed beneath his uniform trousers, either. Only the tensing of his jaw and the flicker of muscles around his eyes betrayed his discomfort.

I pulled the car away from the house.

"Did you take the bandages off your leg, too?" I asked casually.

"No. I just put on a smaller dressing and taped it up tight. Feels fine that way."

The neighborhood we drove to had reached its social peak two centuries earlier, during a time when wealthy merchants built their houses near the river. Moss-hung oaks overhung the street, dwarfing the large houses built of yellow Savannah brick. The trees created an overhead canopy that filtered the moonlight. I'd seen the area in the daylight. Most of the houses were subdivided, a multitude of telltale mailboxes and utility meters marring the exteriors. Wealth had not disturbed the area for a long time.

Flashing lights and a roadblock marked the edge of the crime scene. Before we came to a full stop, a young, uniformed black woman moved a barricade aside and waved us through. In the rearview mirror, I saw her speak into a walkie-talkie.

A few yards farther along, I stopped the car across from one of the largest houses on the block. Tommy stood by the front walk, obviously expecting us. He crossed the street.

Equipped with his cane and a mulish expression, Alex was already pulling himself from the car. Tommy nodded coolly to him, then walked around to lean into my open window.

"I offered to send a driver, and he called me a fucking nursemaid. What's the secret of your success?"

"I called him names and promised to wait in the car."

Alex held on to the door frame, poked his head back into the car.

"Look, Tommy, I'm sorry for being rude. But you had enough to do without organizing transportation for me. And, Jane, all kidding aside, I won't have you waiting here. This could take all night. Go home. Get some sleep. I'll get a lift back to the station when we're through. Then I'll drive one of the patrol cars home."

"Damn it, Callaghan—" Tommy and I both began.

Amused, I turned to look at him and caught a flash of teeth as he gave me a quick grin.

"This po' white boy's a real slow learner," he said, exaggerating his drawl.

"Yeah," I replied, mimicking the accent. "He sho' as hell is."

"Shit! You're both impossible!" Alex snarled.

He stepped back from the car and slammed the door.

Tommy lingered beside my window. We watched Alex walk toward the house—a tall, limping figure eerily illuminated by the flashing blue lights of the squad cars blocking the ends of the street.

Alex paused to talk with a patrolman.

"He saved my life in 'Nam, you know," Tommy said mat-

ter-of-factly. "We'd escaped from the Vietcong and Alex,
well, they'd hurt him real bad. So I was the one who carried
him out of the jungle. Made me look real heroic. But he was
the reason we got through. The pigheaded bastard refused to
give up. 'It'd be mighty embarrassing,' he kept telling me, 'if
two Georgia boys got killed by a swamp that doesn't even
have gators.' Then he'd offer to carry *me* for a while. That was
such a goddamned impossibility that I'd laugh and—"

Alex shouted from across the street.

"Hey, Grayson! I sure as hell could use a little help over
here!"

Tommy grinned.

"He'd be lost without me. You gonna wait?"

I nodded.

"Thanks."

His long strides carried him quickly to Alex's side.

I waited, spending my time alternately catnapping and watching the procession of people and vehicles moving to and from
the crime scene. Press cars and television vans with logo-em-
blazoned side panels—WJCL, WTOC, WSAV—arrived
shortly after Alex and Tommy disappeared into the yard behind the house. Soon a sidewalk full of reporters, photographers, and cameramen blocked my view of the young
policewoman standing duty by the barricades. The ladies and
gentlemen of the press moved aside only once, jockeying ea-
gerly for position as a covered body was removed to a waiting ambulance. Then the ambulance sped away, and the
newspeople settled down to wait. Anticipation kept them restless. I dozed.

About an hour past dawn, I was awakened by an excited
murmur from the crowd. Reporters and onlookers surged forward as Tommy approached the edge of the police line.
Though his back was to me, his deep voice carried clearly.

"Chief Callaghan will have a statement for you in a few minutes."

Ignoring their shouted questions, he turned on his heel, went to a nearby squad car. He talked briefly with its driver and was handed a thermos. Then he walked over to my car.

"Coffee?"

I gestured for him to join me. As he slid into the car, I reached under the front seat and pulled out my abandoned mug. I steadied it as he poured. Then I took the plastic thermos cup from his hand and held it so that he could tip out some coffee for himself.

"What's going on?" I asked.

"In just a few minutes, the Chief will read a statement that he's prepared. It will say, basically, that another woman has been brutalized and strangled, that her identity is being withheld until the next of kin are notified, and that no, we don't have any new leads. Or clues. Or suspects. Or any fucking thing to get this bastard."

The flow of agitated words stopped abruptly. Tommy slammed the stopper back into the mouth of the thermos, gave it a violent twist, dropped it onto the floor. He took the thermos cup from me, turned away, stared at the crowd.

His voice was more controlled when he spoke again.

"This is victim number five, and there's no end in sight."

Alex read his statement, then answered the reporters' pointed—and, I thought, frightened—questions before returning to the car. His back was to the dispersing crowd, so only Tommy and I could see the exhaustion in his face as he tried not to lean too heavily on his cane. Tommy started moving from the car to help him. I put a restraining hand on his arm.

"Don't spoil the illusion."

Tommy looked at me for a moment, then nodded.

"Okay." He continued measuring Alex's progress. "But once he's in the car . . ."

I laughed.

"You knock him down. I'll steal his cane."

"And if you don't mind my riding along, maybe between us we can convince him to eat a hot meal."

"Agreed. But you know what he'll call us?"

"Fucking nursemaids?"

"Bloody right," I murmured as Alex pulled open the rear door.

Breakfast was nixed.

"Too much to do," Alex said quietly from the backseat. "If you wouldn't mind dropping us at the station, Jane. And then, please, go home. Make sure the door is locked. The alarm is on. Try to get some sleep."

His voice, which had become progressively weaker as he spoke, faded completely.

Tommy twisted quickly, reaching over the backseat to grab his friend's shoulder.

"Alex! Are you okay?"

Unmistakable fear colored Tommy's voice.

I glanced away from the traffic, looked at Alex, understood why. His head sagged against the car window, his eyes were closed. Every bruise and scrape was livid against the sudden pallor of his skin.

Alex opened his eyes.

"I'm fine," he murmured. "Just resting." He clasped his hand briefly over Tommy's outstretched arm, smiled weakly. "Relax. Don't you remember what they told us in boot camp? Marines don't bleed." Then he shifted his back into a corner, propped his injured leg along the seat, closed his eyes again. "Wake me when we get there."

Tommy settled back down beside me, but continued watching Alex anxiously in the rearview mirror.

"You're wrong, man," I heard him mutter under his breath. "Marines bleed plenty. They're just afraid to let it show."

22

22

Weeks passed. Blustery spring weather gave way to summer heat. Jax had been paid, in advance, for several surveillance jobs. Each involved getting proof of infidelity, but he'd decided to take them anyway. They were good money. If he was cautious and relied on his telephoto lens, he could pay his bills without collecting any bruises.

Everything was going fine until one day Jax found himself watching Millicent with more than lust. She was standing, back to him, putting folders in the battered green filing cabinet. She paused, turned her head, noticed him staring at her. She smiled sweetly, went back to work.

He didn't like the way he felt when she smiled at him that way. She's a broad, he told himself. A skirt. Something to be used and discarded.

Nothing more.

The sound of limping footsteps drifted up the narrow back stairs, awakening me very late that night. I lay in bed, listening to the alternating rhythm of footsteps and cane.

The sound was difficult to ignore. I gritted my teeth, reminded myself that I was already too involved, tried not to think of the pain Alex was in. I, too, had felt the raw compulsion to keep moving in spite of injury, to push body and mind beyond exhaustion. I knew just how counterproductive it was to push too far.

I listened to him crossing and recrossing the kitchen floor until I could bear it no longer. I left my bed and walked barefooted down the back stairs.

Moonlight glowed through the back window. There, outlined against it, was Alex. He had paused in his pacing and perched on the edge of a kitchen stool. His back was to me. His left elbow was braced against the window frame, his forehead was against his palm, his fingers were laced through his hair.

"Hey, supercop," I said softly, letting him know that I was there.

Then I joined him by the window, briefly touching the hand that rested on his cane. He didn't look away from the yard. He just lifted his head from his left hand and moved his cane so that his right arm extended behind me, encircling my waist.

In silence, we contemplated the world outside the window. And I waited.

"He's out there somewhere and he's content," Alex said finally. His voice was a cool whisper against the quiet night. "I *know* he's content. Almost peaceful. There was a guy just like him in 'Nam. A Marine who carved up nurses. I helped hunt him down, volunteered for escort duty when he was moved to Saigon. I wanted to talk to him—to find out *why*. He never made it to trial. Hung himself in his cell. I wasn't really surprised when I heard." He moved his chin in the direction of the river. "That guy out there, he's the same. For a while he'll convince himself that it's over, that he'll never need to kill again. But for him, it'll never be over. His need will grow, eat him alive. And when he can't stand it any longer—"

Abruptly, he stopped speaking. The arm around my waist tightened, the muscles along his jaw tensed, his body vibrated with ill-suppressed agitation. He swallowed hard, then became very still.

I knew that, but for my presence, he would have returned to his pacing.

"When he's finally stopped, I think he'll be relieved," Alex said finally. His voice was unnaturally calm.

"You're feeling sorry for the bastard? What about his victims?"

Come on, Alex, I thought. Let the feelings out. Then you'll be able to rest.

"I'm not trying to excuse the guy. Just trying to understand him. He's got to be stopped. Only—"

He stopped speaking again. His body jerked involuntarily.

This time, I didn't give him a chance to regain his composure.

"Only what, Alex? Only what?"

"Only I don't know if I can stop him." His voice trembled with nervous exhaustion and anger. "All right? Are you satisfied? Is that what you wanted to hear?"

I shifted in closer, wrapped my arm around his shoulders.

"Tell me about it."

In reply, I received only silence. Somehow I had mishandled him, I thought. There wasn't anything more to be done. Best to leave him alone, return to bed, snuggle down—

"If I were a better cop, maybe people in my town wouldn't be dying," Alex said slowly. "Maybe those young girls . . ." Then his words began pouring out, one on top of the other, each sentence more agitated than the last. "All day long, their faces look out at me from the bulletin board. Black-and-white glossy prints. Night after night, I see them in my sleep. And others, too. Girls I know. Joey. Her friends. Women I've dated. Made love to. And Jane, I've warned them to be careful. Warned them again and again and again. You know what they do? They smile at me. They say 'Sure, Alex honey. Sure.' They don't take me seriously 'cause they're convinced I'm some sort of hero who can keep them safe. Well I can't. *I can't!* I've got no leads, no chance to catch this guy. All I can do is wait, hoping that he'll make a mistake, knowing that he'll strike again. And then there'll be another one dead, God damn it, dead!"

He turned from the window, wrapped his arms around my waist, pressed his face into my shoulder.

I held him. I stroked his back, whispered soothing words, waited for him to relax. Then, I knew, his body's demand for sleep would become overpowering. I stood staring past him, out into the darkly shifting shapes of the trees, and held him tight. Eventually, his body sagged against mine.

I waited for a few minutes, then pressed my lips to the top of his head.

"Hey, supercop, it's time we both went to bed."

With a little sigh, he straightened.

"Yeah, I think you're right." Still holding me within the circle of his arms, he added, "You must be awfully tired. You know, it's a long way up to that second-floor bedroom. Since the bed that I'm sleeping in is really yours . . . Maybe we could share it. Tuck each other in. I know a wonderful bedtime story."

I laughed. He *was* feeling better.

"Not in the script," I said.

I landed a chaste kiss on his forehead and sent him hobbling off to bed.

23

The moon-faced, grey-haired policeman smiled when he saw me.

"Hey, Miz Nicols."

I matched his drawl.

"Hey, Randy. How's it goin'?"

The question was purely rhetorical. Randy was three months away from a much anticipated retirement and staffed the front desk during the relatively peaceful seven A.M. to three P.M. shift with enthusiastic good humor.

His smile widened.

"A couple weeks hangin' around the station, and you're startin' to talk without an accent, Miz Nichols."

Two weeks, I thought, as I laughed at Randy's joke. Two weeks since driving Alex and Tommy from the murder scene to the station and staying to share strong coffee and warm donuts with them. Two weeks since Tommy's suggestion that the best way to understand cops was to observe them as they worked. Two weeks, and the faces populating each shift were now familiar. So were investigation techniques and patrol patterns.

Bless Tommy Grayson. Thanks to him, I felt secure enough to kill Jim O'Neil. Not, as I'd originally thought, from the rooftop overlooking his riverfront warehouse. Savannah's cops, I discovered as I rode around in the uniformly uncomfortable rear seats of their patrol cars, were solicitous of their town's businesses. Frequent and overlapping patrol patterns in the area of the warehouse made O'Neil's residence a better risk for escaping undetected.

"Is the Chief in?"

"Sure is." Randy's smile wavered. He jerked his head toward the doorway behind the desk. "He and Detective Sergeant Grayson are having a discussion."

I peered past him, saw the two men standing in Alex's glass-enclosed office. The body language was unmistakable.

"Who's winning?"

Randy's grin reemerged. "Not worth my job to say, ma'am."

I grinned in return. Leaving a personal message with the desk sergeant was as effective as taking out an ad.

"Well, I'd planned to invite them to join me for lunch before I drove down the coast to play tourist. But I think that, under the circumstances, I'll just be on my way. If you wouldn't mind, though, would you remind Alex that I'll probably spend the night at a motel somewhere near Beaufort? I don't want him worrying."

"I'll tell him, Miz Nichols. Have a nice drive."

Actually, the drive took only minutes. It ended on West Liberty, in a crowded public parking lot adjoining the Savannah DeSoto Hilton. I parked in a middle row, walked several blocks. I planned on spending Saturday afternoon in Forsyth Park.

I sat for hours with a drawing pad and an assortment of colored pencils in my lap. Azaleas splashed the park with color—an impressionist painting in hues of pink, crimson, orange, and white. I'd chosen the drawing pencils to match, then added a range of greens and browns for trees and foliage. The sunny afternoon had drawn crowds of tourists and picnickers to the gardens and central fountain.

Nestled in one corner of the park was a playground—a child's delight with climbable sculptures, a wading pool, sandboxes and swings, and brightly enameled slides. I sat on the wooden bench facing the largest slide.

Over the hours, a parade of children climbed the tall ladder to the top of the slide and disappeared into its covered upper platform, only to be disgorged seconds later—dizzy and laughing—at the bottom of the enclosed, corkscrew-shaped chute. I drew, answered friendly inquiries about my artwork, and watched the elegant rowhouse across the street from the playground.

The view through the upper half of the lenses I wore made nonsense of my sketches, but effectively closed the distance between the bench and the house. I was almost certain that O'Neil lived in the rowhouse, but by seven o'clock, I feared that belief wouldn't be confirmed. Over the past hour, joggers had steadily replaced the families and tourists populating the park. Now, with dark clouds and a chilly breeze making rain imminent, even the joggers' numbers were dwindling. I was in danger of becoming the park's sole visitor, a situation inadvisable when maintaining a low profile. Fifteen minutes longer, I thought. Then I'd abandon my vigil.

Five minutes later, a white BMW drove past and pulled into the carport adjoining the rowhouse. A large man in a business suit got out, glanced at the threatening sky, rushed to the rear of the car, took a sack of groceries from the boot. Even without my special lenses, his bright red hair was clearly visible. I watched, with hatred tightening my chest and making breathing difficult, until he went into the house.

I stood, tucked pad, pencils, and glasses into my shoulder bag and walked toward O'Neil's house. I intended only to memorize the BMW's license number. But as I approached, he pulled open the drapes that covered the tall, narrow front windows. He stood for a moment, gazing out at the park, with a well-lit room behind him.

Weeks of deadly intention crystallized into a workable plan. I've got you, you bastard. I've got you.

I reached the car only moments ahead of the rain. Mac had provided the slim canvas bag that was in the boot. It contained a pair of thin cotton gloves and a sniper's rifle. With its optical sight, the 7.62 mm Dragunov had a range of thirteen hundred meters. The distance from the playground to O'Neil's living room was not nearly that great.

I took the canvas bag and a long, hooded raincoat from the boot, then locked myself into the car. I needed full darkness for my plan to work. Full darkness, open curtains, and a cool head. I kept my hatred under control as, shielded by the steady flow of water down the windshield, I transferred the Walther from my shoulder bag to the raincoat's right pocket. Then I moved the car closer to the park.

At nine o'clock, I slipped into the raincoat and unzipped the canvas bag. I put on the cotton gloves before removing the rifle and its magazine from the bag. If need be, I could abandon the rifle. It was of Russian manufacture and was clean—no fingerprints, no identifying marks. Nothing to connect it to me or the organization.

I slipped the Dragunov's rectangular magazine into my left pocket. Then, leaving the rifle's hollow butt folded, I hid it inside the raincoat, beneath my left arm. I pulled my hood down so that it concealed much of my face, got out of the car, and walked back towards the park in the rain.

Half a block later, I spotted a squad car cruising slowly down Barnard. Although I knew it was a routine patrol, I sought shelter in the shadows of a tall hedge. The officers in the car—Merle and Dave, if I wasn't mistaken—would feel compelled to warn a woman walking alone that she was in jeopardy. Like most of the cops I'd talked with in the past weeks, they had expressed the hope—but not any real belief—that vigilance would prevent the next murder.

Inconvenient if they recognized me. Also bloody inconvenient if the strangler were to turn up in the park tonight. I'd have to delay killing O'Neil.

Not unexpectedly, the playground was deserted. I walked back to the place where I'd been sitting and noted, with relief, that rectangular patches of light still glowed from the house on Whitaker.

The ladder to the top of the slide was slick with rain. I climbed it carefully, then crawled, feet first, into its covered platform. Inside the cramped interior, I lay on my side with my legs dangling down into the chute. I pulled the Dragunov from my coat, unfolded its butt, and snapped in the magazine, which held a standard ten rounds. I loaded one round into the chamber.

I doubted I'd need more than one shot to kill O'Neil.

I rolled so that my belly was pressed against the wet metal, steadied the rifle with my left hand and elbow. Ignoring the water dripping steadily onto my back, I put my right eye to the scope, let the crosshairs drift until they were centered on the rowhouse's front windows. I settled in to wait. After a few minutes, the wind-driven rain brought thoughts of another wet night.

Brian Hurst was late, and I was tired of waiting.

I stood in the darkness of an alley in Manchester, in the icy rain, with my back pressed into the questionable concealment of a very damp brick wall, and cursed the man. I'd been waiting for a long time. Long enough that the bricks had leached every bit of warmth from my body. Long enough that my violent, uncontrollable shivering threatened to betray my position to anyone who happened by.

Why send me as a messenger? I wondered bitterly. Certainly Mac knew that, where Brian Hurst was concerned, I was the wrong choice. Although training with the man had improved my survival skills dramatically, those weeks did little to endear us to each other. And if Mac thought that assigning us to the same team would force us to reach some kind of accord—well, six months had more than demonstrated that we didn't work well together. Even Mac had finally grown tired of our constant bickering. Certainly I'd felt nothing but relief when Hurst left London to work undercover. And now . . .

Damn him, I thought, peering down the darkened street as a gust of icy wind whipped the rain almost vertically against me. No bloody Brian Hurst.

For a few minutes, just for distraction, I worked on being philosophical. I tried to convince myself that there were advantages to being thoroughly drenched and nearly hypothermic. Impossible to tell, for instance, how much of the liquid soaking my clothing was water and how much was blood. Comforting, that. And the gash inflicted by a switchblade skittering along my ribs—unchecked by the wholly inadequate windbreaker I wore—bothered me less now that I was thoroughly cold.

The kid had come up behind me on rubber soles. I'd heard him almost in time. Nothing more than a murderous little thief, I thought disgustedly. My bad luck to be chosen as his victim. His bad luck that I'd broken his arm taking his knife away. Thinking about how I would explain the incident in my report provided another few minutes of distraction from my thoroughly miserable state.

Then I thought of Brian Hurst again. I'd just begun another heartfelt mental recitation of every rude word I knew when the object of my ire appeared. He emerged from a nearby alley, lingered there for a moment, then walked slowly down the street.

The fleece-lined collar of his leather jacket was pulled up against the bite of the rain. I hated him all the more because he looked warm.

He passed the place where I stood.

"I have a message," I said.

Without breaking stride or looking in my direction, he nodded.

I stayed where I was until I was sure he wasn't followed. Then, avoiding the headlights of passing cars and detouring around the weak illumination of the area's few unbroken streetlights, I joined him at the prearranged place, in the shelter of a storefront several blocks away.

I huddled into the relative warmth of the recessed doorway. Brian stood opposite me. He was within arm's reach but, in the darkness, was little more than a murky figure.

"Mac says abort."

"No." His resolve was unmistakable even in that single, quietly spoken word. "I'm too close to quit now. You tell him that."

I loaded as much antipathy into my voice as I could muster.

"Mac says, and I quote, 'Tell Hurst that he may not do personal penance at the organization's expense. His situation has deteriorated dangerously, and I will not condone suicide. Tell that young bastard that I want him back. Now.'"

I wondered if my voice sounded as odd to Brian as it did to me. I was beginning to feel truly ill, but I'd be damned if I'd let him know that.

Brian spaced out his words for emphasis.

"I am not coming back."

"Mac directed me to bring you in forcibly if necessary."

His laughter carried from the darkness where he stood.

"You? How exactly did he expect you to manage that, M'lady?"

The last word was delivered in the same offensive drawl he'd used so often in the past. This time, I was beyond caring.

"I don't fucking know. But he *does* expect it, and I'll fucking do it."

My voice cracked as a violent shudder caught me unprepared. Suddenly, I was hurting terribly in spite of the cold. Damn it, Mac, I thought wearily, if this fuckwit wants to die, let him.

I left the shelter of the storefront. The icy wind hit me full force. Shuddering uncontrollably, I staggered another step forward, into the wash of headlights from a turning car. Cursing my carelessness, I turned so that the driver would catch only a glimpse of my back, stepped back into the recessed doorway as the car swept past.

I found myself face-to-face with Brian.

"My God, woman, you're hurt! Why the hell didn't you say anything?"

He stripped off his jacket, wrapped it around my shoulders. I tried to shrug it away.

"I don't want your help. And I won't have you blaming me for ruining your jacket."

"Sod the jacket." He put an arm around my shoulders, pulled me into the shelter of his body. "Be grateful you're so incompetent. You've blundered yourself into the only situation that could make me return to London."

I pressed my eyes shut for a moment, resting them as I forced the memory away. I refocused on the room beyond the windows.

Waiting.

O'Neil stepped into my sights. I kept the crosshairs on him as he walked across the room. He bent to get a magazine from the coffee table, then stood. The crosshairs were on his back.

I took a deep breath, released it slowly through my mouth,

imagined my bullet speeding toward its target. I began squeezing the trigger as I envisioned the bullet slamming into his body, splintering his ribs, tearing through his heart, exploding from his chest . . .

A wave of nausea swept over me. The crosshairs wavered. I breathed rhythmically, willed my stomach to settle down.

Waiting.

Mac had been wrong. I didn't need to see O'Neil's eyes when I killed him. My desire for revenge no longer ran hot and violent, as it had in the first months after Brian's death. It had become part of me—a cold, dark place in my soul.

I steadied the rifle against my shoulder again. O'Neil was pacing the floor, thumbing through the magazine. He stopped, stood reading with his head centered exactly in my sights.

I had seen someone else die that way.

That memory, detached from time and circumstance, brought with it the sure knowledge that O'Neil's head would fragment into bits of hair and flesh and bone, that clots of blood and brains would darken the glass of the windshield, drip from the steering wheel, spatter my face and hands—

My stomach cramped violently, banishing thoughts of the past. Urgently, I put the rifle aside. I sought the edge of the platform, vomited into the darkness. Then I pulled back into the shelter, lay with my forehead pressed against the platform's cool metal surface, waited for the trembling weakness to pass.

I picked up the rifle, peered through the scope.

O'Neil was still reading.

No more waiting.

I took a deep breath, concentrated on my target, exhaled slowly.

I held my breath, began squeezing the trigger.

A little more pressure—

I wrenched my face away from the scope.

I couldn't do it. God damn my inhibitions to hell, I couldn't.

I was not an assassin.

I lay the rifle down on the platform, put my head down next to it. For a time, hot tears of shame and frustration mixed with the cold puddle beneath my cheek.

With a heart filled with regret, I clambered stiffly down the ladder.

"It's about time, Janie."

Startled, I jerked around. An old woman detached herself from the shadows at the end of the slide's corkscrew chute. My blind spot.

There was something about the way she stood, something I recognized.

"John?" I said in a strangled voice. "John Wiggins?"

"One and the same, dearest Jane. Now suppose we get in out of the rain?"

24

I stepped from the shower, began toweling myself dry.

"Exactly how long have you been in Savannah?" I asked loudly.

John had a suite at the Hilton—a bathroom, a sitting room and two bedrooms. He had checked in, I supposed, as two people. Elderly mother and middle-aged bachelor son, unless I missed my guess. From the park, we had separated briefly, each driving our own car the few blocks to his hotel. The parking lot adjoining the Hilton was the same one I'd parked at earlier in the day. I wondered if the coincidence had amused John.

The room's accommodations included a well-stocked bar. John had helped me out of my dripping raincoat and immediately fixed us each a drink—tonic water for himself, Scotch for me. I'd pretended to take a sip, then accepted his offer of a clean, dry shirt and the use of the shower.

John raised his voice so that I could hear him from the next room.

"Actually, I arrived before you did. I didn't need to wait,

you see, for a courier from London, and I was concerned that it might take a little time to set up surveillance. But if the job had been any *easier*. Doesn't your friend Alex ever lock a door? And that alarm system! Even *I* got past it. The other morning, I temporarily disabled the exterior alarm and by-passed the phone line, went inside, and took the back door off the circuit. Bloody inconvenient not to be able to fix myself the occasional cuppa while you two were out."

I dropped the damp towel over the side of the tub, stood naked, shaking my head. Hard to know whether to be impressed by the man's cheekiness or appalled that I hadn't noticed his invasion of the house. After a moment, humor—and the thought of John having afternoon tea in Alex's kitchen—won out. I snickered.

I pulled my damp underwear and jeans back on, took the Walther from the shelf beside the tub, and tucked it against the small of my back. I buttoned on the dark blue dress shirt John had provided, left its tails hanging loose. After using John's comb to pull the tangles from my damp hair, I joined him in the sitting room.

John had changed, too.

An old lady had accompanied me through the lobby. She wore sensible shoes, a boxy dress in a shade of pale lavender, and matching gloves. On the way to the elevator, she'd clung to my arm, chattering in a high, breathless voice and an accent reminiscent of the Queen Mum's. She'd admired the Oriental vases and crystal chandeliers in the lobby, talked about the importance of afternoon tea as we traveled to the sixth floor. We'd entered the suite, and I'd left her sitting on the edge of a chair with her ankles primly crossed.

She had been replaced by a slim, sandy-haired man in slacks and a dressing gown. He looked much as he had years earlier when he, Brian, and I had spent the evening together.

When I entered the room, John stood. He handed me my drink with a gracious smile, waited until I was seated comfortably on the couch, then settled back into a nearby armchair.

I set the drink aside.

"You bugged the house."

"The house, the phone, your car. How is Alex feeling, by the way? Since that girl died, the tapes have been quite boring. Far more interesting those first few days. Now, with the two of you popping in and out all the time, it seems that all I've done is listen to the front door slamming, dodge headlights as the two of you drive back and forth through that mosquito-infested front yard, and follow you as you wander around—how did you phrase it? Oh, yes—soaking up local color. Then, just as that poor, beleaguered cop of yours settles back into something resembling a normal routine, you decide to kill someone else on his turf. Had you managed it, your Alex would have been very upset."

"Well, I didn't manage it. And you didn't try to stop me when I made the attempt. So I can only assume that Mac sent you to make sure there were no embarrassing loose ends left *after* I'd killed O'Neil. Were you going to take me back, John? Or were you instructed to eliminate me here?"

John stared down at his drink. Grey silk gloves had replaced the old lady's lavender lace. He swirled the glass gently. Ice tinkled softly against the sides of the tumbler.

He looked up, calmly met my eyes.

"If you really think that, then what the hell are you doing here with me?"

"Trying to find out what happens next. Has Mac reserved a locked room for me in that nice little clinic north of London?"

I pulled the Walther from my waistband, pointed it at him.

John's composure was finally shaken.

"Jesus Christ, woman, you really don't trust anyone, do you?"

"Not a soul."

"Well, then, it's time you learned who your friends are."

He put his drink on the table next to mine, picked up my tumbler of Scotch, took a healthy swallow, and grimaced before setting it down again.

"First, I did not drug your drink."

Then he stood. Holding his hands away from his sides, he moved deliberately toward me.

I rose from my chair, leveled the Walther at his belly.

"Don't come any closer."

He stopped.

"If I'd wanted to take you, I could have stepped up behind you in the dark this evening and done just that."

"Risky. Mac must have told you that I had a side arm. It's no secret that I'm good with a knife. Even if you'd managed to subdue me, it's bloody inconvenient to remove a body—dead or alive—from a public place. And it would have been counterproductive to leave my body behind for the Americans to ID. My Alex, as you call him, would have eventually traced me back to the organization."

"My, my, my. Brian told me once that you were more like Mac than you knew. Fire and ice, he said. Now it shows."

He took another step forward.

I kept the Walther steady.

"I'll kill you."

"Not in cold blood. You're not put together that way. Mac knows that. So do I. So did Brian." He tilted his head, narrowed his eyes. "Brian never told you what caused his nightmares, did he?"

If he wanted an emotional response, I disappointed him.

"Brian has nothing to do with this."

"Did you know that Brian was determined to die? That before you came along, nothing—nothing—mattered enough to stop him?"

"Leave it alo—"

John stepped forward so that his abdomen touched the barrel of the Walther, nearly startling me into pulling the trigger. I fought the impulse, discovered that his maneuver had trapped me. The backs of my legs were against the couch. If he attacked, there was only one way I could stop him.

I didn't want to kill him. He was one of Mac's people—one of *our* people—and Brian's trusted friend. And I would have as much problem disposing of a corpse as he would.

"Move your hands and you're a dead man."

"I just want your full attention."

"Believe me, you have it," I said harshly. I watched his outstretched arms for any flicker of movement. "For the last time. Why . . . are . . . you . . . here?"

"Because Mac suggested I contact you as soon as you realized you couldn't assassinate O'Neil. And because I owe you for every moment of life you gave my closest friend. I try to pay my debts."

"All you owe me is an explanation of your presence in Savannah."

"Whether you approve or not, the explanation involves Brian."

He paused. When I didn't speak, he continued.

"It actually begins several months before you met him. We had infiltrated a gang that was expanding, violently, into the drug scene. Everything was going well until I—"

John's lips compressed into a tight line, his pale eyes flickered away from my face. I moved the Walther slightly against his abdomen. His attention shifted abruptly to it, then back to me.

"Suffice to say, I made a mistake—a stupid, trivial mistake—and was found out. I was snatched from my digs, stuffed into the boot of a car, and driven to an abandoned house in Liverpool. There, in one of the upstairs rooms, my captors began extracting information—and revenge—with a great deal of enthusiasm."

John's arms wavered.

"Don't!"

He froze. For the first time, something resembling fear touched his eyes. For all his bravado, I was an unknown factor. If I panicked and pulled the trigger, he would certainly die.

I looked at him, wishing I could put some distance between him and the Walther without weakening my position. But he'd given me no options.

"It would be most regrettable if, instead of killing O'Neil tonight, I killed you."

"That would be unfortunate. So with your permission, dear Jane, I'll put my hands behind my head. We'll both be more comfortable that way."

I nodded. He linked his gloved fingers behind his neck.

"Even among professionals, your Brian was good. He had brains and he was fast. Damned fast. He discovered what had happened, guessed where I had been taken, called for assistance, and decided not to wait until it arrived.

"When he found me, there was just one man with me, keeping watch. Not that there was any chance I'd escape, you understand. But I kept passing out. The sodding bastard would call the others back whenever I came to.

"Brian slipped into the room just as that sod discovered I was conscious again, was leaning over the bed with one hand twisted in my hair. Brian cut the fellow's throat, lowered the body to the floor. Then he cut the ropes that bound my wrists and ankles to the bedposts.

" 'Hang on, John,' he said. 'I'll be back for you.'

"I knew then, knew from his voice, from his dark, empty eyes . . ."

John's voice trailed off. He tipped his head back, pressed his eyes shut, exhaled slowly as he lowered his head and looked at me.

I wanted to look away. I wanted to be away from this place, away from this man, away from his manipulations.

"Very dramatic," I said. "Did you rehearse with Mac?"

"No, I didn't."

The words were almost whispered, but I heard an undercurrent of anger. I wondered why John cared what I believed.

I prodded him with the tip of the Walther.

"Intermission's over. The play must go on."

John's lips compressed.

"Brian left me," he snapped. Almost immediately, he looked mildly embarrassed. "Mac warned me about you, but I didn't expect—" He took a breath, fixed his eyes on mine, and repeated more moderately: "Brian left me there. I lay for a long time, concentrating on the silence. Then I heard an automatic firing. Two shots. An Uzi clattered. There was another shot. After that, more silence.

"I was convinced that Brian was dead. Convinced that they would return, that they would continue . . . But when the door swung open, he was there. Wounded, bleeding, holding an automatic clenched in his hand.

"He said, 'There, John. You're safe now.' "

John paused. He looked at me expectantly, as though I should have found something significant in his words.

"It's getting late. What's your point?"

John sighed.

"My point is that Brian saved my life, probably saved lives among those who came to rescue us, by killing everyone he found in that house. He eliminated the sadist who guarded me, and a man and a woman in a nearby room. Another woman and two men were downstairs in the kitchen. One of the men made a grab for the Uzi. Brian killed all three of them.

"Afterwards, he found out that the young woman in the kitchen was working for us. He was devastated. He wasn't a killer by nature. He believed in the system, in British law and British justice. Our superiors felt his actions were justified. So did our peers. But that didn't matter. Brian knew that he'd lost control, stepped over the edge.

"'I murdered that girl,' he kept saying. 'I went into that house looking for revenge, and I murdered that girl.'"

I kept my face composed, my eyes on John, my weapon steady. But I wanted nothing more than to pull the trigger. I remembered too vividly Brian's nightmare-driven cries and the anguish that lingered when he awoke.

"You were his friend. He wouldn't have left you alone if you had asked him to stay. Why didn't you try to stop him?"

John regarded me with washed-out blue eyes.

"Stop him? Yes, perhaps I could have. I let him go, and that is something *I* have to live with. But I wanted that bloody, brutal, mindless revenge. Wanted it more than . . ."

Abruptly, John looked away. He took a deep breath, fixed his attention on the Walther that threatened his life. Ignoring my growled threat, he moved his hands deliberately from behind his neck. He held them between us, fingers pointing upward, palms toward me. His dressing gown sagged away from his fine-boned wrists. Pale, twisted lines of scar tissue crossed and recrossed his forearms.

"When Brian found me, I'd been tied to that bed for hours. They started with my hands. After that . . ."

John choked. Through the gun that I held pressed against his belly, I could feel the shudder that swept his slight frame. But his hands were steady as he peeled off his gloves. They remained unwavering as he held them out for my examination. He turned them slowly so that I could see.

When he put the scarred, nailless fingers of his left hand against the barrel of the Walther and pushed it aside, I didn't resist.

25

I spent the better part of an hour collecting the listening devices that John had planted around Alex's house. He'd mentioned eight bugs, which hadn't taken much time to locate. But well-developed paranoia had prompted me to double-check the rooms downstairs. I'd found four more bugs.

I tucked the handful of devices into a pocket of my equipment bag, locked everything back in the car, then changed into a soft jersey shirt and sweatpants, and sprawled onto my bed. I was right not to trust him, I thought. I was right not to trust anyone.

If I hadn't already been so comprehensively miserable, I would have been furious. But I was too exhausted to be angry. I closed my eyes, willed myself to relax, to get some sleep. The evening had cost me far too much mental and physical energy. I needed to rest, to regroup.

Tomorrow, I thought. I'll make my decisions tomorrow.

John's words kept trailing through my mind, making sleep impossible.

I would make my decisions tonight.

Impulsively, I abandoned my bed, crossed the brightly lit foyer, switched off the alarm, then sought refuge in the darkened living room. I opened the French doors and curled into the far corner of the sofa. The damp, cool breeze blew against my face and ruffled my hair.

I had failed miserably. Mac had known that I would.

I constructed a sentence to add to my personnel file: "Psychologically unfit to eliminate a self-selected target." Nice euphemism for, "She set out to execute a man she hated but was too squeamish to do it."

Not that it should matter to me what was in my file. I had quit the organization. I didn't want to work for Mac again.

I wanted to rest. To write my book. To kill Jim O'Neil.

Earlier, John had outlined what Mac wanted.

I stood looking out at the storm from the window of his hotel room, drinking my Scotch, getting a firm grip on the emotional upheaval his revelations had caused.

"He wants you back," John said. "He also wants O'Neil as badly as you do. If you had been willing to work with us, well, an accommodation could have been reached earlier."

I turned from the window.

"I don't want an accommodation. I want O'Neil."

John poured himself another glass of tonic.

"Mac gave you, quite literally, your shot at him." He picked up the tongs, added ice to his drink. "He suggests that it's now time to do things our way. He's offering you control of the operation. You'll receive whatever support you require to disrupt O'Neil's activities and bring him to justice. If it is acceptable to you, I will assist and liaise so that you can maintain the cover you've established. Mac has already contacted friends in Washington. While you were showering, a signal was sent. The operation is now sanctioned, unofficially, on both sides of the Atlantic."

"And if I refuse to work with you? I can still force O'Neil into a confron—"

"I wouldn't advise that." His eyes met mine over the top of his glass. "Mac has superiors, too. Ones who regard a renegade agent with far less tolerance than he does."

"I see."

And I did see. Suddenly there was something about John— a distant, passionless quality that he undoubtedly intended I see—that made his position clear. If our shared friendship with Brian wasn't enough to gain my cooperation, John would seek other ways to eliminate me as a potential embarrassment to his employers.

I crossed to the bar and freshened my own drink.

"You don't work for Mac, do you?"

He laughed. The warm, slightly affected personality reemerged.

"Let's say, Jane love," he said in his cultivated voice, "that both Mac and I feel a certain sense of obligation where you are concerned. But I do not share your scruples. Or Mac's. Or Brian's, for that matter."

He raised his drink to his lips, then lowered it. For a time, he stood contemplating the gloved hand that held his glass.

"Had the gods been kinder," he said slowly, "it would have been I—not Brian—who roamed the house that night. I would not have felt his pain."

I sat in the darkness in Alex's living room, weighing my options.

Outside, thunder cracked and lightning flashed. With a roar, the rain began again.

The gutters overflowed, creating a curtain of water just beyond the screens. Strobes of lightning seemed to hold the droplets in place, suspending them brightly for a moment in time.

I could stay in Savannah and work for the organization.

I could go home to England and never stop looking back.

"For God's sake, stop fussing." I sank gratefully onto the edge of the bed and kicked off my shoes. "I had quite enough of that at the hospital. It was only a scratch."

Brian emptied a kit bag full of medication onto the bedside stand.

"That scratch was half a dozen inches long and complicated by pneumonia. Bloody stupid of you to stand there in the freezing rain."

"I suppose you would have toddled off to the nearest doctor and left Mac's message undelivered until the weather cleared."

He stripped back the blanket, motioned me to tuck my legs under it.

"On the contrary, I wouldn't have let that little bastard fillet my ribs in the first place. Silly girl, I thought you'd learned something from me."

I looked up at him as he tucked a pillow in behind me.

"Perhaps you should stay in London for a while and conduct another training session. Call it remedial street fighting."

An amused smile touched his lips, lingered for just a moment. Then his lips tightened. The smile was gone.

I thought, as I had frequently during his visits to my hospital room, that laughter was a skill Brian seemed to have forgotten.

Brian crossed the room, pointed at my suitcase.

"Where do you want this?"

"Anywhere."

He pulled a chair nearer the bed, put the suitcase on it, struggled briefly with the clasps before popping the lid open. I lay against the pillows and watched him, wishing that he'd be still for a few minutes. Since we'd gotten to my flat, he hadn't once met my eyes.

"Would you like a cuppa?" he asked over his shoulder. He was already moving toward the bedroom door. "I'll put the kettle on."

I reached the end of my patience.

"No, damn it! There's only one thing I want, Brian Hurst."

My words stopped him mid-stride. He turned slowly, stared at me. He looked much as he had the first time we'd met—an intensely physical man with melancholy brown eyes, dressed in faded jeans and a turtleneck. I wondered how I'd convinced myself I hated him.

"What's that, Jane?" His voice was little more than a whisper.

"You."

He took a step toward me, hesitated. Stood, restlessly running his fingers through his curly brown hair.

"Someone like you . . . You can't want the likes of me."

"I want you. I've always wanted you."

He took another step, stiffened, turned away.

"You don't know a bloody thing about me. You've clearly mistaken my sense of duty for something else."

Too late, Brian, I thought. I've seen the man hidden behind that tough, hostile posturing.

I slipped from my bed, stepped up behind him, touched his shoulder.

"I haven't made a mistake. You care for me."

He shrugged my hand away, swung around, faced me.

"You're wrong. I don't care for anyone."

He was almost believable. His voice was brutal, his expression hard. But he couldn't disguise what was in his eyes. Ignoring everything except what I saw there, I wrapped my arms around him.

He stood rigidly, his hands clenched at his sides. But there was agony in his dark brown eyes.

I touched his lips with mine, desperately seeking to overcome all the carefully nurtured antagonism of the past months.

"Please, my darling."

With a deep groan, Brian wrapped his arms around me. He lifted me from my feet, carried me to my bed, laid me down against the pillows. His kiss betrayed a hunger rivaling my own.

The unforgiving world that was my reality ceased to exist when his hands and lips were upon me, when his lean, hard body moved in rhythm with mine. I touched his face, stroked his angular cheeks, ran my fingertips over his warm lips, brushed my fingers through the dark tumble of curls on his forehead.

I love you, Brian.

The thought brought with it a surge of pure terror. All my life, everyone I'd ever loved . . . My hands tightened convulsively on his shoulders. Please, don't you leave me, too!

The movement of his body slowed. He tilted his head to one side, studied me seriously. Then he brushed his lips across the backs of my hands.

"My lovely Lady Jane, don't be afraid."

He smiled with such reassuring tenderness that my fear didn't matter. He was in my arms and I wanted him—dear Lord, how I wanted him. I stopped thinking, stopped analyzing. I abandoned myself to him, trusting him, loving him. His body's caresses aroused me, nurtured me. His touch pushed me to the limits of my control and then, suddenly, beyond. I arched my body beneath him. He moved against me, and his lips descended, capturing my cries of joy.

*　　*　　*

The sound of an engine and the sweep of headlights across the porch wrenched me back to the present. The car scrunched to a halt, the engine was cut. Familiar footsteps crossed the porch. Alex came in, abandoning his rain gear at the door.

I stayed where I was, huddled wretchedly in the darkness, and watched him cross the foyer. Goodnight, Alex, I thought, willing him to go upstairs. I wanted to be alone. But as with so much else, what I wanted made very little difference.

He paused in the doorway, framed by the light from the foyer, then stepped inside the living room. He extended an arm toward a nearby floor lamp.

"Please, Alex, don't turn the light on."

If he was startled, he didn't show it. He drew his hand away from the lamp as he looked in the direction of my voice.

"Is it all right if I come in?"

No it's not, I thought.

"Certainly," I said.

He crossed the room in his stocking feet.

I was determined to sound casual.

"You're limping. Have you been playing supercop again? Leaping tall buildings with a single bound?"

He sighed as he settled down onto the sofa beside me.

"Nothing quite so glamorous. For the past three hours, I've been sitting on a wooden chair at my dear little sister's kitchen table, eating pizza, sorting receipts, and filling out tax forms."

"That earns you more sympathy than the limp does."

"Thanks. How about you? I thought you were planning to play tourist and drive down the coast today."

"I changed my mind."

"Jane, is something wrong?"

"No. Nothing."

"Makes sense to me. You're sitting alone in my living room, in the dark, in the middle of the night, staring out at a thunderstorm because nothing's wrong." He reached out, lifted my chin with his fingers. "Come on, Max, old buddy, stop being such a tough guy. Talk to me."

At his touch, I trembled involuntarily. Tears welled in my eyes. I swallowed hard, controlling them.

"Nothing's wrong." I was pleased at the conviction I heard in my voice. "I just couldn't face my manuscript. I came in here because—"

I stumbled to a halt. I didn't know why I'd sought refuge in the living room.

Thunder rumbled, shook the house.

I turned my head away, seeking an answer.

"Things aren't going well with my book. I've been thinking of going home."

"Back to London?"

Alex sounded as if the possibility had never occurred to him.

"Yes."

Abruptly, he left the sofa, walked to the open French doors. He looked out across the porch, out into the rain.

"I'd miss you if you went away."

I sat on the sofa, staring at his back, and the terrible, aching emptiness I felt grew intolerable. Ignoring an inner voice that urged caution, I went to him, put my hand on his shoulder.

He turned away from the storm, stood very still, looked down at me through the darkness.

For a moment I hesitated, searching his shadowed face for something I couldn't name.

He didn't move. Simply said, "Jane."

His voice was little more than a whisper.

I laid my head against his chest.

He encircled me with his arms.

We caressed each other in the dark as the storm outside raged on. Moments were spent in quiet laughter, in tentative

touching, in little sighs. His hands whispered pleasingly
against my flesh, his lips explored the sensitive hollows of my
face and neck. I stroked my fingers along his muscular
curves, tasted the exquisite roughness of his cheeks and jaw.
We sought each other's lips, shared the textures of our
mouths—smooth and hard, soft and moist.

I closed my eyes, imagined his face, cried out to him to
hold me tight. Sheltered beneath him, secure at last in his em-
brace, I found a place beyond memory. I found a place of feeling and texture, of pleasure and warmth.

Afterwards, as his gentle fingers traced lingering patterns
against my flesh, I reached out through the darkness to brush
his dark curls back from his forehead.

26

Of course, morning came.

Dawn found me on the back steps, glaring resentfully at the sky. Bright blue. No clouds. No darkness to encourage self-deception. A crystal clear sky. Thoughts to match. And an inner voice demanding to be heard. It was, I supposed, the voice of reason. Too bad it hadn't been a bit more insistent the night before.

How exactly did one go about telling a man that, although your time together had been breathtaking, he wasn't exactly the one to whom you'd been making love? That you had been making love to a memory. That he had merely provided the necessary body.

I looked away from the sky, focused instead on the contents of my coffee cup. As I sipped, I imagined myself distracting Alex from our romantic interlude by telling him I'd abandoned my plans to assassinate one of Savannah's more notable citizens. After that, I would further endear myself to him by explaining that, instead, I would be heading a covert operation on his turf.

If he had been up before dawn, rather than sleeping contentedly in my bed and dreaming of God-only-knew-what, he could have listened in as I gave my first instructions.

As we'd agreed the night before, I had called John's hotel room at five o'clock. He picked up the phone on the first ring.

"Yeah-us," he drawled in a wavery, high-pitched voice.

"Tell Mac that I'll play the game his way. I control the operation, you assist and liaise. Agreed?"

"Absolutely." He slipped effortlessly into a deeper male voice.

"Then there are a number of things I would like you to start on immediately."

"Fire away, Jane dear."

"First, contact Washington. Find out about the importing and exporting Coastal Limb and Orthopedics has been doing. Check back five years. If you get anything, arrange to have it sent to our analysts in London. With luck, they'll come up with some significant pattern."

"Done."

"Second, find us a team. Two, maybe three people. Make sure they're experienced. I want O'Neil under twenty-four-hour surveillance."

"No problem. Anything else?"

"Yes, one more thing. Last night, you told me about eight bugs. I counted twelve. Cross me again, John, and you'll find out exactly how much *we* have in common. You're vulnerable. You have enemies. With a couple of phone calls, I can make bloody certain you'll be watching your back for the rest of your life."

"My, my," John murmured. "Fire and ice." Then, in a voice that sounded more entertained than fearful, "Rest assured, Jane dear, I wouldn't dream of crossing you again. We are, after all, on the same side. In fact, if you'd be kind enough to tell me which bugs you found, I'd be delighted to tell you where to locate the three you missed."

I stifled my grim chuckle in a gulp of coffee.

Damn you, John! I'm finding it difficult to dislike you.

Alex came into the kitchen. I turned my head in time to return his wave as he walked over to the coffeemaker. He'd covered the essentials with red running shorts and a white T-shirt.

I watched him through the screened door as he fixed himself a cup of coffee. I saw his long, lean legs stretch as he reached into an upper shelf for the sugar canister. I noticed the strength in the hands balancing the heavy container on its downward journey. I observed the economy of his movements as he refilled the sugar bowl and spooned sugar into his coffee.

He came out onto the porch, stood for a moment, looked down at me with dark, expressive eyes. Unsolicited, my mind offered images of the night's lovemaking. My body warmed in response.

Perhaps, I thought, Alex had been a bit more than a stand-in.

"Good morning."

"Good morning," he said.

He sat next to me on the top step, his mug cradled in both hands, a dozen inches of space between us. Gratefully, I observed that the expression on his handsome face lacked the moonstruck quality I had most feared. If anything, Alex looked tense.

I studied him very seriously. Then I tilted my head, clearly measuring the gap between us.

His tension deepened toward embarrassment.

I grinned.

"About last night . . ."

Alex flushed.

"Ah, shit! Am I so obvious?"

I reached out, briefly touched the back of his hand.

"Obvious and much appreciated. Thank you for last night, Alex. You made things better."

"I'm glad, Jane." Then he added lightly, "So, when are you leaving?"

"If you don't mind terribly, I think I'll stay."

"Not because . . ."

"No, Alex, not because we made love. Because I haven't finished what I came here to do."

He looked relieved. His face relaxed into a warm smile, a smile that I was certain would vanish had he an inkling about my unfinished business. He shifted so that his back was against the railing and his long legs angled across the steps in front of me. I half-turned so that my back was to the opposite railing and tucked my bare toes in against his thigh.

"I realized, afterwards, how difficult I was making things for you," he said. "I've been worrying about it most of the night. I had no right to pressure you to stay. It's just that over the past weeks, well, sometimes it's seemed to me that you're the only pleasant thing in my life."

I put my coffee cup aside, leaned forward. I put my hand on the back of his neck and pulled him toward me.

"You mean as compared to a concussion, a slashed thigh, and a serial killer?" I landed a kiss on his forehead. "Oh, Alex, love. You do say the sweetest things!"

27

I met the Americans three days later.

John arranged a meeting at a run-down motel just west of Beaufort, South Carolina. In a room furnished with a pair of twin beds, two uncomfortable chairs, and a table with a radio bolted to it, John introduced Smith and Jones.

The two looked very much alike—fortyish, medium build, medium brown hair, medium brown eyes. Unremarkable appearances. Unmistakable characteristics. Each possessed the physical and mental toughness that marks the professional soldier. Smith and Jones were mercenaries.

I sat on the corner of one of the twin beds and interviewed the pair.

Smith spoke with a twang, claimed that he and Jones had a common relative in Montana, smiled warmly and often, and used his hands freely to express himself. He also answered all my questions. Jones didn't utter a word beyond the "howdy" he murmured when he answered the door. Tempting, I thought, to dismiss Jones as the pair's muscle, subordinate to

Smith. Also foolhardy. Jones exuded an aura of unflappable calm and acute awareness.

"But can we trust them?" I asked as John and I drove back toward Savannah.

He was wearing his little-old-lady outfit which, to my surprise, had not disturbed Smith and Jones in the least. Unfortunately, he had adapted his driving to match. He drove carefully in the right lane, well under the posted speed limit. Traffic whizzed past while we remained behind an exhaust-spewing tanker.

"I've worked with them before, though they were carrying Canadian passports at the time," he said. The male voice was most disconcerting coming from a face framed by a flowery voile scarf. "I think they're what we need. They're experienced and capable of taking the initiative."

"I don't like working with mercenaries. Never have. Too easy for them to sell out. Or to decide at a critical moment that we aren't paying enough for what we're asking."

The tanker slowed as it began ascending a low hill. Its exhaust became a dense blue cloud. John made an irritated noise, rearranged his lace-gloved hands to a more businesslike position on the wheel, accelerated sharply, and swung into the left lane. He put some distance between us and the tanker, then moved back into the right lane and slowed to a more moderate speed.

"With them, money's not the primary motivation. They're danger freaks. God only knows who originally trained them. My guess is they're ex-Special Forces. But the work suits them."

"We *could* find out exactly who they are."

"No reason to. They came highly recommended. They're reliable. But if you don't trust them . . ."

I shifted my eyes from his sincere old-lady face and looked

out at the rolling greenery beyond the highway, weighing the risks. "Do *you* trust them, John?"

"More than most."

We crossed the Talmadge Bridge, which links South Carolina to Georgia.

"Do you trust *me*?" John asked.

I flicked my eyes toward him, then back to the ships docked at the Georgia Port Authority's ocean terminal.

"More than most."

He said something extraordinarily unladylike, clearly understanding how little that meant. Then he added evenly, "It's your operation, but I recommend we go with them. It could take weeks to find anyone more suitable."

Smith and Jones walked into the lobby of the Hilton the following Sunday afternoon. They wore expensive three-piece suits with fancy cowboy boots, smoked twisted black cigars, and flashed wads of Mac's money. The two-bedroom suite they had reserved—"Mah lucky number, you know," Smith told the desk clerk—adjoined John's.

That evening, we held our first briefing session in John's sitting room. Jones and I sat at either end of the cream-and-peach sofa. John and Smith settled into comfortable dark coral armchairs opposite. John had abandoned his matronly garb in favor of more conventional male attire.

The remains of dinner littered the coffee table between us. When I'd suggested the shared meal, Smith and Jones had insisted on providing the food. They'd ordered from Billybobs on East River Street, and we'd eaten batter-fried shrimp, barbecue sandwiches, and baby back ribs. At Smith's insistence, John and I also tried armadillo eggs—stuffed jalapeño peppers, deep fried, and topped with salsa and parmesan cheese. I'd managed to finish mine.

I firmly deferred all business until we finished eating. By

the meal's end, conversation among Smith, John, and my-self was comfortable. Personalities were emerging. And al-though he hadn't spoken since he'd arrived, Jones' body language reflected a growing empathy with all three of us, rather than with Smith alone.

After dinner, I played hostess and poured dark, strong cof-fee from a silver carafe provided by room service. I spoke each man's name as I handed him a steaming cup and allowed myself a glimmer of satisfaction at the way each met my eyes. The beginning of rapport. The beginning of a team.

I outlined the operation.

"So, almost eight years ago," Smith said, after I had pre-sented an edited version of my association with O'Neil, "you got a good look at this guy in Chicago. By implication, he got a long look at you. You're a pretty woman. Not easy to forget. Will he recognize you if he sees you here?"

"Unlikely," I said, appreciating both the compliment and the thought behind the question.

"Okay. So he personally disposes of the guy who was his Chicago contact and, because you've seen him, orders his dis-tributor in Rome to kill *you*. There's a bloodbath—"

John flinched at the word, looked sharply at me.

I noticed the movement, met his eyes dispassionately. Im-portant to make it clear that where an assignment was con-cerned, my feelings were irrelevant. I refocused on Smith.

"—one of your agents is blown away, the distributor is killed and, as far as O'Neil is concerned, the stewardess dies, too. O'Neil disappears. Years later, you spot his picture—"

Jones moved slightly and cleared his throat.

The change in Smith was instantaneous. He stopped speak-ing, sat forward on his chair, fixed his attention on Jones.

Jones' eyes flickered over me, returned to Smith.

"Cover blown?" he said in a soft drawl.

"Could O'Neil have known you or your agent in Rome were MI-5?" Smith asked.

I shook my head.

"Brian's cover was solid. It was his operation. He was the one who pinpointed the shop in Rome as the source of the high-grade plastique that was showing up all over the U.K. He was strongly recommended as a very desirable employee—"

Jones interrupted me by tilting his head to one side and raising an eyebrow.

John answered the implied question before I could.

"No leak there. He had relatives in Sicily."

Jones looked satisfied, so I continued with my explanation.

"Once inside, Brian tipped us to the stewardesses acting as couriers. So I became Moura McCarthy, befriended one of the known couriers, and let her know that I had serious money troubles. She introduced me to Joe Green who—because I insisted—exposed his employer's identity. *That's* when things fell apart. Interpol interrogated the six other stewardesses who had ferried packages to Rome. Eventually, each admitted knowing Joe Green, Tony, and Roberto—Brian. None had ever met O'Neil."

Jones stirred again.

"Panic or pruning? Trunk or branch?"

John and I looked at Smith for the translation.

"Jonesy wants to know if O'Neil was so panicked that he abandoned everything. Or did he just prune a small, high-risk branch from a much bigger operation? If it is a bigger operation, is O'Neil the center or just a branch himself?"

I was stunned. For a moment, I just stared blankly at Jones.

"Of course," I whispered. I turned toward John. "How stupid of me. I've always considered O'Neil and Rome as the center."

"Not stupid, Jane. Human. For you, Rome *was* the center."

I shook my head, narrowed my eyes, considered O'Neil from this new perspective.

"Mac believes that O'Neil is just a branch, doesn't he? He's never wanted anything less than an entire network."

I didn't wait for John's confirmation. I didn't need it. But I *did* need to make it clear to the pair of Americans that, fallible or not, I was still very much in control of this operation.

"Jones," I said. I waited until he was looking directly at me. "I owe you one. If I make any other stupid mistakes, you just have Smith speak right up."

Jones grinned at me.

Smith said, "Yes, ma'am."

I asked John to go over the city map with the Americans, then excused myself to go to the bathroom. I splashed cold water on my face and smoked a cigarette before rejoining the men.

"—essential that we know where he goes, what he does, and who he meets," John was saying. "I have equipment for infrared photography. Can either of you handle it?"

"We both can," Smith said. "In fact, if it's acceptable to you all, Jones and I will divvy up the night shift. We like working nights, don't we, Jonesy?"

Jones lifted his coffee cup, which I interpreted as a positive response. John glanced at me. I moved my head in assent.

"Fine," John said. "You have the nights and can sleep by the phone during the days while *I'm* watching O'Neil."

"Alex has settled into the day shift, so for the time being, I'll join you, John," I said.

"Good. And we'll want to listen in on O'Neil's phone conversations. As soon as we get an idea of his routine, I'll scatter some bugs around his home, then—"

"Take one of us as backup," I interrupted. "I won't tolerate another Rome, understand? There'll be no bodies littering this operation."

John nodded halfheartedly, but I was distracted from pursuing my point by Jones. He leaned across the sofa, briefly touched the ring finger of my left hand.

"Brian?"

The man's intuition was appalling.

I managed to keep my voice level.

"It doesn't matter. What *does* matter is disrupting O'Neil's organization."

"Seems to me and Jonesy, little lady," Smith said, "that you might prefer we disrupt the organization by putting a bullet in O'Neil's head. You're the boss. All you have to do is give us the word."

I stood, thinking that this was all too much to bear. I walked to the bar, poured myself a tumbler of Scotch. Holding my drink with an absolutely steady hand, I recrossed the room. Instead of sitting back on the sofa, I ignored John and Smith and stood in front of Jones. He looked up at me.

"Jonesy, I want you to understand me beyond any question. Beyond any doubt. I gave my word to my employer. We'll get O'Neil his way."

I came home late that evening and pounded away at my typewriter.

Alex arrived a few hours later.

I abandoned Andrew Jax and Millicent mid-argument to call "Come in," when he knocked lightly on the library door.

He looked as if he'd had a grueling day, too. His uniform was rumpled, his eyes were smudged with exhaustion. He limped as he crossed the room to my worktable.

"Thought I'd stop by and say goodnight."

He took care not to disturb my notes as he leaned back against the table, near my typewriter. I put my reading glasses aside, shifted in my chair so that I could look up at him comfortably, and smiled.

"Rough day, supercop?"

He shook his head slightly, sidestepped my question.

"How about your day? I saw your light on when I drove up. Figured I'd better remind you that even best-selling authors need sleep."

"I can't believe that I'm hearing this from a man who's been on duty since seven this morning and has just stumbled in at—" I paused long enough to raise my watch dramatically and announced, with just a hint of questioning in my voice, "—two o'clock in the morning."

Alex glanced away, shook his head again. When he looked back, there was a mischievous smirk on his face. I dismissed the possibility of a candid response.

"There's a hell of a lot of paperwork involved in being a police chief," he drawled. "And I read and write *real* slow."

"Somehow, I'm not surprised."

I knew perfectly well that his sense of duty and, I suspected, the misplaced belief that he alone could stop the strangler were responsible for making nonsense of concepts like regular routine and eight-hour days. He kept office hours during whichever shift he felt his presence was most necessary. When he was off-duty, he prowled the streets of Savannah. From Tommy I had learned that, since the discovery of the strangler's first victim almost seven months earlier, Alex's usual ten- or twelve-hour day had lengthened to sixteen or eighteen hours.

Alex attempted to cover a yawn by twisting slightly to touch the page in the typewriter.

"May I?"

"Certainly."

He concentrated for a moment.

"H-m-m, nice dialogue. I really like Millicent."

"Thanks."

He began to say something more and was stopped by another yawn.

"You're pushing yourself too hard, Alex."

"Not really." He rolled his shoulders, grimaced, massaged his neck with one hand. "I just spent a lot of time sitting. There *was* a ton of paperwork."

I motioned for him to lean forward.

"Come here, supercop."

I reached my fingers around the back of his neck, curled them into the muscles along his spine, and began kneading.

With a blissful sigh, Alex moved closer. He rested his arms along the back of my chair for support, put his forehead on my shoulder, turned his head slightly. His breath was warm against my neck and jaw.

"It was a bitch of a day," he said quietly after a couple of minutes. "The kind of day that makes me wish I'd never become a cop."

"Want to talk about it?"

"No. I want to hang up my cape, take a warm shower, and crawl into a soft bed. And I was thinking, just now, of how very badly I want you to join me."

The lights were on.

I knew who he was.

This time I had no excuse.

28

John and I used a rental car to follow O'Neil from his home to the warehouse. We parked out of sight and, because the rooftop of an abandoned building across from the warehouse offered the best vantage point, we climbed its rusty fire escape and settled in to watch. When O'Neil left the warehouse—which he did at noon on Monday, at twelve-thirty on Tuesday, but not until past six on Wednesday—we scrambled back into the car and followed him. At the end of our shift, we'd contact Smith and Jones. One of them would pick up the tail.

For several days, the familiar patterns of surveillance—the long stretches of inactivity, the coffee from Styrofoam cups, the candy bars and cigarettes, even the occasional unexpected bursts of activity—made it possible for me to watch O'Neil with indifference. Viewed from a five-story rooftop or through the windshield of a car parked across the street, he was just another subject. He was not significantly different from the dozens I had followed and observed over the years.

I was working for Mac again, back in a job where emotional involvement was a liability. This was my operation. Its success and the welfare of my team depended on my ability to make clearheaded decisions. Detachment and control were part of my training, essential to the process, and virtually impossible.

By Thursday evening I was in running shorts and a T-shirt, making the trip from Alex's house to the stone pillars at the end of his driveway and back at a dead run. The evening was warm and humid. My lungs burned, my legs ached, perspiration ran in itchy trickles down my back. But still I ran, forcing myself to maintain the pace I'd set. Focus on the movement, on breathing, on muscles stretching, on feet pounding rhythmically against the earth. Focus on the movement, empty your mind, purge your emotions.

Earlier that day, my control had slipped.

Just before noon, O'Neil had left the warehouse and crossed the parking lot to his BMW. It was an easy intercept, even without the homing device John had attached beneath his car. We rushed down the fire escape to our car and fell in behind him at the first major intersection.

We followed O'Neil as he traveled west on Bay Street, across the historic district. He turned left on Montgomery, swung around Franklin Square, then backtracked east half a block on Congress. He pulled up in front of The Lady and Son's Restaurant, emerged from his BMW and casually flipped his car keys to a waiting attendant.

O'Neil's large body was impeccably clad in a tan tropical silk suit, a cream-colored shirt, and a dark brown tie. He went inside the restaurant. Two hours later, he reemerged, accompanied by an attractive dark-haired woman. Her clingy green dress made the most of her considerable curves while exposing a lot of leg.

"She was waiting for him," John muttered.

I heard his camera's motor drive whir.

O'Neil and the woman paused at the curb. He gestured to the attendant, then turned and conversed with the woman again. She nodded, laughed at something he said.

I watched them over the steering wheel.

"Mistress, friend, or business associate?"

"I can't tell."

The attendant whistled for a taxi. As it pulled up, O'Neil placed his hands on the woman's shoulders, stood smiling down at her.

From where we were parked, it was impossible to hear them. But my memory provided the words that had accompanied that gesture years earlier.

"Good fortune to you, Moura, I'll see you next trip."

Suddenly I was back in a small, poorly lit room that smelled of leather and my own fear. I was looking down the barrel of a Luger. Brian was standing behind me, his fingers tightening on my arms.

Abruptly, dizzily, the scene shifted again. I was on my knees in the dust. The afternoon sun was hot against my back, the smell of gasoline hung in the air. A man in a stocking mask pointed his gun at my head.

"Sorry, love. You weren't supposed to be here."

Then I was back in the car, clutching the steering wheel with white-knuckled fingers. The dark-haired woman was getting into a cab. O'Neil was bidding her goodbye. John was beside me. I didn't have to turn my head to know that he was staring at me.

He said nothing as I turned on the ignition and pulled into the traffic.

"We'll follow her," I said. "Perhaps she's part of it."

"Perhaps."

By the time the cab was southbound on Bull Street, I'd unclenched my fingers and my teeth and smoked a cigarette, inhaling the smoke deeply, trying to relax. But the muscles at the back of my neck and across my shoulders remained an agony of knotted tension.

"That's the first cigarette you've smoked today," John said.

"I've been trying to spare your lungs."

We passed Oglethorpe Mall. Bull Street became White Bluff Road. The city of Savannah looked increasingly suburban as the cab continued south. Finally, it turned onto Rose Dhu Way, slowed as it passed a long stretch of manicured lawn and stately oaks, pulled into the driveway of a modern, single-story brick home. We watched from across the street as O'Neil's female associate paid the driver, unlocked the front door, and went inside.

"I'll have her checked out," John said. "And, Jane. It may take time, but we'll get him. I swear."

I met his eyes for the first time since we'd begun following the cab, then I looked away. I resented the sympathy I heard in his voice, hated the understanding I saw in his expression. Most of all, I feared his insight. If he knew I was having flashbacks, he would tell Mac. Mac would undoubtedly compel me to return home.

I swung the car back into traffic.

"I'll pass your assurance on to Mac in my next report. And when you file *your* report, you may remind him that I am one of his key operatives. I may not be capable of cold-blooded assassination, but I can certainly handle an operation as minor as this one."

John stiffened beside me. From the corner of my eyes, I saw the color drain from his face.

"I am not Mac's spy. I do not file reports behind your back."

He fell into a hostile silence.

His reaction reassured me. He wasn't behaving like someone who suspected his team leader was going a bit mad. Which left the problem my accusation had created. Counterproductive to work to build a team, then destroy it with a few words.

I swung the car off the roadway, into the parking lot of a fast-food restaurant, and cut the engine. I shifted so that I was facing John.

"That was a stupid thing for me to say, John. I apologize."

John pursed his lips, stared at me narrow-eyed, and slowly shook his head. His voice was a painful reminder of Brian's most offensive drawl.

"If you want to be more believable, try lifting your eyebrows and widening your eyes a fraction more. And shake your head slightly on the word 'stupid.' Your sigh was good, though. Very effective."

"Go to hell."

I reached for the keys dangling from the ignition.

John snatched them away.

"What the—"

"Ah, indignation. Excellent. I couldn't have done it better myself. Of course, you have the advantage of a pretty face. Can you do tears on command?"

I wrenched my eyes away from him as I worked for emotional control. I was infuriated by his arrogance, confused by his sudden antagonism. All of it was out of character. Or, at the very least, it was a far cry from the character I'd experienced to date. I knew John was manipulating me. I didn't know why.

I met his eyes.

"You don't really want tears. What exactly *do* you want?"

"Perhaps a little honesty between us. For instance, did you know that Mac trained us both? Ah, very good. Virtually no reaction. But your eyes flickered—a dead giveaway. You might try practicing in front of a mirror, my lovely Lady Jane."

He drew out the last three words. It took all my restraint not to flinch. It was Brian's pet phrase, and John knew it. He'd used the words deliberately, cruelly, intending to hurt.

I allowed nothing but the mildest curiosity to touch my voice.

"Why are you doing this?"

"Jesus, you're good." His expression was contemptuous. "Perhaps the best of Mac's elite little group. Brian, by-the-by, wasn't one of us. Far too normal. But you and I—bright, socially adept and, from a very young age, outsiders. A tragically orphaned little girl with little memory of her past, raised by a retired admiral. The odd, artistic son of a blood-and-guts regimental commander and his socialite wife. Mac chose us, dear, and encouraged us to become the calculating, manipulative, bloody-minded professionals we are today."

I shrugged.

"So, Mac's a bastard and we're not very nice people. No surprises there. May I have the car keys back now?"

John ignored my request.

"Mac's not totally to blame, though. He just exploited what was already there. I never liked all those messy, disruptive emotions. They tended to make one vulnerable at the wrong moments."

He stopped speaking and sat staring at me, probing my features for a reaction. I didn't give him one.

He dropped the keys into my lap.

"We do have much in common," he said. "Two of Mac's own. Brian's closest friends. Working side by side and struggling to keep our every emotional response under control. Still missing Brian terribly. Still feeling guilty as hell that he sacrificed himself for us. Still hurting, God damn it, Janie, *hurting*."

The haughty mask wavered. John turned away.

"But it's easier to lie about the way we feel," he continued softly, "because most of all, what we are is afraid. Afraid of trusting, of being hurt, of being abandoned again. But we can't be afraid, either, can we, Jane? Because that just wouldn't be professional. And God knows, we're professional."

He pushed the car door open.

"I've got to have a slash. I'll get us some coffee on my way back."

A few days later, John and I were once again lying side by side on the rooftop that gave us a clear view of Coastal Limb and Orthopedics. Except for Thursday's detour, Smith, Jones, John and I had followed O'Neil constantly for a week.

If only he'd actually *done* something, I thought irritably. As it was, the four of us were less likely to die from overwork than we were from frustration. Or—at least where John and I were concerned—from heatstroke. By the weekend, Savannah's weather had become unseasonably hot. Today's noontime temperature made the black, unshaded rooftop blisteringly uncomfortable. The smell of the warm, sun-softened asphalt just inches from my nose was overpowering.

I rolled onto my back as much to break the monotony as to escape the smell. The movement sent salty drops of perspiration rolling into my eyes. Scowling, I rubbed my face against the shoulder of my T-shirt. Then, shading my eyes with my arm, I glared up at the cloudless sky.

John laughed.

I shifted slightly to include him in my scowl. He had turned his head away from the camera and was grinning at me. A cap covered his head and shaded his face, but he was as uncomfortable as I was. Perspiration created glistening rings beneath his pale blue eyes and beaded on his upper lip. He'd been watching through the camera's telescopic lens for almost an hour, occasionally looking away to avoid eyestrain.

"Mad dogs and Englishmen go out in the midday sun," he quipped. He blotted his face on a handkerchief, then returned to the camera.

"Anything happening down there, mad dog?" I asked, not optimistic.

His smile broadened.

"The river behind the warehouse is a lovely stretch of sparkling water. Several slow-moving barges in the distance. The street in front of the warehouse is filled with unoccupied cars. A mob of children are playing in an open fire hydrant on the corner. Lucky little bleeders. The empty lots on either side of the warehouse are just that—empty. And if you are not careful, my dear, you will get a sunburned nose."

"I wish I knew what he was doing in there." I rolled back onto my stomach and groped in the duffel bag for a tube of sunscreen. "For God's sake, it's Sunday afternoon. He should be at home. We could be watching him from under a tree."

"He could be at church. We could be watching him from a back pew."

"Unlikely," I said flatly. I smeared another layer of sunscreen on my face. "Lightning would strike."

"Us or him?"

"Both."

He turned his head, looked at me again.

"You believe that, don't you?"

I shook my head—not a negative, rather a postponement of an answer—and dropped the sunscreen back into the bag. Then I pulled out two cartons of juice. They had been frozen when I had packed them. Now they were blood warm. John's attention had returned to the camera, so I stuck a straw in his carton before pressing it into his hand.

"Thanks," he said around the straw. "So, *do* you believe that?"

"Do you think," I said between sips of apple juice, "that God keeps a body count?"

"Unfair answering a question with a question. But if He does, it's instant immolation for me."

I did some quick sums in my head. Except for Jim O'Neil, I'd never deliberately set out to kill anyone. Still, the number was high.

"Me, too." I glanced back up at the sun. "I think this rooftop is a down payment."

"Undoubtedly." He wiped a lens tissue across the eyepiece. "I hope God also counts the ones we've saved."

I grunted in agreement.

We drifted back into another of the comfortable silences that had begun to characterize our working relationship. John kept his attention on the warehouse. I stared at the sky, considered our progress to date, and tucked away a bit of dialogue for Andrew Jax.

"So, what have we learned by lying in the blazing sun and watching this creep for an entire week, Millicent?" Jax would say.

"We've learned," she would reply brightly, *"that suntan lotion is essential to surveillance work."*

"This is getting us nowhere," I said about an hour later.

John looked at me, made a noncommittal noise, went back to his camera.

"Let's review what we know, okay?"

"Sounds jolly," he muttered.

"Between the time I spent watching him before you arrived on the scene and what the four of us have observed over the past week, we've got a pretty clear idea of O'Neil's schedule."

"Such as it is."

"Such as it is. We—rather, you—have bugged his car."

"And his girlfriend's house."

"And from that inspired bit of detecting we've discovered that the lady at the restaurant is guilty of nothing more than extraordinarily poor taste in men."

"And that O'Neil has ghastly taste in music and is more polite in public than he is in bed."

"Too true."

I'd been the one to screen that set of tapes and had been sickened by its contents. The woman had forgotten to hang up his suit jacket. At first, the accusation had sounded silly. I'd thought perhaps it was a joke. But before too long his loud, spiteful words were punctuated by the sharp crack of open-handed blows. She was sobbing, crying for him to please, please stop. Then he had raped her. Whether with her consent or not, I could think of no better word for the brutality of the act.

My thoughts skipped back to Chicago, to stupid little Joe Green who had died a horrible death at O'Neil's hands. O'Neil *liked* to hurt people. Even his lover.

Then I thought of Brian. Of stolen moments between assignments. Of passion enfolded by tenderness. Of friendship intertwined with love.

Of violent death on a sunny afternoon.

"Jane?" John's tentative voice interrupted my thoughts.

As I looked toward him, I automatically schooled my face into an expressionless mask. I realized what I had done when I saw his concern harden to indifference.

I reminded myself of John's value to our mission's success and acted to keep our team intact. I quickly twisted my lips into a bitter smile.

"Sorry. Old habits die hard. That tape. The way O'Neil abused her. Hard to imagine. Brian was so . . . gentle. He used to leave notes in the refrigerator. Said that way he was sure I wouldn't miss them."

John returned my smile, then went back to the camera.

"I'm glad to know he finally started writing his own. We used to collaborate. He'd fall in love with the girl, I'd provide the literary allusions. When we were about fourteen, he fell madly in love with one of my cousins. We plagiarized Thomas Lodge—'her paps are centres of delight, her breasts are orbs of heavenly frame'—and scandalized her entire family."

"I think he used that line in the note he stuck in the marmalade."

Silence drifted in between us, a silence full of memories. I allowed John a little time to savor the past before I tainted it with the present.

"We also bugged O'Neil's house."

"Right," John said. "And we learned absolutely nothing."

"Oh, I don't know about that. We found out that *you* don't follow orders and that *he* keeps a nasty little dog that bites."

I chuckled as the color crept up John's cheeks, turning them a blotchy red. He hadn't expected that I'd find out that he'd gone—without backup—into O'Neil's empty home and returned with a painfully chewed calf. Smith had dressed the wound, provided tea, and laughed as he reported the incident to me.

"Embarrassed, are we?"

John kept his eyes steadfastly on the street.

"Too bad he doesn't talk to the sodding little beast. Then perhaps there'd be something on those tapes worth listening to. There was certainly nothing in his house worth looking at."

"There's only one possibility left, you know."

John nodded. "The warehouse."

"I'm going in tonight. I can do it carefully, so I don't alert him. I think that if—"

"Heads up. Movement along the river." John quickly adjusted the focal length of the camera, then his hands relaxed and he sighed. "It's our bag lady. Already have *her* picture."

I peered over the roof's edge at the large, lumpy figure of a woman dressed in layers of flapping rags. She wore a dark babushka tied under her chin and pulled down around her face. Dismembered doll parts—primarily arms and legs— were strung from a rope belt at her waist.

"When I write my memoirs, I'm including her," I said.

A cracked, weed-ridden pavement separated the warehouse from its nearest, equally deteriorated neighbor. The bag lady walked slowly across it, paralleling the river's edge. She paused frequently, gesticulating wildly at an invisible companion and readjusting the burlap sack she carried on her back. When she reached the mound of sandbags and broken cement that protected the private area beneath the warehouse, she stood staring down into the shadows surrounding O'Neil's speedboat.

Undoubtedly, it would be cooler down there near the water and out of the sun. But I knew that a heavy galvanized fence woven with barbed wire made the dock inaccessible from the riverbank. The fence was securely attached at top and sides to the massive vertical pilings and horizontal beams that supported the warehouse. It extended—barbed wire and all—to at least my arm's length below the waterline.

Entry to the dock was possible from only two directions. Within the caged area, an imposing steel door at the top of a short flight of concrete steps connected the dock to the warehouse. A vertical gate, powered by a heavy-duty motor bolted onto the underside of the warehouse, allowed a boat in from the river. The gate—more fencing woven with barbed wire— was electronically activated by signals from a transmitter that

I assumed was inside the speedboat. Typically, the number, sequence, and duration of the activating signals on that type of device were programmed by the owner. The wide range of signal options made accidental—or unauthorized—opening of the gate extremely unlikely.

I'd found the docking area a wholly inhospitable environment. Apparently the bag lady and her invisible friend agreed with me. After consulting loudly with thin air, the bag lady turned and walked along the windowless length of the warehouse in the general direction of the street.

"I'll bet she's going to go through the dustbins again," John said. "Though I doubt there's anything in there today. Yesterday, while you were off playing writer, she found a cracked artificial *leg* and put it in her bag so that the calf, ankle, and foot stuck out at right angles. It was lovely. She's probably keeping it as an objet d'art in her digs."

I shuddered. I'd visited her "digs." The first time we'd seen her lingering near the warehouse, I'd been suspicious enough to leave John on the rooftop and follow her. She lived in a moldering lean-to of driftwood and debris built between the pilings of a railway bridge. Rotting fish and vegetation surrounded the structure. The smell was beyond description. She'd gone inside. I'd gone back to the rooftop.

I watched as she circled the dumpster and then squatted down in the shade of the warehouse's side entrance. "Poor old bird. I wonder how long she's—" I stopped speaking, stared down at the street. "What the hell do you make of that?"

The old woman had opened up her burlap sack and taken two adult-sized artificial arms from it. As we watched, she laid them down in front of the door, dropped a ragged piece of burlap over them, kicked the door twice, then walked ponderously away.

"Has she ever *left* anything before?" I asked.

"No, not that I've noticed. I'll check with Smith and Jones this evening."

"Probably just more bizarre behavior."

"Probably."

The side door opened.

"John—"

"I see him."

O'Neil stepped into the doorway, scooped up the rag and the arms beneath it. He retreated back into the building, closed the door. Minutes later he reappeared empty-handed, locked the door behind himself, and got into his car.

"When *we* go into the warehouse tonight," John said as we hurried down the rickety fire escape, "we should make a point of locating that pair of arms."

29

"The water moccasin," John read loudly, "is a large, olive-brown poisonous viper with dark crossbars, related to the copperhead and found along riverbanks and swamps of the southern United States. That's where we are, isn't it, dear? It's also called a cottonmouth because of its characteristic whitish—"

"Button up, John," I said, emerging from the bathroom. I'd exchanged the afternoon's sweaty, tar-stained clothes for an elegant white-on-white embroidered cotton dress.

John had showered first. Fortified by a glass of tonic with a slice of lime and dressed in a pale grey linen shirt and stylishly baggy charcoal slacks, he had settled into one of the suite's overstuffed chairs to wait for me.

He looked up from the book on snakes that Alex had given me. I already regretted lending it to him.

"It is a sad day," he said in a haughty voice, "when a young woman has no respect for her betters."

"That's *elders*, John." I lifted the hem of my dress to strap my knife high onto my thigh. "It's a sad day when a young woman has no respect for her *elders*."

"Ah, a young woman with a viper's tongue—so appropriate to the evening's activities."

I laughed as he grinned at me. Then I checked my shoulder bag. My Walther was secure and accessible.

"I'm off, then. I'm going to join Alex for dinner, play sweet lady author for a couple of hours, then leave him to the evening shift."

John nodded.

"I'll bring Smith as a lookout, and meet you at the warehouse at midnight." Then he added, and there was very real doubt in his voice, "Don't risk going in there alone, Jane."

I thought about the way he had described us days earlier. Bright, socially adept, and outsiders, he'd said. Chronic outsiders. A lonely place to be.

I extended my hand.

"Never fear, John. I wouldn't consider going in without my partner there to protect my back."

Surprise, then pleasure touched his eyes. He hesitated only a moment before linking his gloved hand with my bare one.

No matter who his masters were before, I thought, he worked for me now. Mac had taught me well.

Along the desolate stretch of riverbank, the Savannah River was little more than a shifting ribbon of darkness between me and the glimmer of lights on the far shore. I had wedged myself down between two huge chunks of concrete breakwater. With the river tugging constantly at my feet, I slipped out of my dark windbreaker and jammed it into a crevice in the rocks.

"Ready?" John whispered from a similar spot just a few feet upriver.

"Ready."

I adjusted my goggles snugly against my eyes, bit down on the mouthpiece of my snorkel, and slipped down into the river. For a moment I lingered—clinging to an outcrop of rock and treading water as I waited for my body to adjust to the cold—and listened for the telltale sound of John following me into the water. Only then did I strike out in the direction of the warehouse.

The best combination of access and concealment had been several hundred yards upriver. At first I let the current carry me toward the dark spill of rocks that distorted the riverbank and marked the mouth of O'Neil's boat landing. Then the undertow caught me and I swam hard, resisting its pull toward the river's center.

I was a strong swimmer but the undertow created another layer of anxiety—one that was more immediate than my fear that I would be unable to get us into the warehouse. I glanced back over my shoulder toward John. He was carrying the waterproof bag that contained our equipment. It was a troublesome burden under the best of circumstances. I feared that he might not swim as well as he had claimed. By day, the tiny stretch of water hadn't *seemed* particularly challenging.

I was relieved to see that he was just behind me, using long, smooth strokes against the current. He lifted his head for a moment. The pale oval of his face was distorted by the dark vertical slash of his snorkel and the horizontal lines of his mask.

Don't worry about him, I told myself. I chose to worry instead about the identity of something that stroked lingeringly along the length of my bare leg. It inspired me to greater efforts. I reached the gate well ahead of John.

While I waited, I clung carefully to a section of slimy fence and uncoiled the flexible nylon cord that was wrapped around my waist. John joined me as I was anchoring one end of the cord to the fence just below the waterline. After checking to be sure that the other end of the rope was still secured loosely around my waist, I took a deep breath and plunged into the water.

No light penetrated the muddy water below the river's surface. With my eyes wide open, I swam blindly, using my outstretched right hand to keep track of the huge gate beside me, touching its surface lightly as I swam downward. As I'd hoped, algae had covered the barbs woven into the fencing with a soft, cushioning layer. If one was careful . . .

My momentum slowed, the current tugged at me unexpectedly. I grabbed the fence. That was a mistake. Stupid to impale one's palm on a piece of wire. Impossible to cry out when one's very limited oxygen supply would be imperiled. I bit down hard on my mouthpiece, lifted my hand, put it in a safer place. Then I distracted myself from the discomfort by considering that someone smarter than I would have worn gloves.

I berated myself for not being smarter as, more carefully, I moved hand-over-hand down the fence. Without further painful incident, I reached the steel tube that marked the gate's bottom edge. I moved along its base, searching between the gate and the mucky river bottom for a gap large enough to accommodate my body. I tried several possibilities. Just as I was beginning to feel dizzy from lack of oxygen, I found a space large enough to wriggle through.

With lungs burning and bright dots of light floating before my oxygen-starved eyes, I raced upwards. The nylon rope trailed behind me, creating a guideline for John. I touched a smooth fiberglass hull and followed its upward curve, breaking the water's surface inside the dock area. With one hand braced against the stern of O'Neil's speedboat, I waited, treading water and taking ragged gulps of fresh air, until my vision cleared.

When the last exploding dots of light disappeared, I was

left in a darkness nearly as impenetrable as the one below the water's surface. Only the mouth of the docking area showed light. I could see John vaguely silhouetted against the gate. Two strokes put me just opposite him.

I shifted the rope from my waist to the fence.

"Mind the barbs," I whispered.

I swam back into the darkness, found the floating dock by bumping into it, then clambered up onto it. I checked to see that my knife was still in its sheath against my leg, and shivered in my black tank suit as I waited for John.

He popped to the surface like a cork. I called his name softly so that he could orient himself. A few strokes brought him up next to the dock. He pushed the dripping bag onto it, lifted himself out of the water, huddled in next to me, and began unpacking.

The first item out of the bag was a walkie-talkie.

"We're in," John murmured into it. Smith would alert us if anyone came near the warehouse. Jones was tailing O'Neil who, I hoped, was spending a quiet evening at home.

We blotted ourselves on a towel that John pulled from the bag's interior. The sticky wetness of blood spread across my palm after I'd dried it. I tore a strip from the towel, wound it around my injured hand, and dismissed to nerves the bit of Andrew Jax dialogue that drifted through my mind.

"An important rule of clandestine breaking and entering," Jax would say, *"is to avoid leaving wet footprints or bloody handprints behind."*

My holstered Walther was in the equipment bag, too. I strapped on the shoulder holster, adjusted it so that it was snug against my damp suit. Then I asked John for my tool kit.

Briefly, I'd tried the pickgun, a mechanical lock-picking device much touted in the intelligence community. But I'd found it bulkier than the hip-pocket-sized case of tools I usually carried, and not nearly as precise. In the end, I'd gone back to my set of tiny picks and tension wrenches. The compact tool kit was also packed tight with the electronic devices I'd found most useful over the years. My current favorite was one that clipped into an alarm system's keypad. In under a minute, it ran all possible combinations of numbers until it hit upon those that deactivated the alarm.

I was surprised when John didn't immediately pass me my tool kit. It wasn't difficult to pick out, even in the dark. It was attached to a webbing belt.

"Hold out your hands first," John said.

His warm, gloveless hands closed around mine. He discovered my makeshift bandage.

"As I suspected. A clumsy burglar with hands like ice. Not terribly confidence inspiring."

I thought it was just as well he hadn't been around when I'd located the dock with the top of my head.

He carefully retied the knot on my bandage and gently kneaded essential warmth and sensitivity back into my fingertips. Only then did he press the kit into my hands.

I slung the belt around my waist, left John on the dock. Focusing the narrowest possible shaft of light at my feet, I moved carefully up the stairs. I knelt so that the tumbler lock embedded in the steel door was at eye level, clamped the rubber-wrapped penlight between my teeth, and began working.

John, I knew, would join me after removing his own equipment from the waterproof bag and sealing our towel, masks, and snorkels within it. Then he'd tether it on a short line and drop it into the water.

He came up behind me, leaned over my shoulder.

"Rumor has it," he breathed next to my ear, "that you dismantle locks and alarm systems the way the rest of us open cereal boxes."

I took the flashlight from my mouth, flexed my neck and shoulder muscles, answered him.

"Exaggeration. Now belt up so that I can concentrate."

And it did take concentration. Not so much on the lock as on a mental picture. Feedback from fingers and ears let me visualize what was happening inside the lock as I coordinated pressure and torque with the movement of the pick. I used the rake tip, aligned the pick on each pin, carefully applied pressure, and set each pin at the sheer line. Five heartbreakingly tense minutes later, with all obstacles removed, the plug cylinder rotated and I opened the lock.

We were inside.

The room that John and I stepped into looked like a home workshop gone mad. Half a dozen sturdy workbenches were crammed haphazardly into the room. Each sprouted power strips, soldering irons, and dozens of hand tools. Wire of varying lengths and thicknesses, leather and plastic scraps, strips of rubber, and empty circuit boards tumbled from bins hanging on every wall. Underneath each bench was a bank of small drawers filled with nuts, bolts, screws, and tiny, brightly colored electronic components.

We moved forward carefully, John following slightly behind me. We used the narrow illumination of our penlights to examine the room thoroughly.

"He's customizing wheelchairs," John murmured. He pointed his light at a tiny, cushioned wheelchair that rested on one of the benches. Colored wires erupted from one of the wheelchair's arms and a disemboweled joystick lay on its seat.

I picked up a clipboard from a nearby stool.

"This is assigned to a technician named Clint. The wheelchair's owner is a five-year-old girl with cerebral palsy."

John focused his penlight on another clipboard, then flickered the light over the adjoining work area. Another small wheelchair—this one on its side—lay on the bench.

"The child who uses this is having trouble breathing," he said. "The physiotherapist seems to think that adjusting the seat position will help."

John lifted the miniature camera he'd brought as part of his equipment. Its telltale motor had been whirring almost continuously since we'd entered the room. We went from bench to bench and bin to bin, methodically examining and photographing everything.

John moved past me, his attention captured by a handful of electronic components. Intent upon getting a closer look at them, he stepped fully into my flashlight's beam. For one mind-numbing moment, it illuminated his bare arms and torso. I saw that John's cruelly mutilated hands had, indeed, been only the beginning.

Even the long-healed evidence of the torment he had endured filled me with outrage. If I had found a friend tortured that badly . . . I knew suddenly and beyond doubt that, even had he tried, John could not have kept Brian from his revenge.

John stepped quickly out of the light.

"I'm sorry. I hadn't intended that you ever see . . ."

In his shattered voice I heard the all too familiar echoes of a deeper trauma. Guilt, humiliation, shame, fear—barbs that pierced the soul. Those wounds, it seemed, were the slowest to heal.

With that in mind, I directed my light toward him again, almost faltering in my purpose when it touched his body and he flinched. But then he stood rigidly, like a wild animal caught in the sweep of headlights. I kept the beam moving steadily until it lit the Browning 9 mm pistol hanging from the webbing belt at his waist. I let the light linger there briefly. Then I turned away and used my penlight to examine another clipboard.

"I can certainly understand why you'd be embarrassed to be caught wearing nothing but a miniature cannon," I said dryly. "The sexual connotations are appalling."

After a moment, John's ghostly chuckle drifted out of the darkness.

"Better get your eyes checked, Janie love. The real cannon is covered by the bathing costume. And it's not a miniature."

We worked our way through to the doorway at the end of the room.

"Nothing in this lot," John muttered.

"Unless we've missed something."

I checked carefully along the door's frame for alarm wires and contact points. Nothing. I opened the door, used my flashlight to gesture John through.

By contrast, the next small room was neat and orderly.

Injection molding and vacuum-forming machinery dominated the room's center. Stowed carefully beneath the machines were molds—lower legs and feet; forearms and upper arms; jointed fingers, wrists, elbows, and ankles. Hinges and switches of graduated sizes were stored in plastic bins. Several delicate myoelectric control devices in padded, dustproof wrappers lay on a nearby shelf beside a couple of tiny electric three-fingered hands. Within reach, in an unlocked metal cabinet, was an assortment of hands and arms, feet and legs, and flesh-toned latex gloves.

"The arms aren't here," I said flatly after we'd checked the lot.

John's camera whirred.

"I'm not surprised. Don't you notice anything odd about all of this?"

I put down the myoelectric device I'd been examining.

"It's good technology."

"No, not that. The sizes."

I moved my penlight around the room again, confirming what my eyes had registered but my mind had neglected to find significant. I also thought about the first room we'd examined.

"There are no adult prosthetics here. Everything is for children."

Hundreds of five-gallon metal canisters—two rows deep on all four walls and stacked from ceiling to floor—made the adjoining storage room claustrophobic. The canisters were labeled in English and Chinese. The English identified the contents as acrylic powder, assorted shades, product of Taiwan.

"Probably used in the injection molding process," I said. "Though there's a hell of a lot of it here. More than I can imagine an operation of this size using in several years. I wonder if the Chinese says the same thing."

John peered through his camera, snapped a frame, then said, "It does."

"Ah, hidden depths." I began prying off a canister's lid. "Any other languages, my friend?"

"Oh, the usual German, Spanish, and French," he said airily. "A little Italian. Some Dutch. A smattering of Russian. And of course, Arabic and Hebrew."

The lid popped off the can abruptly. John's quick intervention kept it from clattering to the floor.

"Good catch. I don't suppose you brought sample bags?"

He handed me one.

"Damn it, John. It's bloody difficult working with the perfect operative."

"You'll get used to it."

I took tiny samples of the coarse powder from several of the canisters. Then we moved on to the reception area that ran parallel to the front of the warehouse. Except for the quality of the alarm system we found there, that room proved to be businesslike and boring.

"He's invested some heavy money here," I said to John, flickering the flashlight over the alarm's control panel. "Coming in undetected through the front or side doors or through any of the windows would have been difficult."

"Wonder why he neglected the back door?"

"Probably figured that a strong current, poisonous snakes, a fence strung with barbs, and a locked steel door would put anyone off."

"Stupid bugger."

The receptionist's desk and the file cabinets were locked. After I unlocked them, John and I rifled them systematically. Nothing seemed particularly significant, but John's camera whirred anyway. Then he planted a handful of electronic bugs.

"Did you know that U.S. Customs cracked down on forty spy shops last year?" he said as he lifted the telephone from the cradle on the receptionist's desk. He used a small screwdriver to open it, slipped a pea-sized transmitter behind the earpiece, then reassembled the phone. "Seems they sold illegal bugging devices—more than four thousand of them over a year and a half—to anybody who was interested in buying them. They made more than three million dollars."

"Nice business."

"That's what I thought."

Five doors led away from the reception area. We'd come in through one of them. Two went directly outside—one to the street, one to the parking lot. A fourth was labeled with a brass nameplate that read J. O'NEIL. The last one opened onto a narrow staircase.

I glanced at my watch's luminous dial. "Let's split up. Do you want the loft or the office?"

"I'll do the office," John said. "More likely to need the camera there. First one finished joins the other."

The loft was a nightmare—a jumbled storehouse for generations of discards. O'Neil had owned Coastal Limb and Orthopedics for fifteen years, but the company had been in existence for almost a century. If the tiny, skin-toned myoelectric hands downstairs were the "after," the contents of the loft were definitely the "before." The most remote area of the loft was a tangle of crudely carved legs and feet, wooden arms ending in unwieldy hooks, canes and crutches of every description, and impossibly heavy wooden wheelchairs with caned seats and backs.

I searched the loft carefully, looking for the adult-sized arms the bag lady had abandoned at the front door. I was on my hands and knees on the floor, examining the tangled stack in the room's center, when something scuttled over my bare foot. I didn't shriek, but I didn't have to like it. I finished my inspection and went back downstairs.

I joined John in O'Neil's windowless office, where he had apparently decided that there was little risk in turning on a lamp. After an hour spent in almost total darkness, even the single dim bulb was blinding. I pulled the door carefully shut behind me and stood, letting my eyes adjust.

"Sorry about the light," John said from the shadows behind the desk. "I have no problem planting bugs in near darkness, but I'm not as good at picking locks as you are. I find that being able to see them helps."

Actually, he had managed the locks on the desk quite nicely and had removed the drawers to check behind and beneath them. I had interrupted him in the process of putting the drawers back. The center one was giving him trouble. I started across the room to help. The texture of the woolen rug against my bare feet was a pleasant change from the worn linoleum throughout the rest of the warehouse.

If I'd had shoes on, I wouldn't have noticed the trapdoor.

"John," I said urgently, bending over to grasp the rug's edge.

I heard the drawer slip back into place. Then John was on his knees beside me, helping me roll back the rug. He whistled softly and reached out to grasp the handle we'd exposed.

I grabbed his wrist, yanked his hand away.

"No! Don't!" Then, more moderately, I added, "Humor me."

With painstaking care, I checked the area around the trapdoor and found what I had feared most. I heard the breath catch in John's throat and knew that he, too, had recognized the fine copper wire for what it was.

"Booby trap," I said, thinking aloud for John's benefit. "Wired to something beneath the trapdoor. But assuming that he wants easy access, there has to be some straightforward way . . ." I sat back on my heels, moved my flashlight slowly around the perimeter of the carpet. "Ah, what have we here?"

The connection was concealed in the base of a floor lamp. I disengaged the trap, unclenched my jaw, took a slow, deep breath. Then I turned back to John.

"It's safe now."

Without hesitation, he grabbed the handle, pulled the door open. We lay on our stomachs and aimed our penlights into the inky darkness. The gap between the office's floor and the smooth slab of concrete below was something more than twelve feet.

"It's a frigging bunker," John muttered.

We systematically swept the room with our flashlights' twin beams and found what we'd been looking for. A pair of artificial arms lay beside a dozen five-gallon canisters.

There was no ladder. I didn't remember seeing one in the other rooms, and didn't want to take the time to search.

"Lower me down. I'll have a closer look," I said.

John wasn't thrilled with the arrangement.

I kept the impatience from my voice.

"I don't see any alternatives. I might be able to get you down there, but I sure as hell couldn't get you back up. Besides, I'm in charge of this operation, remember?"

John threw me a quick salute.

I stripped off my weapons and abandoned them beside the trapdoor. Then I clenched my flashlight between my teeth, held onto the edge of the doorway, and eased myself into the hole.

I dangled there, still supporting my weight with my own hands, and turned my head slowly, using the flashlight to probe the area around me. It was completely enclosed by cinderblock walls and extended from beneath O'Neil's office to what I guessed was the end of the injection molding room.

"It's a bloody big room," I said around the flashlight.

I moved the beam along the wire that came in through a corner of the trapdoor. When I saw where it ended, I gasped, nearly opened my mouth and dropped my light.

"What do you see, Janie?"

"Not certain. Hang on to my left wrist."

With his comforting grip strengthening my left hand, I grabbed the splintery horizontal support beam nearest the trapdoor with my right. I pulled myself in close to the shadows where the wire ended.

A fist-sized lump of plastique was packed into the intersection of subfloor and beam. It was enough explosive to level the building.

"Holy Mother of God," I murmured through clamped teeth. The words were a prayer of thanks for my life and John's.

My muscles were beginning to object, but I hung on long

enough to examine the bundle carefully. It was also wired with a heat-sensitive fuse. Double jeopardy.

You owe me one, John, I thought.

I hung by my left arm long enough to pinch a tiny sample from the deadly lump and pass it up through the opening. I was tempted to disarm the device, to disconnect both the booby trap and the heat-sensitive fuse. But that would risk O'Neil's discovering our presence prematurely. As long as there were no accidental fires . . . I'd have been willing to bet that Coastal Limb and Orthopedics had the best sprinkler system money could buy and a strictly enforced no-smoking policy.

I grabbed for the edge of the doorway with my right hand. When I was secure, John clamped a hand around each of my wrists. He gave me a minute to rest.

"Ready whenever you are, Janie."

"Now."

Slowly, he lowered me, extending his upper torso well into the hole.

"Release," I said.

I dropped the remaining distance to the floor, then glanced up at John's face framed in the trapdoor above me. If he abandoned me, I'd have a devil of a time getting out. I looked away, unconcerned by the thought.

I carefully walked around the perimeter of the subterranean room. It contained nothing besides the canisters and the twin arms. Nothing, unless you counted the lump of plastique overhead. The lids on the canisters were loose. I carefully probed through each container's powdery contents. Nothing hidden *in* the powder so, although it looked much like the powder I'd collected upstairs, I called up to John for a few more sample bags. He dropped them through the opening, and I filled them with the powder. Then I tucked the tiny bags securely into the top of my suit, sat down on a canister, and picked up one of the prosthetics.

When I saw what had been jammed into the hollow upper arm, I said "Bloody hell," loudly enough that John immediately leaned back down into the hole.

"What's wrong?"

I put the arm down beside me, held up one of the five-hundred-dollar bills, spotlighted it for him.

"We're rich."

"Too bad there's no time to count it," he said rather pointedly.

"Yeah, too bad."

I tucked the bill back in with its mates, twisted the hook at the end of the arm until it separated from the forearm. I probed the exposed space with my thumb and forefinger, immediately encountering a soft, malleable substance. I pinched off a piece, examined it in the light, then tamped it back inside the arm. I didn't need to take a sample. I knew what it was. The first limb's hollow forearm and every inch of space in the hollow second limb were packed with plastique. Enough plastique to make me dismiss the lump above me as insignificant.

John watched me put both artificial arms back on the floor of the bunker and carefully check their position.

"Find anything?"

"Get me out of here and I'll tell you."

"Righto."

He dangled by his knees from the edge of the hole, extended his arms. With an easy jump, I grabbed his hands. I crawled up his body until the edge of the trapdoor was within reach, grasped it, and pulled myself through. Then I held John's ankles as he righted himself, breathed a sigh of relief when we were both finally kneeling above the trapdoor, looking down.

As I reconnected the booby trap, I told him what I'd seen.

*　　*　　*

We backtracked through the warehouse, detouring briefly to search O'Neil's boat. We found nothing, retrieved the water-proof bag and placed our samples carefully inside, exchanged our weapons and burgling equipment for our snorkels, and got the hell out.

The bag lady was there, waiting at the front door. She was dressed in her usual layers of clothing and wore the grisly belt we'd seen so often.

Smith, who'd been watching the warehouse from a nearby alley, reported that she'd shown up just after we'd gone in-side. For most of that time, she'd been standing beneath the security light at the front entrance.

"Stay here and watch her," I said. "Don't make contact, but spend the night following her. I want to know exactly where she goes."

30

With a loud sigh, I dropped the last handful of black-and-white photographs onto the floor next to me and sourly contemplated the hundreds of glossy 8 x 10 prints that were already scattered across the sitting room's thick carpeting.

It was Friday, late. Or—more accurately—Saturday, early. On Friday morning, I'd kissed Alex goodbye and told him that I'd be meeting my literary agent in Atlanta that afternoon. Afterwards, I said, I planned to check into a hotel and possibly spend the next morning shopping. Actually, I was sitting on the floor in John's suite, comfortably dressed in my inelegant grey sweatpants and a T-shirt, and surrounded by the photos we'd taken during the past two weeks.

John was sprawled in a nearby easy chair with a set of stereo headphones pushed down around his neck. He was using bamboo chopsticks to eat sweet and sour chicken from a carryout container. On the table at his elbow were a tape player and audio cassettes that represented hundreds of hours worth of electronic eavesdropping.

Earlier, he'd paused in his fast-forward screening of the

tapes to call a Chinese restaurant whose main claim to fame seemed to be that it was open all night. When his order arrived, he had abandoned the tapes and attacked the food with considerable gusto.

He was growing more comfortable with me, I thought as I looked over at him. At midnight, when he'd exchanged his street clothes for dark blue silk pajamas, he hadn't bothered putting on his gloves.

I leaned forward, examined the contents of the carryout containers on the coffee table.

"How do you stay so skinny when you're such a greedy bastard?" I asked good-naturedly. "Did you eat the last egg roll, too?"

John tapped his chopsticks on the edge of a box I hadn't looked in yet.

"I saved you one. Knew you weren't serious when you said you weren't hungry."

I settled back against the sofa, nibbled at the egg roll until my thoughts drifted back to the contents of a manila folder that lay on the sofa behind me. I finished my egg roll in two quick bites, then twisted around to retrieve the folder. I thumbed through its contents one more time.

The photocopied news stories it held called O'Neil a hero.

"It's justice," he was quoted as saying, "that as a citizen of the most blessed nation on the face of this planet, I use a portion of my wealth to help those children who are the innocent victims of war—mankind's worst sin against itself. I consider it my duty to serve them."

O'Neil, the newspapers reported, arranged for children maimed by war to receive state-of-the-art prosthetic devices and lightweight, customized wheelchairs. Using personal wealth and business-derived income, he visited refugee camps throughout the world, seeking out those children who might otherwise be overlooked.

The photos that accompanied the stories were much like the one that had caught my attention in the Atlanta newspaper. In one, O'Neil stood with his arm over the shoulders of a young Iraqi boy—the child was lifting his loose robes, showing off his new leg to the world. Another was taken in a refugee camp in Bosnia—a pretty little girl waved at the camera with a myoelectric hand.

A report from London was also in the folder. Though I already knew that the information I sought wasn't there, I reread its typewritten pages.

The report noted that the market for the prosthetic devices sold by Coastal Limb and Orthopedics was the United States and Canada. No sales were made overseas. But—and this paragraph was highlighted by a vertical slash of yellow down the right-hand margin—donations of children's lightweight wheelchairs and child-sized artificial limbs were shipped regularly to hospitals in hotspots throughout the world.

I stopped reading, referred to the stack of photos we'd taken in the warehouse. I glanced at one of the small wheelchairs we'd photographed and thought of how easy it was to ship timers and detonators in the guise of joysticks and control devices, to fill the core of rubber-coated wheels with plastique.

I picked up a magnifying glass and carefully examined each of the injection molding forms. A few had already been circled with grease pencil. I looked at them once more, envisioning the finished product—imagining tiny artificial limbs whose hollow interior spaces could be packed with plastique.

Hard to detect and easy to use, the explosive was a longtime favorite of terrorists worldwide. One hundred grams, properly placed, could bring down an airliner. The destructive potential of the plastique hidden in the bunker was incalculable.

I laid aside the warehouse photos, fanned through the photocopies in the folder, paused when I located the face of a boy from Cambodia. He'd lost his leg when a land mine had detonated in a field his family was planting. The shipments to him and to the other children were legitimate. O'Neil had truly helped them.

What logic was there in repairing a handful of fragile lives while providing the means to destroy hundreds more? Even as I asked myself the question, I knew the answer. There was no logic. Simply profit.

Death as a high-profit enterprise. The business suited O'Neil.

He was not just exporting death. He was importing it, too. The lab found the contents of the dozen canisters to be a mixture of three parts acrylic powder to one part heroin. Sift and sell. Another product of incalculable destructive potential.

I looked up at John.

"Do you think he's marketing the drugs himself?"

My question caught him between bites. He ignored his pineapple-laden chopsticks long enough to answer me.

"Not his style. He's a middleman by choice. My guess is that a partial shipment of drugs went out to one major dealer via that artificial leg I saw the bag lady carry off on Saturday afternoon. And a partial payment—in money and explosives—was what we found in the arms on Sunday night. He banks the money, gets rid of the plastique—and the heroin—as quickly as he can."

"There were twelve containers stored beneath the floor. If hollow limbs are the only method of transport, we're talking about at least another half a dozen trips to clear out his present drug supply. Is he getting it past us some other way?"

John shook his head.

"We've watched the warehouse and the old woman constantly. I'd be willing to swear that nothing's gone out of that place."

"So why hasn't that crazy woman made another pickup?"

John shrugged, said, "Maybe O'Neil's *not* in a hurry," and popped the piece of pineapple into his mouth.

"Thanks a hell of a lot," I muttered.

I refocused on the report from London and reread Mac's page-long, typed postscript. Skimmed the "good-show-but-I-expected-nothing-less-from-you" paragraph, then slowed as he outlined the activities he was coordinating from London. Oddly enough, it was his understated language that reminded me how influential my employer actually was. He'd managed to generate cooperation on both sides of the Atlantic, on both sides of the Channel, and in Asia.

For a moment, I closed my eyes, trying to derive some satisfaction from the outcome, to date, of our operation. Employees of the acrylic manufacturing plant in Taiwan and all receivers of those shipments were being closely watched. Mac anticipated that within weeks the specific supplier and his network of overseas buyers would be a matter of record. That information would be turned over to key personnel in various nations' drug enforcement agencies, enabling them to shut down the distribution networks within their countries.

If our operation continued for any length of time, we'd be disrupting some terrorist organizations, too. For the duration of our investigation, any overseas shipment made by O'Neil or Coastal Limb and Orthopedics would be intercepted, examined minutely, then hurried on its way. Each shipment, Mac assured me, would be watched carefully until it reached its final destination.

Not bad for a fortnight's work, I told myself. I opened my eyes and refocused on the report. I was a well-trained operative. This was the work I did best. Just like the assignment in Belfast. Just like the dozens of assignments I'd had over the years. Identify the source. Target the network. Follow the lines of distribution. Identify the end users. Terrorists and big-time drug dealers were an unpopular lot—given names, addresses, and evidence, most governments would prosecute them.

The problem was that, in spite of our accomplishments of the past two weeks, the Savannah operation was running out of time.

My team was exhausted. We desperately needed more operatives. The four of us had spent the past five days attempting to keep tabs on O'Neil, follow the bag lady at all times, *and* watch the warehouse constantly. It was a frustrating task that often demanded difficult, spur-of-the-moment decisions about whom to follow. At this point, O'Neil was most often abandoned. It also meant that John, Smith, Jones, and I were all working grueling schedules without backup.

At Jonesy's suggestion, we subscribed to an answering service and all of us now carried beepers. Combined with a call-in schedule and the simple codes we'd devised, they provided some regular communications. But the system would be useless in an emergency, and we all knew it.

On a personal level, I didn't know how much longer *I* could endure the strain. As team leader, it was my duty to maintain a balanced perspective on the operation. For the most part, I was managing well. But I was paying a price for my professionalism. My few hours of sleep were plagued with nightmares, my stomach ached constantly, and I was visibly losing weight.

That, and my cover was becoming difficult to maintain. In spite of his preoccupation with his serial killer, Alex had commented on how little time I seemed to spend writing. He'd meant the comment as little more than gentle teasing, but I wondered how much longer I could explain my odd work habits as "trying to get a few more ideas." I was also terribly aware that the time I spent maintaining my cover placed an additional burden on Smith, Jones, and John.

But the critical time pressure was coming from the Americans who had "unofficially" sanctioned our operation. They were becoming impatient. I wouldn't be allowed the time necessary to regroup, to pull in a few more people, to establish a new cover at a different location. The sentences that Mac had scribbled in red ink on the bottom of the report said it all. The Americans needed something immediate in return for tolerating a British operation on their soil.

"The Americans want to know how much longer, Janie," Mac's note read. "My impression is that they've reason to believe there's a U.S. military connection to O'Neil. I passed on your information about the pilferage from Fort Stewart, just in case the information hadn't reached their level. No reaction to that, but one of the Americans went so far as to suggest that the inquiry be abandoned in an attempt to avoid embarrassing their government. He's only one voice—the others seem to want the problem cleaned up. But as a whole, they see little benefit to themselves in what you've gotten so far. They are only interested in who's receiving the heroin and where the plastique is coming from. Get me that information, Janie!!"

"God damn it!" I flung the folder aside with far more vehemence than I'd intended, sending a scatter of papers sliding across the sofa. "Doesn't he think I'd tell them if I knew who was doing it? It's not like the bloody Yanks are *giving* us any help."

John looked at me expressionlessly before going back to his contemplation of the food he held. After some deliberation, he selected a morsel of chicken, deposited it carefully in his mouth, and chewed it slowly. Then he looked up at me again and swept his chopsticks so that the motion took in the scatter of photos, the report, and the cassettes.

"If there's something more here—some secret signal, some alternative drop—we'll find it," he said mildly. "But we've been at this for the past twelve hours, Janie. It's time to step away from it. Relax. Stare at the telly. Get some sleep."

He was right. We both knew it.

With a disgusted sigh, I got up, gathered the papers back into the folder, and put it carefully aside. Then I stretched out on the sofa, pillowed my head on a bolster, and lit a cigarette. I stared up at the ceiling as I inhaled deeply, hoping that the smoke would subdue the gnawing pain in my stomach. I already regretted eating the egg roll. I could either eat or I could think about O'Neil. It seemed that my stomach didn't understand detachment well enough to allow me to do both.

At some point, I butted my last cigarette, curled up on the sofa, and slept.

It was dark and, in my dream, I could hear the river in the distance. The clearing was in that direction, so I walked toward the sound, unafraid of the brooding shapes of the moss-hung trees and the sinuous ripple of moonlit scales among the branches. The path was swampy and the mud grabbed wetly at my shoes, making a sucking noise each time I took a step. After a while, a warm breeze from the river began to stir the trees surrounding me, bringing with it a whiff of dampness and vegetation.

I kept walking. The sun rose and I could see my way clearly, could see the ribbon of red mud that was my path. The day grew warmer, and the smells that were carried on the breeze became more pronounced. The damp, green smell of the river. The odor of hot tar and gasoline. And something unidentified but very familiar.

The path angled downward, grew muddier. The red clay caked thickly around my shoes, making them heavy, difficult to lift. But I struggled forward, toward the sound of the river. The smell on the hot breeze grew stronger.

The trees before me thinned, then finally parted. Somehow I found myself on a rooftop, peering down at the solitary figure of the bag lady trudging along the bank of a slow-moving river.

The unidentified odor rose to surround me. Then I knew it for what it was. Reluctantly, I dragged my eyes from the river below and gazed around the rooftop. In a nearby corner, I saw a mound of human limbs, decaying in the heat. A foot, still encased in a polished black boot, lay on top of the mound. Blood and corruption oozed from the raggedly amputated leg, flowed sluggishly toward me through the fissures in the soft tar, mixed with the red clay that coated my shoes, mingled with the innocent smells of the river.

I heard a child's voice, recognized it as my own.

"Can Stavros still be our driver, even without his leg?"

Behind me, I heard deep laughter, then a mocking voice.

"Moura, me darlin'."

I turned.

Two men were walking toward me along the wooded path. The first man's face was hidden by shadows. Behind him, grinning wickedly over his shoulder, was Jim O'Neil. His arm was uplifted. Sunlight glinted off the knife he held. The flashing blade plunged downward.

I screwed my eyes shut, not wanting to see.

"Moura, me darlin'." The voice came softly.

I couldn't help myself. I opened my eyes.

He had severed his victim's head. With a triumphant cry, he lifted the grisly object. His bloody fingers were threaded through its dark brown hair. He laughed as he rotated the head slowly.

It had two faces. Brian's. Alex's.

I pressed the back of my hand against my mouth, bit

down hard. The scream I couldn't control emerged as a whimper.

A comforting voice beside my ear murmured my name.

I opened my eyes and was treated to an unfocused view of upholstery fabric. For a moment I panicked, unsure of where I was and remembering, too clearly, what I had left behind. I was afraid to turn my head.

Sofa, a more rational part of my mind volunteered. John's suite.

"You're safe, Janie." A cool hand touched my cheek. "Go back to sleep."

Because the voice was one I trusted, I muttered, "G'night, John," and did what it said.

I awoke to the thin light of dawn creeping in through the window and to the smell of strong coffee overlaid with rotting fish.

Smith was sitting in John's chair, sipping coffee from one of the hotel's delicate china cups. A silver carafe and a second cup were at his elbow. He smiled when I opened my eyes.

"Room service just delivered the coffee next door. I brought it in here, figuring that if you were ready to get up, the smell would wake you. Did you sleep well?"

I sat up, stretched, and reached for my cigarettes.

"I slept," I said succinctly.

"Yeah, I know how that is. You lie awake, wishing you could sleep. Then you sleep and wake up wishing you hadn't."

I nodded appreciatively, lit my cigarette, took a couple of drags.

"Where are Jonesy and John?"

"Jonesy is following the bag lady. John's watching the warehouse. He told me to report to you and suggest that a stint as lady author might inspire you. I'm supposed to get myself a shower and catch a few hours of shut-eye."

Smith poured coffee into the second cup, leaned forward to put it on the table in front of me. I wrinkled my nose at him. The odor of rotting fish had gotten stronger with his proximity. I was grateful for my cigarette.

"Not meaning to be indelicate, but you stink."

"No shit! That fucking bag lady of yours—" He caught himself, shifted his eyes quickly to the floor. "Uh, sorry. Didn't mean to talk to you like that."

"My dear Smith, you may talk to me however you like, as long as you tell me what's on your mind. I gather that *my* fucking bag lady is a bit of a problem?"

He took a pack of cigarettes from his shirt pocket, lit one, and inhaled deeply. Then he took the cigarette from his mouth and examined its tip as he answered.

"I spent last night squatting in fish guts so that I could watch that old derelict sleep in her hovel. It's not the first time. In fact, it's one of the nicer smells Jonesy and I have had to put up with lately. We've been taking turns following her for days and, I'm telling you, she hasn't done shit. I want to know why we're wasting our time on her."

"You know why. John and I saw her deliver two artificial arms, packed with explosives and cash, to the warehouse."

Smith looked straight at me, defiance glinting in his eyes. "I figure you're lying to us about that."

I was genuinely surprised.

"Why would I do that?"

Smith shrugged, scowled.

"Maybe you Brits think Jonesy and I are nothing more than the hired help. Stupid American muscle."

"I don't feel that way. Neither does John. The four of us are a team. You and Jonesy are as important to the success of this operation as John and I are."

"Then why the hell would you want us to believe that some crazy old fucker who shits in the street and talks to thin air would be trusted with such valuable merchandise?"

I leaned forward, crushed my cigarette out in the ashtray, met his eyes squarely.

"Damn it, Smith. I want you to believe it because it's true."

31

31

I left the hotel, drove to O'Neil's house, pulled into a parking space at the end of the block. It was well within the range of one of John's listening devices. From the sound of O'Neil's snoring, I confirmed that he was still in bed. His alarm went off, the dog barked, the shower ran, dishes rattled in the kitchen. An hour later, I followed his BMW to the warehouse, then joined John on the tenement's rooftop.

He watched through the telephoto lens of the camera as I repeated my conversation with Smith.

"You can hardly blame them for feeling that way," John said. "If we hadn't seen it for ourselves . . . Did you put him straight?"

"I hope so. But if he doesn't take my word . . . It's one hell of a time to have our team fall apart."

"A good team doesn't fall apart that easily, Jane. We're a good team."

We lapsed into a long silence that John interrupted with a yawn.

I consulted my watch.

"Here, give me a turn. You get some sleep."

We traded positions. John rolled onto his back, pulled his cap down over his eyes. Soon his chest was rising and falling in the gentle rhythms of sleep.

I had to wake him at ten-fifteen.

"John," I said softly, not looking away from the camera.

I was immediately rewarded by the quiet sounds of movement beside me.

"He's on his way out. Do you want to go or stay?"

John sighed.

"I'll stay and watch the warehouse. As you're enjoying the car's air con, don't forget that you're now in my debt forever."

O'Neil drove to a bakery.

Customers sat at small tables outside the bakery, in the shade of a blue-and-white striped awning. I parked across the street, watched O'Neil go inside and emerge within a few minutes, carrying a white paper bag and a hot-beverage container.

Perhaps it had been a pickup, I thought. It was a small bag, but it could hold money. Or detonators. I watched him carefully, hoping I'd discovered another point of contact.

He sat alone at one of the tables, opened the bag, sipped his coffee as he ate the donuts he'd purchased. He crumpled the bag before tossing it and the coffee cup into the trash.

I sighed, cursed, followed him back to the warehouse.

"Anything significant?" John asked.

I resisted the urge to throttle him.

We watched from the rooftop for a few more hours. Then John suggested that I should spend some time strengthening my cover.

"We can't afford to have your Alex get suspicious," he said when I objected. "Not at this point."

"Must you be right all the time?"

John kept his face serious, except for his lips quirking slightly at the corners.

"It's a habit I've cultivated over the years."

"Along with humility?"

"If I wasn't humble, I wouldn't be perfect," he said solemnly. "And we both know—"

"Don't say it," I interrupted, smothering my laughter. "Don't say another word. I'm leaving. I'll contact Smith and have him join you here. You can work your charm on him for a while. You stay on the warehouse, have him tail O'Neil. And when Jonesy reports in, tell him I'll relieve him tonight. I think it's about time I took a turn smelling like rotten fish."

I arrived to an empty house, took a quick shower, put on clean clothes. Then I called the station to invite Alex to join me for dinner.

Randy was at the desk. He chattered obligingly away.

"The Chief's in one foul mood, Miz Nichols. He's been in since dawn, lookin' at everything we've got on the strangler, meetin' with everyone involved in the case. Been stormin' around, sayin' there's got to be somethin' we all have missed. Grayson finally told him he was pushin' too hard, ordered him to get some lunch. Away from the station. Before some cop shot him. For a minute, I thought the Chief would deck him. Instead, he made some crack about another good reason to wear a vest, then he headed out the door. Matter of fact, he said he was goin' home. Should get there anytime now."

I thanked Randy, disconnected, spent a few frenzied minutes making my work area appear worked in. Then I settled into my chair. As Alex pulled into the drive, I quickly typed a few lines.

"Millicent," Jax said, "I don't like smart broads."

"Especially ones who tell you when you're wrong,"
she snapped.

"Yeah, especially."

Not a bad bit of dialogue, I thought as I heard Alex in the foyer.

"Fuck it all!" I said loudly. I snatched the paper from the typewriter, balled it up, threw it across the room. "I don't need this right now!"

I heard Alex's throaty chuckle, looked up to see him lounging in the doorway.

"Ah, the creative process. A joy to behold. But such language!"

He clucked his tongue, shook his head.

"Drop dead."

"If I do, my body will fall into the library. You'll have to work with my corpse lying across the doorway, looking pathetic."

He hung his head limply to one side, lolled out his tongue, did his best to look like a pathetic corpse.

"That's quite all right," I said, choking back laughter. "You won't disturb me. I'll just toss a rug over you and stomp out the lumps."

Alex shook his head again.

"My, my. We are certainly cranky today."

Then he crossed the room, stood next to my chair.

I looked up at him.

"You are interrupting the creative process."

"Yeah, I know. But I won't be here long—"

"Good."

"—because we are going out for a walk."

"No, I can't," I wailed. I propped my elbows on the typewriter and leaned my head into my hands. "I need to finish this chapter."

Alex began rubbing my shoulders.

"Headache?" he asked softly.

"Yes. A bloody awful headache. I couldn't sleep last night, so I got up at dawn and drove home. Been typing ever since."

"Look, honey. I've got no right to tell you what to do, but I'm going to give you the same advice Tommy gave me half an hour ago. You need a break." He gave the ashtray next to my typewriter a gentle shove with his index finger. "If not for the sake of your mental health, for the sake of your lungs. Come on. Let's go for a walk. We can follow the path that goes down to the Ogeechee. I'll show you what Savannah was like before it got so civilized."

I uttered a little sigh, then got up and moved toward the bedroom.

"I have to go to the loo first."

Alex dropped into my abandoned chair.

"I'll just wait here, between you and your typewriter."

Once inside the bathroom, I closed the door behind me, looked in the mirror.

"Coward," I muttered at my image.

I'd never liked walking into unfamiliar territory unarmed. But more than that, the thought of walking into the swampy forest behind Alex's house truly frightened me. It was a silly fear, one that I thought I had outgrown. I'd been terrified of the forest behind my grandfather's estate—as a child, I often dreamt of dark, terrible creatures pursuing me through it. That old fear had returned after Michael's death in Ireland.

Fortunately, there was an easy remedy for it.

I opened the small cupboard above the toilet, pushed aside an extra roll of toilet paper and several bars of soap, and took down the box of sanitary napkins I'd stored there. Hidden beneath the second layer of napkins was a 10 cm. semiautomatic—a .25 caliber Beretta no larger than a pack of cigarettes. I took it out, left my sheathed throwing knife angled through the bottom layer of napkins.

I removed the tiny, lady's Beretta from its compact holster, checked its load, strapped it below the calf of my right leg, wishing all the while that the weather was colder. I preferred the firepower of my Walther, which I kept hidden and easily accessible behind the wardrobe in my bedroom. But the larger weapon would be impossible to conceal beneath my lightweight khaki slacks and sleeveless white top.

When I returned to the library, Alex stood quickly and grabbed my hand. Grinning enthusiastically, he half-dragged me through the house to the back steps. Then he stopped.

"Forgot something. Stay here. I'll be right back."

I propped one hip against the railing and waited, deliberately not thinking about O'Neil. I wanted to enjoy my time with Alex. Within minutes he reemerged. He handed me a sandwich.

"Bologna and mustard on white," he announced proudly. "I actually stopped back here for lunch. Thought we could eat as we walked."

He walked down the steps, happily munching his sandwich.

I took a taste of mine and shuddered.

"Only a man," I muttered as we crossed the yard.

"What?" said Alex, opening the gate for me.

"I said, 'Be careful not to get mustard on your uniform.'"

"Sure." He grinned.

We walked along the path that wound down to the river. Birds and insects called from the massive, moss-draped oaks that lined the way. The breeze barely rustled the branches overhead. The air beneath the green canopy was damp, close. Our footsteps were muffled against the soft red earth.

As we walked, Alex rested his hand on my shoulder. I constructed bits of dialogue in my mind, then tried out one of the better lines.

"I'm going to kill off Andrew Jax if he doesn't start cooperating with me."

"Good solution. A new twist in the Andrew Jax mystery series—no Andrew Jax."

"Doesn't matter. I created him. I can get rid of him. Right?"

"Right."

"He's too macho, anyway."

"Yeah, right."

"And stubborn."

"I couldn't agree more."

"And smug. I hate smug."

"I know," said Alex smugly.

"Besides, he's not cooperating!"

"You're right, Jane. Kill him off."

Alex stepped over a rotted log that lay across the path, turned, and extended his hand. I took it, didn't bother releasing it after I scrambled to join him.

"You know, I really can't kill him."

Alex arched an eyebrow at me.

"Why?"

"I like him."

Alex laughed. After a moment, I laughed too.

We continued down the path in companionable silence. It began to rain. A fine, warm rain. But the wind had picked up. Between the swaying branches of the towering trees, I could see storm clouds building. I could hear the rumble of distant thunder.

Alex followed my gaze.

"We'll have to turn back soon."

"Yes, soon."

He laughed softly.

"Okay, we'll walk a bit farther. But I won't be held responsible for the soaking we'll get on the way back."

"Afraid of a little thunderstorm?"

He shook his head, his dark eyes serious. Then he gathered me into his arms.

"Thanks to you, Jane Nichols, I'll never think of thunderstorms in the same way again."

His kiss was one of gentle invitation that ended much too soon. For a while, we stood together in the rain, holding each other close. I rested my head against his chest, listened to the comforting throb of his heart. You'd be easy to love, Alex, I thought. So easy to love.

Inevitably, reality crept across my moment of happiness. My body must have tensed, because Alex looked down at me questioningly. He pulled back slowly, took my hand.

"Come on," he said gruffly. "Let's go as far as the dock, then head home. I've got to get back to the station and you have to find an alternative to killing your main character."

"Now I'm sure I'll keep Andrew Jax, Alex. He reminds me of you."

"Nice compliment. Macho, stubborn, and smug. Thanks a lot."

"You're welcome."

We emerged from the forest at the edge of a marsh, and I saw the dock that Alex and his father had built. It was a sturdy-looking structure of thick, weathered planks that extended more than ten meters out over the tall marsh grass and ended at the deep, fast-moving water of the Ogeechee River.

We walked out to the end of the dock.

"What you're seeing is pretty much what the early settlers saw. A wilderness—uncivilized, unspoiled. I used to come here a lot. I'd just sit with my eyes closed, listening, imagining a world without people or traffic or crime."

He shut his eyes for a moment. His jaw relaxed, his shoulders sagged, he sighed. He was smiling when he looked at me again.

"We'll come back sometime when the sun is shining. Watch the birds—we get land *and* sea birds here. Maybe we'll even do a little fishing. Would you like that?"

I nodded, knowing that it was a fantasy, liking it anyway.

It began drizzling. We walked back to shore. Alex paused just before we left the dock, swept his hand in the direction of the marsh.

"There's a hidden world out there. Beautiful. Dangerous. Sometimes violent. If you watch carefully, sometimes you'll see the grass move opposite the wind. Then you know that something is moving through. Usually a snake, searching for prey. Hey, look here. See the turtle?"

I looked where he pointed, near one of the dock's log footings. Beady eyes above a pointy nose and a nasty-looking hooked mouth peered back, didn't like what they saw. The turtle moved away through the tall grass, in the direction of the tree line.

We both followed it with our eyes.

That's how we found her.

A naked woman face down in the mud only a few meters from the dock. Her outflung arms and long, tanned legs were streaked with long, bloody scratches. Blonde hair clung in muddy, wet tendrils to her bare shoulders and back. Her head lay at an unnaturally acute angle. Dark bruising ringed her neck.

I stayed where I was, looked out over the marsh, scanned

the shadows beneath the trees, alert for some indication of the murderer's presence.

But Alex, seemingly oblivious to the physical evidence he was damaging, flung himself from the dock. He waded through the tall grass, dropped to his knees beside the body. With a strangled cry, he touched the blonde hair, gently turned the woman's head. He used his fingers to wipe the mud from her bulging and distorted face.

"Thank God!" he gasped.

Then I understood.

He let her head slip gently from his grasp. Her swollen cheek pressed back into the sticky mud. Alex lifted his arm to his face. With his mud-coated hands still stiff with tension, he rubbed his face against his sleeve. Abruptly, he turned from the body and saw me. Our eyes met.

I could hear the lingering terror in his voice, see the fear widening his eyes.

"I thought . . . The hair, so much like Joey's . . ."

Then he caught himself. His face composed. He stood, stepped back from the body, looked down at it. He pulled a handkerchief from his pocket, wiped his hands as he surveyed the scene with the cool, cynical detachment essential to his job.

His sweeping glance took me in again. This time I watched his eyes narrow as the cop realized that the writer wasn't shocked by what she saw.

A touch of hysteria had been called for. Even some terrified sobbing would have been acceptable. But the murderer's trail was fresh, time was precious, and I was supposed to be one of the good guys. I wouldn't deliberately impede his murder investigation.

"I'll walk back and call the station," I said.

Four scrambling strides carried Alex back to the dock. He pulled himself onto it, stood, grabbed my arms.

"What the hell's wrong with you? This isn't a scene from one of your books. It's real!"

Reaction, I thought, flinching as his fingers dug into my biceps.

He noticed, stopped abruptly, stood for a moment just staring at me. The sky had darkened. Rain was now coming down steadily, soaking his hair and running in rivulets down his cheeks. He gently rubbed my arms.

"I'm sorry. I didn't mean to hurt you. It's just that whoever did this may still be around."

"Look," I said reasonably, "this rain is going to sweep away any physical evidence long before the lab crew arrives. You're a cop. It's your job to stop this psycho. You can't afford to let potential leads be washed away while you walk me safely to my door. Besides, the fellow's gotten his victim. You said it yourself. He'll be satisfied now, at least for a time."

His fingers tightened again. "No. I won't risk you."

"It's the only way."

He glanced down at the body, then up at the thunderheads—searching for alternatives that didn't exist.

"I can take care of myself. Believe me."

He hesitated, released my arms, nodded. He unclipped his holster, drew out his service revolver.

"Okay. Take my gun. Use it if you have to. Hold it with both hands, point, and squeeze the trigger."

I ignored the butt of the .38 he extended toward me.

"Do you have a backup?"

"Funny thing," he said grimly. "It didn't occur to me that I'd need one. I left it locked in the glove compartment of the patrol car."

I suppose I could have taken his .38, left him without a weapon, avoided the questions I knew would inevitably come. But I couldn't leave him unarmed, any more than he could let me walk away without protection. So I bent over and retrieved the pistol I had strapped to my leg. I straightened, held the Beretta point up, my right index finger already threaded through its trigger.

"Put your gun away, Alex," I said quietly. "I have my own."

For a few seconds, he stared at me, openmouthed. Then he snapped his jaw shut, turned, went back to the body.

Within twenty minutes, the red pickup truck I recognized as Tommy's pulled into the drive. It was followed in quick succession by two squad cars, an ambulance, and the coroner's station wagon. After I'd called, I had abandoned the very damp Beretta in favor of the Walther, which I had tucked discreetly into the deep pocket of the yellow slicker I'd put on. I'd gone out to the front porch to await Tommy's arrival. Deliberately bareheaded, I ran through the downpour to meet him as he stepped out of his vehicle.

"Oh, Tommy," I sobbed, "we found a girl and she's been strangled and Alex is down there all alone and . . . and . . ."

I shuddered dramatically. He wrapped a protective arm around my shoulders.

"It'll be all right, Jane," he said in that patient tone policemen worldwide reserve for lost children, hysterical women, and the mentally deficient. "I know you've had a terrible shock, but I need you to tell me exactly where Alex is and exactly what you saw. Take a deep breath, think about how much Alex needs your help, then tell me all about it."

I took a long, trembling breath, and managed a little hiccuping sob. Then, because the image of Alex standing guard over a corpse was not a pleasant one, I allowed Tommy to draw a coherent account and straightforward directions from me. After assuring him that it was, indeed, all right to leave me all by myself and that I would, absolutely, be sure to keep the door locked, Tommy and his crew gathered up their gear and slogged quickly across the yard, toward the path that would take them to the river.

I didn't go inside right away. Instead, I stood within the shelter of the porch, lit a cigarette, and stared out at the rain.

32

By early evening, the front drive no longer resembled a parking lot. The coroner's wagon had taken the victim's body to the morgue. The photographers and camera crews had finished taking shots for the late news and the early edition. The reporters, who had trailed mud up the front steps for Alex's statement and my firm "no comment," had rushed away to file their stories. Most of the patrol cars and even Tommy's red pickup truck were gone.

Alex was the last to leave. When he'd returned from the murder scene, I was back at my typewriter. I called out to him as he walked through the foyer, but he ignored me. He went upstairs, traded his sodden, muddy uniform for a clean one, then walked back through the foyer. He paused in my doorway, jaw set, face grim, car keys already in hand.

"Popgun or not, I won't have you here by yourself. One of my men is sitting in a patrol car in front of the house. He won't bother you unless there's an emergency. When he goes off shift, someone will take his place. They'll stay until I get home."

"Really, Alex, there's no—"

"If you have a problem with it, pack your bags now. I'll take you to a hotel."

I didn't argue.

After Alex left, I called the answering service.

"Please have my salespeople call me at this number when they phone in," I said to the operator. I left a combination of numbers that would prompt John to contact me.

"Would you like me to page them, Mrs. Murdock?"

"No need."

Smith called an hour later.

"Where's John?" I asked.

"I was hoping he got ahold of you."

"No. I left him at the warehouse. With you, I thought."

"Yeah. I was there with him. That was when we saw the bag lady. Just like last week, John said. She retrieved a limb from the dumpster."

"Fantastic. Jonesy's still following her?"

"Uh, no."

The hesitation in Smith's voice made my stomach lurch.

"That's why I called. Jonesy's here with me."

"Damn it, what happened? Where's John?"

"We spotted the bag lady, but we didn't see Jonesy. John didn't want to risk losing her. So he said he'd follow her, too. Figured Jonesy would see him and make contact. I was on the rooftop. I watched through the telephoto lens as she and John made their way up the river. Thing is, I watched long enough to realize that Jonesy wasn't anywhere nearby. So I got worried. Called the service from the nearest phone booth and had Jonesy paged. Got your message for John at the same time. Jonesy called the service and they relayed his location. So I

drove there and picked him up. He was miles away from the
riverfront, following the bag lady. He hadn't taken his eyes
off of her all day."

"What?"

"Yeah. There must be two of them, Jane. Identically
dressed. Except one is crazy and one is our courier."

"And John's following the courier."

"Yeah. And he's not answering his pager."

Damn it, John! I thought.

"He probably turned the bloody thing off," I said. "He'll call
when he's ready. You and Jonesy stay together. Maybe back-
track the route he was following along the river. Perhaps you'll
get lucky and find him. If not, take the car and park so that you
can keep an eye on the warehouse tonight. Take turns getting
some sleep. Odds are that the courier will be back tomorrow
with the payoff, and John will be in tow. At that point, one of
you can relieve him."

"Will you stay there or come back to the hotel?"

"I think I'd better stay here tonight." I briefly outlined what
had happened. "I'd rather not add to Alex's suspicions. But I
want you to call me if anything at all happens."

After I hung up the phone, I sat for a long time in the darkened kitchen.

The rain continued.

John didn't call.

Alex didn't return.

My anxiety-driven thoughts chased themselves around in
my head, echoing the staccato beat of the rain on the windows
and rooftop, wearing on my nerves, building themselves into
wild, fearful fantasies.

Finally, I lit a cigarette and roamed Alex's house, seeking
distraction. In the living room, a rectangular wooden box
caught my eye. I crossed the room and tiptoed to remove it
from its place on an upper shelf. It was a chessboard. I stood

for a moment, running my fingers restlessly over the alternating squares of inlaid ebony and alabaster. Then I slid out the shallow drawer that was cut into one of its ornately carved sides. The chess pieces lay nestled in the padded interior. I picked up the white king, remembering something Mac had told me ten years earlier.

"How can you just sit there?"

I sprang from my chair, moved compulsively toward the opposite end of Mac's office. He leaned back in his chair, lifted his eyes from the chess game I'd just abandoned.

"What would you have me do, Janie?" he said around the stem of his pipe. "Together, we analyzed a situation, formulated a strategy, and assembled a team capable of carrying out that strategy. Based on reliable information, we decided that the intercept should be tonight. Has the situation changed?"

"No, damn it! Nothing's changed."

I turned on my heel, walked over to the window. I looked out at London's late-evening traffic and imagined eight darkclothed figures—eight people that I had personally selected—hiding among the jagged rocks on an isolated, storm-tossed beach.

"Then sit down and conserve your energy. You'll need it. Particularly if something goes wrong."

I recrossed the room, stood over the small walnut table where the chessboard was laid out.

"I hate waiting, doing nothing. For God's sake, Mac! Our people are out there. My *friends* are out there."

Mac touched the crown of the black queen.

"Friends? Where an operation is concerned, Janie, you have no friends. You can't afford them."

He moved the piece across the playing board.

"Checkmate."

He raised his eyes to look at me, then slowly touched each dark piece I had taken from the board as we played.

"I lost quite a few pieces to develop a strategy that would defeat you."

He picked up the white king—my defeated white king—and held it out toward me on his open palm.

"Like it or not, Janie, the people out there tonight are nothing more—or less—than valuable playing pieces. You do your damnedest to preserve them, but you do what you must in order to win the game."

I turned away from the sight of his outstretched hand.

"No! I can't accept that. I won't be that cold-blooded."

"Janie, my dear, you would be amazed what you can do—what you can be—if the stakes are high enough."

I put the box back on the shelf, took a deep breath, told myself that the stakes *were* high. For better or for worse, my pieces were in play. I could do nothing more than await the outcome.

I went back to the library, went back to my typewriter. As I had so often in the past, I forced myself to concentrate on Andrew Jax.

He lay with his left cheek against the cracked linoleum floor.

The bullet had torn a jagged hole in the flesh of his upper arm. Blood oozed steadily from the wound, ran in a trickle down along his biceps, dripped into the red-brown puddle surrounding his shoulder and head.

It's time to try again, thought Jax.

He raised his head and shoulders, strained against the rope binding his hands and feet behind him.

The rope didn't give.

Jax's upper body collapsed back against the floor. A

newly swollen stream flowed from the wound, adding to the sticky, warm puddle surrounding him.

Soon, Jax thought, he would bleed to death.

He shut his eyes.

Doesn't matter. No point fighting it. Not enough time, not enough energy.

His failure would mean Millicent's death.

The thought, sudden and unwelcome, wrenched him back from the edge of unconsciousness.

Jax tensed his muscles, strained against the rope again.

At midnight, I called the service to check for messages that weren't there. Then I went to bed. I was still awake when Alex came in an hour later. I lay listening to the sounds of his measured footsteps crossing and recrossing the kitchen floor.

I listened to him pace for a long time. I was certain that, except for the events of the afternoon, he would have sought me out, talked to me, held me tight. Because he didn't, I knew that part of his analytical cop mind was busy putting fact and conjecture together. At the very least, he knew I had misrepresented myself. At worst, my cover was completely blown.

I lay staring at the ceiling, remembering how harshly I had judged Dora, how bitterly I had condemned Mac. Unlikely that Alex would tolerate betrayal any better than I had. Unless I went to him, explained what I was doing, and why, he'd never trust me again. Impulsively, I pushed the blanket aside and sat up. I slipped my legs over the edge of the bed, touched my feet to the cool floor, hesitated.

I sat on the edge of my bed and thought about who I was. I thought about my job with Mac and the things I had done— the things I would be willing to do—to stop the likes of

O'Neil. I thought about the laws I'd ignored over the past few weeks, about breaking and entering, about unreported bombs and unregistered weapons. About running a covert operation on American soil.

My commitment to my job stopped just short of cold-blooded murder.

Then I reminded myself that Alex was a damned good cop, as committed to his job as I was to mine. He could never accept the rules by which I played. Slowly, I lay back against the pillows, pulled a blanket over myself, and curled into the bed.

Losing Alex was an acceptable price to pay for my operation's success.

Eventually, his pacing stopped.

Eventually, I slept.

I dreamt of a riverbank where bodies lay like driftwood.

In an agony of fear, I knelt beside each corpse in turn, wiping mud from bloated grey faces, searching for someone my dream-mind couldn't remember. Each newly revealed face—each gaping mouth, each pair of bulging, sightless eyes—brought with it the hope that the one I sought was not among the dead. Still, I kept searching. Searching. Until there was just one more body, one more face covered in a mask of mud. I knelt beside it, too. Gently wiped the mud away. And saw that I had found him after all.

I awoke with a gasp, covered in cold sweat, my stomach twisted into a painful knot. I lay very still, breathing deeply, until I had controlled undefinable fears.

By the time I'd showered and dressed the next morning, Alex was gone. He'd left a note taped to the coffeemaker. It wasn't a love note.

"I'll be back at noon," it said. "Be here."

Bloody cop, I thought. Bloody nuisance, more like.

I called the service again, left a message for someone—
anyone—to call me. Then I sat on the back steps, lit a cigarette, and smoked it between sips of coffee.

John finally called.

"Where the hell have you been?" I asked.

He laughed. "I gather this means you can talk freely."

"Bastard!"

"So glad to know you care. I *am* sorry I didn't call sooner,
but I've been busy. I'm calling from a phone belonging to a
lady of ill repute. She charged me twenty dollars. Have you
talked to Smith?"

"He told me what happened at the warehouse. Jonesy
didn't lose her, John. There are two of them—two bag
ladies."

"Not unexpected, considering what I've seen. The one I
followed went into the back door of Harrys—you know, the
pub where you and Alex had dinner that first night."

"I remember."

"Well, I lay on a rooftop all night, waiting for her to
come back out. She never did. The patrons all staggered out
around four A.M. The kitchen crew left a few minutes ago.
The whole place is shut down now. Like a tomb. Sunday
morning. Perhaps they're all at church." He allowed himself a brief chuckle, then continued, "She's either inside—
which I doubt—or she's not a she at all, but one of the
fellows I saw leaving. In which case I've lost her . . . er,
him."

"Not lost. Just misplaced until she shows up at the warehouse. Smith and Jones are there, keeping watch. Are you too
tired to join them?"

"Not at all. Though I thought I'd do a spot of breaking and

entering before I left here. Check out the restaurant and maybe scatter a few bugs about."

"Don't you dare! That's an order. We'll go in together, with backup."

"Seems to me that you already have enough to keep your hands full. Did yesterday blow your cover?"

"I'll find out soon. I'm hoping the situation is salvageable." Then the implications of what he'd just said hit me. "How do *you* know what happened yesterday?"

He laughed again.

"I borrowed a phone from a literate prostitute. The morning edition is right here in the middle of the kitchen table. Have you seen it?"

"No."

"I think you'd better read it, dear." Then he disconnected.

I jogged to the mailbox at the end of the drive and arrived breathless. As I took the tightly rolled newspaper from the box, I considered giving up cigarettes. I leaned against one of the stone pillars, opened the paper. My own face was front page, center. Below it, much smaller, was a high school yearbook photo of Melissa Adams.

I lit a cigarette and smoked it as I read.

One of the *News Press* reporters had managed to find a unique angle on what would have been another routine—albeit gruesome—story about the strangler's latest victim.

Yesterday afternoon, British mystery writer Jane Nichols found herself involved in a real mystery. In a strange twist of fate, Nichols and Savannah police chief, Alex Callaghan, discovered the body of 25-year-old Melissa Adams, latest victim of the Savannah Strangler. Nichols, author of the popular Andrew Jax mystery series penned under the name

Max Murdock, has been staying with Callaghan as she works on her latest novel.

"Oh, damn!" I muttered. Then I shrugged philosophically. Dora would be happy. That kind of publicity inevitably boosted sales.

33

Jax ignored Millicent's cheery greeting, flung his hat and jacket in the direction of the coat rack. He thumped the camera into the metal In basket on the corner of his desk, dropped into his chair, wrenched open the bottom drawer, pulled out the open fifth of bourbon. He dumped the dregs of his morning coffee into the wastebasket, filled the mug from the amber bottle, took a gulp.

Millicent followed him into the room.

"Bad day?"

He topped off the mug, took another swallow of bourbon.

"Bad day? Bad week. Bad month. Bad life."

Her eyes widened.

"Why?"

Jax found himself suddenly, inexplicably wanting to tell her. He crushed the impulse, narrowed his eyes, pointed to the camera.

"Life is nothing more than thirty-five-millimeter

black-and-whites of some sleaze sleeping with another guy's wife between grubby sheets in a run-down motel."

Millicent came around to his side of the desk, looked down at him with sad eyes.

"You might try aiming your camera at something else."

The confrontation came, as promised, at noon.

Alex came slamming in. I looked up from my typing as he paused at my doorway.

"I'd like to talk to you, Jane. Please join me in the kitchen."

Not unexpectedly, the easygoing manner of the man I'd lived with for more than a month was gone. Undoubtedly, the person who now confronted me was used to absolute authority. His words were polite, his tone chilling.

"Sure, Alex," I replied brightly. I preceded him into the kitchen. "I could use a break, and if there's something I can help you with . . ."

He yanked out a chair, pointed at it.

"Sit."

I understood interrogation technique as well as he did. Probably better. Mac had taught me well. The key was to determine what a subject knew without giving anything away. And to stay in control.

So I smiled inoffensively, went to the counter, and carefully poured myself a cup of coffee. I spent some time adding just the correct amount of half-and-half.

"Can I fix you a cup?" I asked when I had finished. "Or perhaps a sandwich?"

"No, thanks," he said levelly.

I sat down in a chair across from the one he'd indicated. Alex chose not to notice.

"You look upset," I said. "What's wrong?"

Instead of answering, he parked one hip on the kitchen

table, then took a pack of cigarettes from a pocket. Though I'd never seen him smoke, he lit one and inhaled deeply. Almost as if it were an afterthought, he offered me the pack.

"Cigarette?"

Choke on it, I thought.

I took a sip of my coffee.

"No, thanks. I didn't know you smoked."

Alex stared blankly at me. He leaned forward so that my line of vision was effectively blocked by his body, put his cigarette in the ashtray and shifted it so that it was within easy reach of my right hand.

"Comfortable?" he asked, knowing damned well I wasn't.

"Yes," I lied.

I slid my chair back slightly from the table, tilted it back on two legs, met his gaze with a cool expression and just a trace of a smile. I allowed the silence to lengthen, compelling him to speak first.

"At the station last night," he said finally, "Tommy told me how terribly upset you were about poor Melissa Adams."

"I read in the paper that you'd identified her."

He ignored me.

"Tommy said that even though you were crying and practically incoherent at first, you did a first-rate job of describing the spot where I was waiting. He said I should be proud of you."

"Tommy's kind."

"Tommy's gullible. So, now, let's talk about you, Jane. Who, exactly, are you?"

"That's silly, Alex. You know who I am."

Without warning, he slammed his hand down on the table-top.

Startled, I dropped my chair forward onto its four legs.

Alex leaned forward. He clamped his right hand around the back of my neck, grabbed the collar of my T-shirt with his left. He yanked the shirt downward, exposing my right shoulder and the swell of my breast.

"Don't—" I gasped involuntarily.

It's a bluff, I told myself, fighting instinctive fear. He's a decent man doing his job. Concentrate on his interrogation technique!

He touched the slightly puckered, inch-long scar above my right breast.

I held my breath, managed not to recoil.

"Entry wound," he said coldly.

He stared down at me, his eyes betraying no feeling, as he slid his hand around until he located the large, ragged scar just below my shoulder blade.

"Exit wound. Large caliber, close range. The other night, you said something about an accident. Now I want the real explanation."

His left hand remained on my bare shoulder. His fingers pressed uncomfortably into my flesh. Intimacy and physical threat. It was a combination intended to throw any female interrogation subject off balance. Time to let him know that it wouldn't work with me.

I let some hostility creep into my voice.

"Just who the hell do you think you are?"

Then, as if I was touching something distasteful, I put my left thumb and index finger on either side of his wrist and lifted his unresisting hand away from my shoulder.

"Nicely done," he said. "A touch of fear and just the right amount of offended dignity. Though I'm afraid that your dramatics are wasted on me. You see, beyond being Savannah's chief of police, I'm an ex-Marine with friends in Interpol, Naval Intelligence, and at the Bureau. And you are a British agent. More specifically, you work for MI-5. Just what the hell are you doing in my town?"

"Don't be an ass, Callaghan," I said, damning my luck.

He'd gotten more than I had expected. "I didn't come here to do anything but write."

He shook his head.

"I don't think so. Not after what I was told this morning. You've got quite a reputation, lady. One of my buddies said, 'If that hard-assed bitch from MI-5 is involved, something big's in the works. I wouldn't get in her way.'"

Good advice, I thought.

I parted my lips slightly, allowed just a hint of sadness to touch my widened eyes.

"Alex, please listen to me," I said quietly. "Reputations change. People change."

He was leaning forward, his hand braced against the table. I reached out, lightly touched his fingers.

He wrenched his hand away.

"Bullshit! No one changes that quickly. From the first day I met you, there have been inconsistencies. But because I liked you, because I trusted you, I brushed them aside. But no more, lady. You're into something and it sure as hell isn't fiction. If you're running an operation in my town, I want to know about it."

"Believe me—"

"No! *You* damned well better believe *me*. I will not have some foreigner fucking around on my turf without keeping me informed. I've got a call in to the Feds. In the meantime, I'm going to clip your wings. I'm going to have you watched around the clock. If you even breathe wrong, I'll have your little British butt kicked out of this country so fast that your head will spin."

I looked at him, knowing what was at stake. There were people in Washington who could force him to leave my operation untouched. In the United States, locals inevitably lost in turf wars with the Feds and—at some level—I was sanctioned. Alex would be told to back off. But that could take time—time I didn't have. My operation was at a critical point. I had to be mobile *today*. I couldn't afford to have someone as smart and determined as Alex Callaghan obstructing me. So I chose my words deliberately, made them brutal.

"Don't you threaten me, Callaghan. *If* I were working on your bloody turf—and I tell you I'm not—*you* sure as hell wouldn't be able to stop me. You're working way out of your class. You're not even capable of finding a psycho who leaves girls strangled in your backyard!"

Alex's head snapped back as if I had slapped him. The color drained from his cheeks.

"You manipulative bitch," he said slowly. There was genuine hatred in his voice. "You've been using me all along. Well, I may be nothing more to you than an incompetent local cop, but this is still my town. So unless you'd like to file a *formal* complaint, someone will be assigned to *protect* you at all times."

But it won't be you, will it, Alex? I thought. It's your skills and perceptions I fear most, and I've made sure you'll stay well away from me.

I loaded venom into my voice.

"Thanks for your kindness, supercop."

Alex turned on his heel, stalked from the room.

I followed him. I went into the library, stepped through the open French doors, walked along the shadows of the porch until I was near enough his car to listen as he radioed the station.

"Callaghan, here. I'm at home. Send Harris and Stevens out here ASAP."

He signed off, walked over to my car, tried the door.

I'd locked it and wasn't about to offer him the key.

Alex squatted down beside the right front fender of my car, pulled something out of his pocket. His body blocked my view, but the hiss of air told me what he was doing. When he stood, the tire was flat. He walked around the front of the car, repeated the procedure with the left tire.

Damn! I thought. I hadn't been concerned about being watched as long as I had a car. I could easily lose a tail in a town like Savannah. But I hadn't thought he'd try to detain me at the house.

I stepped from the shadows, went out onto the front steps.

"You can't detain me like this without charging me."

Alex stood, leaned back against the fender, scanned the length of the screened porch.

"I assure you, Miss Nichols, you're not being detained. It's unfortunate, though, about your car trouble. Tell you what . . . 'Cause I'm such a good ol' boy and since you've been such a fine houseguest, I'd be delighted to drive you to the airport right now. You just pack your bags, and I'll put you on that plane myself. *And* I'll have your car fixed and returned to the rental agency."

"I have no reason to leave," I said flatly.

"It's more likely you have a reason to stay. I want to know about your operation."

I shook my head.

"My book's not finished."

Alex shrugged.

"Well, then, I guess you'll just be stuck here with my other houseguests. You'll like them. They're fine Southern gentlemen who will keep you company constantly."

"You can't do this, Callaghan," I said, knowing that, in effect, he already had. "I've done nothing to deserve this treatment."

He gave me a smile that sent chills up my spine.

"Feel free to call the police and file a complaint."

"Rot in hell," I said.

I retreated into the library.

A short time later, two burly cops arrived. I heard them pull up. Once again, I walked through the French doors, stood quietly on the porch. I watched carefully as they emerged from the car. One had short-cropped blond hair and was clean-shaven. The other had short-cropped dark hair and a bushy black mustache. The cop with the mustache had been driving. He pocketed the keys.

I slipped back inside and sat down at my typewriter. When Alex brought the pair into the library, I stood, smiled, and extended my hand.

"Hello. I'm Jane."

Like a pair of well-trained Dobermans, they ignored me and looked to Alex for direction.

"This is Miss Nichols, boys. Watch her. Don't let her out of your sight—not even for a minute. If she goes to the john, stand in front of the door. Don't trust her. She's a real actress—Academy Award material."

Then he turned to me.

"I could demand that you give me that little popgun you carry, but I'm sure you have backups. So I'm going to save myself the aggravation of a search by assuring you that if you pull a weapon on the boys here, they'll shoot back—whether they have a chance of getting you or not. Those are my orders and these boys are damned good at following orders. You'll have to kill them to get past them, and I doubt that even *you* can justify killing a cop."

Alex got into his car and drove away.

34

Blondie made a point of answering the phone when it rang. When the call was for me, he sat nearby and unabashedly eavesdropped on my half of the conversation. On the plus side, I thought, it hadn't occurred to him to listen in on the extension.

Calls trickled in throughout the afternoon. I worked on my book in between them.

Joey called, asking if Alex and I would like to join her for dinner. I said no, I didn't think so. A woman claiming a psychic link to the strangler phoned, explained his motivation to me, and asked that I pass the information on to Andrew Jax. Instead, I relayed it to Blondie who, with a disgusted snort, passed it along to Alex. A local talk show host called and invited me to be a guest on his show. I refused politely.

The call I was waiting for came at five o'clock.

"Your publisher's on the phone," Blondie announced. "Says there's a problem with printing your book jacket."

"Damn, always something going wrong," I muttered appropriately. I took the phone from him, leaned back against the kitchen counter. "Yes, John. What seems to be the trouble now?"

"It's rather complicated, Miss Nichols—"

Smith's voice. Where the hell was John?

"—Would you mind if I explained in detail?"

"Go right ahead. I want to know exactly what's going on."

"I assume you can be overheard?" Smith said in a rushed voice.

"Absolutely," I said, glancing at Blondie. He was cleaning his fingernails with a pocket knife.

"The bag lady showed a few minutes ago. Dropped off another pair of arms. No sign of John, so Jonesy's following her."

"But, John, when I talked to you earlier, you told me you knew what the problem was. You assured me you'd supervise that part of the printing operation yourself. What happened?"

"John called you and said that he was joining us?"

"Yes, that's what I understood."

"Well, he hasn't shown and he's still ignoring his beeper. He's in some kind of trouble, isn't he? When he called, did he say where he was?"

"It seems to me that this could have been worked out over a good meal and a few drinks—"

"Restaurant or bar," guessed Smith.

"Well, you bloody well go to Harry and tell him." Harrys wasn't too far from the warehouse. Certainly he'd noticed it.

"Harrys," he said.

"Too bad he has such a loyal following. Perhaps you and all your cronies could learn from him."

There was a pause on the other end. Come on, Smith. Stay with me. I heard a quick intake of breath.

"You think John will be at Harrys and that Jonesy and the courier are headed there too."

Good man, I thought.

"Yes, that's the idea! Get the union leadership to join you, but let them think *they're* making the decisions."

"You'll meet us there. When?"

"If it were up to me, I'd tell them that those presses had bloody well better be up and running. Within the hour. Two at most."

"Got you. Two hours, max. Just east of Harrys. If you don't show or if things get critical before you arrive, I'll call the shots. Okay?"

"Thank you. I'm relying on you."

I hung up the phone, allowed myself a moment to be anxious about John, then dismissed him from my mind.

I glanced at the clock—5:15—and announced that I was taking a shower. As Blondie and Mustache watched, I gathered a change of clothes, then went into the bathroom.

Alex was far too provincial, I thought as I locked the door between me and my guards. He shouldn't have allowed me so much privacy.

I stripped, stuck my head in the running shower long enough to get my hair damp, then dressed quickly in a dark T-shirt, comfortably loose black cotton slacks, and dark socks.

I sat down on the lid of the toilet, put on one of my black, rubber-soled oxfords. The other I kept in my lap as I dismantled a disposable razor. I threw the plastic bits in the wastebasket and carefully embedded the sharp blade into the tip of my shoe, between sole and upper. I took my time, angling it carefully so that a sharp, virtually invisible edge protruded. Finally, I used a wad of cotton and a layer of adhesive tape inside the shoe to secure the blade and protect my toes. Then I slipped the shoe on. After testing the blade against a corner, I turned off the shower and waited for a few minutes before emerging from the bathroom.

Making an effort to walk naturally, I went into the kitchen. I made fresh coffee and wiped up the grounds that I spilled on the counter near the telephone. A few minutes later, I wandered upstairs. I paused to straighten the picture that hung above the phone stand in the hallway. I gathered a stack of magazines from Alex's room, stood beside his bedside table as I thumbed through one of them. Then I went down the narrow back staircase with my double escort still in tow. I abandoned my magazines on the kitchen table, then went off to the bathroom again.

Once the door was locked, I removed the razor from my shoe. After that, I took the sanitary napkin box down from its shelf and considered its contents. I weighed the odds, shook my head as I decided against the Beretta. And my Walther wasn't an option either. Even if I could get to it unobserved, Alex was right. I wouldn't risk killing a cop.

I settled for my knife, strapped it securely to my calf.

I returned to the kitchen with my bodyguards close on my heels. Ignoring them, I sat down at the table, thumbed through the magazines. I waited until Blondie was on the other side of the room.

"Damn, it's not in here," I muttered.

With an irritated noise, I snatched up the stack of magazines and moved quickly past Mustache, toward the back stairs.

Predictably, he was fast on my heels. About a third of the way up the stairs, I tripped, cried out as I lost my balance. I flung my arms wide as if I were trying to catch myself. The movement sent magazines scattering in every direction. Then I fell heavily backwards against Mustache.

Between my weight and the magazines littering the steps, he found it impossible to remain upright. We landed in a painful heap at the base of the stairs. Before Blondie was able to untangle us, I had the keys to the squad car in my pocket.

I let Blondie help me to a chair. Tears rolled down my

cheeks as I sat rubbing my bruised left forearm with my right hand and sniffing noisily.

God! they were unfeeling bastards!

Mustache, who was limping painfully, filled a dishtowel with ice and handed it to me.

"Doubt it's broken. If it swells too bad, we'll call the Chief. See if he wants you taken to the hospital."

With a resentful sob, I flung the ice pack in Mustache's general direction, stood, and walked to the back door. I stepped outside, sat down heavily on the back step.

"Everyone hates me!" I wailed.

I pulled my knees up, wrapped my arms around them, and pressed my face against them. Then I began interspersing my wailing with racking sobs and surreptitious glances at Mustache and Blondie.

Not surprisingly, my crying didn't elicit any sympathy. But the noise drove the men away from me. Blondie stationed himself near the back gate at the far end of the yard. Mustache retreated to a chair in the kitchen.

I carried on, varying my cries from shrill and piercing to low and painfully hoarse, until I thought their nerves were stretched about as far as they were likely to be. Suddenly I lunged to my feet, pointed in Blondie's direction.

"Snake!"

Startled, Blondie's attention shifted to the ground near his feet.

In that moment, I put a hand on the railing, vaulted over the side of the porch, and—praying hard that no snake would actually appear—did another quick vault over the fence. I ran around the house to the front drive.

The squad car was already moving when Blondie and Mustache rounded the corner of the house. I floored the accelerator. Through the spray of grit the tires kicked up, I watched as the pair paused, then raced up the front steps.

They'd be frustrated when they got to the door, I thought. To get back inside, they'd have to return to the back door. *That* was their own fault. Blondie had locked the front door and bolted all the French doors. And once they were back in the house . . .

I pressed down on the accelerator with the toes that had, for a time, shared space with adhesive tape, cotton, and a razor blade. The ease with which phone wires could be surreptitiously cut never failed to amaze me.

I drove directly to Riverfront Plaza. With the visor pulled low, I cruised down River Street until I was in front of the Bayou Cafe. Its sign advertised live entertainment, seven nights a week. I thought the patrons might enjoy an extra free show. And I owed Alex a little aggravation. I double-parked, left the keys in the ignition, turned on the rotating Mars lights, and quickly slid from the car. I locked the door behind me.

I walked the few blocks to the parking lot near Warren Square and shopped for a car to steal. I started my search in the center of the lot. The rows of cars screened me from curious eyes.

If I only had my lock pick set, I thought. Or a screwdriver. Or even a wire clothes hanger. As it was, if I couldn't find a car with an unlocked door, I'd have to break a window. That was a noisy, risky business better avoided.

I spotted an unlocked rear door on a copper-colored Buick LeSabre. I opened it, slid into the front seat. Cursing such a crude use of my delicately balanced throwing knife, I stuck its point in the gap where the steering wheel fit to the steering column and broke the metal collar off the column. Peeling away the column's left side exposed the ignition activating rods. I manipulated them and was rewarded by the hum of the LeSabre's engine.

It was a good car, well taken care of and very responsive. I drove it to within a few blocks of Harrys, parked it near the railyard, used the edge of my shirt to wipe away my prints. As I walked away, I wondered if the car was insured.

35

By six-forty, I was walking rapidly toward Harrys. Smith was waiting in the car on the east end of the street. I slipped into the seat beside him, pulled down the sun visor. It had a mirror mounted on it. I adjusted the angle until I had a good view of Harrys.

"Anything happening there?"

Smith kept his eyes on the rearview mirror, which was also adjusted at an odd angle.

"Nothing. No one in. No one out. And I've been watching for over an hour."

"Where's Jonesy?"

"He hasn't shown yet. I shouldn't have let him follow her."

I wondered, briefly, how many lifetimes of regret were attached to the words "shouldn't have." Dismissed the thought and concentrated on the problem at hand.

"If the courier stays in character, she'll take a rambling, roundabout route."

"You're sure they'll end up here?"

I hope to God they will, I thought.

"John told me that he saw the bag lady go into Harrys last night and never come out."

"Maybe they killed her."

And Jonesy, too. Smith's tone made the unspoken postscript clear.

I shook my head, annoyed that his fear for Jonesy was making him irrational.

"If they'd killed her, she couldn't have shown up at the warehouse today, could she? So let's just be patient. Maybe drive past Harrys, take a closer look."

Smith flushed at the rebuke.

He started the car and we circled the block, drove through the alley. We passed the restaurant's back door, then cruised slowly up the block, past the opaque glass door and the single window with Harrys spelled out in neon letters. At the moment, the sign was unlit. Harrys was closed on Sundays. That, I suspected, severely affected the neighborhood's only other visible income-producing business. It was almost dark and a solitary, bored-looking prostitute walked the street. She didn't bother to raise her head as Smith and I drove past.

We rounded the corner and neared the mouth of the alley again.

"Pull over," I said. "I want to take a closer look at that back door. I didn't notice any windows, but perhaps they're hidden behind that dumpster."

"You think they've taken John, don't you?"

Taken him and killed him, I thought. I looked at Smith, understanding his feelings for his partner, sharing them as I thought of John's intention to break into Harrys. I'd allowed him to get away with ignoring my orders before. I shouldn't have.

I put my hand on Smith's arm, gave it a brief squeeze, managed a tight smile.

"Let's take it one step at a time, shall we, my friend?"

* * *

A single steel door, with a wire-enclosed light above it and a peephole through it, linked Harrys with the alleyway. Beside it was a dumpster. Like all the other containers up and down the alleyway, it overflowed with a week's refuse. The top of the dumpster was within a few inches of the windowless brick wall. But at the base, there was about a foot of clearance.

I got down on hands and knees on the cobblestones, in a mound of rotted vegetables heaped between the wall and the container. I peered behind the dumpster and saw the protruding bars that indicated the presence of a window. I dropped onto my stomach, angled my head and shoulders so that I could wedge them behind the dumpster. Trying to breath as shallowly as possible, I slid forward. I hoped for a view of an interior room, hoped to see John, alive and well, the embarrassed captive of a benevolent captor.

The space covered by the corroded iron bars was filled with bricks and mortar. I lay there, in the stink of rotting vegetables, and ground my teeth in frustration. How the hell did you plan to get in, John? Through the bloody front door? Then I realized that, with John's limited burgling skills, that's exactly what he would have done.

I guessed that that was how we'd have to get in, too.

I was still extracting myself from behind the dumpster when I heard a noise in the alley. Not from the east, where I knew Smith would be waiting inside the car, but the sounds of footsteps from the west.

There were a few more footsteps, a faint rustling, then silence. I lay very still, afraid that any movement would give me away. I heard a second set of footsteps. Their weight and cadence were distinctly different from the first. They belonged to someone in a hurry.

The footsteps stopped abruptly, replaced by the unmistakable sound of one body colliding with another. Someone grunted as breath was forcibly expelled. An overturned trash can clattered.

I scrambled from behind the dumpster, glanced in the direction of the noise. Jonesy and the bag lady were just down the alley from my hiding place. They were under the alley's single light post, locked in a silent, life-and-death wrestling match. Jonesy was on his back. The bag lady was on top of him, her legs straddling his chest, pinning him down. She was gripping a silenced automatic in both hands. Jonesy's arms strained upward. His hands were clamped around her wrists, forcing the lethal muzzle up and away from his body.

I pulled my knife from its sheath and raced forward.

Jonesy arched his body, tipped the bag lady from his chest. With each combatant clinging unrelentingly to the gun, they rolled beyond the pool of weak light, into the alley's uneven shadows. They struggled on, their bodies merging and separating in the uneven light.

I paused, trying to sort out a safe target, and heard the muffled cough of a silenced gun.

Both bodies bucked violently.

I dove for cover behind the nearest garbage cans and waited. I had to see who had lost the struggle. I had to know who would emerge armed.

Jonesy shoved the limp body aside, staggered to his feet.

I called his name softly, then stood and walked over to him. Together we rolled the rag-encased body over and looked at what was left of the face. It was the white Harry.

"I'll get Smith," I said. "You pull the body behind those trash cans, strip off that belt and some of the clothes. Go for the layers underneath, not the blood-spattered stuff."

"Another ringer?"

I nodded. Jonesy grabbed Harry's arms and pulled him into the shadows.

Odds were that the black Harry was inside, waiting for the

bag lady's return. The bag lady costume offered a way in that would minimize the risk to John.

If he was inside.

If he was still alive.

Smith and Jonesy's reunion celebration was brief.

Smith cuffed Jonesy on the shoulder as he knelt beside the body.

"You scared the shit out of me, you motherfucking bastard."

Jonesy looked up at Smith, grinned affectionately.

"Oh ye of little faith," he intoned.

He handed me the last item of the clothing he'd stripped from Harry's body. I slipped it on, tied the rope belt strung with dolls' limbs around my middle, and moved my sheathed knife so that it was at my calf, on top of my slacks. I rubbed a handful of mud, scraped from between the cobblestones, into my face.

"I'll need something to cover my hair. And give me Harry's automatic. I had to leave my Walther behind."

Smith folded the bag lady's empty burlap sack diagonally and secured it, shawl-like, around my head. Jonesy handed me the Ruger.

"If John is in there, we have to get in with a minimum of fuss," I said. "The back of the place is like a fortress, but that seems to be the way this bastard planned to come in. So anyone inside will be expecting him. I'll have to knock, but if I stand just right—"

"Key?" Jonesy interrupted.

He held up a bright object.

"Asshole," his partner muttered.

I smiled as I snatched the key from his hand.

"Yes, this just might make things a bit easier. I'll go in first.

With luck, we can get in unobserved and find John. If not, we go in hard and fast. Understand?"

My two Americans nodded.

I slipped the key smoothly into the lock, slowly opened the restaurant's back door. I shuffled into the kitchen, into the whimpering aftermath of a deep, wailing cry. It echoed off the pots and pans hanging in the empty room.

Jonesy was the last one in. He closed and locked the door behind us.

Black Harry's deep voice called from the open doorway to my left.

"That you, Harry?"

As he spoke, the wail began again. It grew in volume.

I pointed at Smith, who was right behind me.

"Yeah," he said hoarsely.

He let the word dissolve into a cough that was buried within John's trailing scream.

"That shit you traded the Navy pharmacist for is wonderful," Harry said loudly. "This British bastard's got O'Neil's hide nailed to the wall. I just got off the horn with him—told him he'd better torch the warehouse. Not sure how much the fucker's got on us, though. The shit's wearing off. I'm giving him another—"

I held the Ruger out of sight as I came, left shoulder first, around the edge of the door. Smith and Jones were close on my heels.

Black Harry had his back to us. His body blocked my view of John. I could see little more than his right arm. It was bound tightly at wrist and elbow to the arm of a heavy wooden chair. Harry was plunging the contents of a hypodermic needle into a vein that bulged purple against John's pale flesh.

As I stepped through the doorway, I aimed the automatic at Harry's head, squeezed the trigger—

The rope belt at my waist caught on the doorknob. It stopped me short.

Smith, close on my heels, ran heavily into me.

The impact abruptly snapped the snagged belt.

Hopelessly overbalanced, I fell headlong into the room. The back of my right hand slammed against the corner of a stainless-steel counter. My shot went wild as the Ruger was flung from suddenly numb fingers.

Harry left the hypodermic needle embedded in John's arm, dove for shelter behind John's chair. He did a half-roll, snatched an automatic from his belt, came up kneeling. He wrapped his left arm around John's neck, began firing over his right shoulder.

I flattened myself on the floor.

Smith and Jones returned Harry's fire from the shelter of the doorway.

John—his bare upper torso checkerboarded with bloody gouges and his pain-crazed eyes stretched wide—arched against the ropes that bound him. He let go another blood-chilling scream.

Harry didn't react except to tighten his hold.

I was without a gun, so Harry was concentrating on Smith and Jones. They were at a disadvantage. They wouldn't risk hitting John. But their gunfire distracted Harry and covered me.

Feeling was tingling back into my fingers. I snatched my knife from its sheath, lunged violently to my right, turned my momentum into a roll that carried me to a spot parallel to John's chair. It gave me a side view of Harry.

He saw me coming. Ignoring Smith and Jonesy's impotent firing, he brought his right arm around the front of John's face. He leveled his weapon at me.

I stared down its barrel, knowing that I couldn't release my knife in time, knowing that I was going to die.

John plunged his teeth into Harry's forearm.

Shocked by the unexpected assault, Harry leaned away from John as he wrenched his arm free. He presented me with a target and died with my knife in his throat.

I ran to John, pulled the empty hypo from his arm. I dragged my knife from Harry's body and cut the ropes that bound John to the chair.

He began screaming again, his body growing rigid with the pain.

I held his head pillowed against me until the moment passed.

"Sorry, love," he gasped. "I told . . . everything. O'Neil knows. Found drugs . . . plastique. Here. Pantry. Freezer."

Then he screamed again, loud and long. His eyes bulged, the cords on his neck stood out. He fainted mid-scream, leaving the room suddenly silent.

"I'm going after O'Neil," I said to Smith and Jonesy. "There might still be time to stop him. You two drag the other Harry in here. Wipe the Ruger clean. Leave it with his body. Clean away our prints. Remember to wipe the hypodermic needle. Find the drugs and the plastique. Put them somewhere obvious. Call the cops. Ask for an ambulance. Then get in the car and drive away. Don't look back."

"No way," said Smith, violently. "We won't leave you with this mess."

"You need us," added Jonesy.

"I don't need you, and I've no time to argue. I'm protected. You're not. You fellows are the best. I hope we'll work together again some time. But for now, you're fired. Clear out. And bury my knife somewhere between here and the great state of Montana."

36

I ran the few blocks to the warehouse, stripping off the more cumbersome rags as I went. As I ran, a sudden eruption of sirens and an unnatural glow of light in the vicinity of the warehouse confirmed my worst fears. O'Neil had set it afire. He had set in motion a sequence of events that would end in death for those working to put out the blaze.

I cut through the railyard, ran through the darkened alleys that were the most direct route between Harrys and the warehouse, praying that I would be able to keep the plastique beneath the warehouse from claiming innocent lives.

I ran, dodging discarded boxes and leaping over heaps of refuse, knowing that there was little hope of catching O'Neil. As I ran, I wondered about my operation's success. Was what we'd accomplished worth the pain John had endured? Worth the lies to Alex? Could I justify the deaths of both Harrys? And my decision to leave a heat-sensitive bomb unreported *and* intact?

The answers came readily. They came with abrupt, soul-chilling clarity. Yes, on all counts. Regrettable, but yes.

I rounded a corner, saw the warehouse. Flames and black, acrid smoke poured from the roof of the narrow two-story building. I imagined the blaze inside eating away at the tangle of limbs and wheelchairs in the attic storeroom, then imagined the heat triggering the fuse beneath the first-floor office. I found the energy to run faster.

The crowd of onlookers in front of the warehouse slowed me. Drawn by the fire, an excited, unruly mob was gathered between me and the people I needed to reach. I pushed my way through the crowd, breathlessly demanding that they move aside. Reduced to a terrifyingly slow pace, I elbowed the more reluctant bodies out of my way.

"It's a fucking bag lady," a male voice cried. "The goddamned bitch pushed me!"

Without warning, a portion of the crowd surged around me. A fist rammed into my stomach. I doubled over, retching with pain. A heavy blow between my shoulder blades knocked me to the pavement.

For a moment, I lay stunned with my cheek against the muddy cobblestone street and a kaleidoscope of feet swirling before my eyes. Then I began crawling, pushing my way through the jungle of legs, struggling blindly toward what I prayed was the front of the crowd.

The ground was a good place to be. There was less smoke and more oxygen down low. My head cleared. I could see that I was almost there. I could see the flickering, raging firelight through one last row of legs.

There was an eye-catching movement beside me. I turned my head in time to see a foot, clad in an expensive leather shoe, pulling back—poised to deliver a kick. I tried to dodge its forward swing. Desperately, I flung myself against the front row of legs, catching the first row of onlookers behind their knees, sending people tumbling to the ground. But my assailant's foot still caught me, rammed a toe into my left kidney.

I cried out at this new explosion of pain. Cried out until concerned faces, friendly hands, pulled me from the tangle of arms and legs. I staggered forward, grabbed the nearest firefighter by the sleeve of his black rubber slicker. He looked up from unrolling a hose.

"Who's in charge?" I croaked.

He gestured distractedly toward the crowd.

"Get back, lady!"

I tried to sound authoritative, knew I looked anything but.

"No! I must speak to someone in charge."

He ignored me, went back to his hose.

I glanced quickly around, searching for anyone giving orders. The wind changed, blowing a cloud of acrid smoke over the street. When the smoke cleared, bodies had shifted. I saw someone in the midst of the firefighters and their equipment, someone shouting and gesturing broadly with his arms. Another gout of smoke swirled through the street, simultaneously obscuring the scene and shielding me from those assigned to contain the crowd behind the barricades. Trusting my instincts, I stumbled forward through the gamut of uniformed bodies and writhing hoses, straining to pick one man, one voice, out of the chaos—trying to reach him. And then he was there, just a few yards in front of me.

"Inside!" he was yelling. "I want a team inside. Check those first-floor offices, fast! Make sure no one's there."

Four helmeted firefighters moved determinedly toward the burning warehouse, fire axes in hand. Their commander abruptly turned and jogged away from me, toward an arriving aerial ladder truck. I knew I'd never catch him in time. I ran to intercept the firefighters.

Flames were licking up the sides of the building, shooting towards the roof. But the offices at the near corner were still intact. Hoses directed water in that direction, soaking the walls and the door, seeking to save that which I knew to be unsalvageable. Heat poured from the building. It wouldn't be long before the heat-sensitive fuse was ignited. And then . . .

I used my shoulder to knock the man nearest the door violently aside.

"Get back! Don't go in there. It will explode!"

The firefighter recovered from his stumble, grabbed me roughly by the arm, shook me.

"You're nuts, you old wino!" He shouted to someone behind me. "Frank! Get this crazy broad out of here!"

He shoved me aside. Then he and his companions began moving back in the direction of the fire.

His push overbalanced me. I staggered backward, caught my heel on one of the hoses, and fell. I lost valuable time scrambling to my feet and stumbling after them, calling for them to stop. They ignored me, simply kept moving. I grabbed at the backs of their slickers, tried to slow them down, to keep them back.

I was seized from behind.

"Just relax, lady," a deep voice muttered near my ear. "The cops will be here soon. They'll take you somewhere safe. Somewhere full of nice people who will take good care of you."

"I'm not crazy! Please! Listen to me!"

"Now, let's not start again!"

Still holding me crushed within the vise of his arms, the firefighter turned his back on the fire. He shifted his stance to the right, then to the left, looking for assistance.

A squad car came squealing to a halt inside the barricades.

"Here comes the cavalry," the firefighter muttered beside my ear.

He moved in that direction.

A familiar figure emerged from the squad car.

"Hey, Chief! I've got a live one for you!"

"Alex!" I screamed. "The building is wired with explosives! For God's sake, don't let anyone go inside!"

Alex sprinted past us.

"Listen to her!" he said.

Abruptly I was free.

"Heat-sensitive fuse," I blurted. "Explosives beneath the first floor. Enough to level the building."

The firefighter raced to alert his commander.

I turned back toward the fire, looking for Alex.

The squad of firefighters I'd tried so hard to intercept had shattered the door with their axes. They were already inside.

Alex plunged into the blazing building after them.

"No!" I cried. If the plastique was ignited . . .

My voice was lost in the roar of the flames.

I watched, counting the seconds. My mind babbled a terrified litany. No! Please, God! No! Not Alex too!

Then he was out, running from the building with the squad of firefighters strung out behind him. The commander intercepted them, activity erupted all around them as commands were shouted over the roar of diesel engines.

I stumbled away, sobbing with relief, and sought shelter behind the truck parked farthest from the warehouse. It was far enough away that I doubted they'd need to move it.

Then I waited. I sat on the running board that extended along the truck's side, pressed my aching body against the cool, chartreuse-enameled metal, and waited. I watched as an invading army of uniformed police pushed the crowds back, moved the barricades to a safer distance. Watched as smoke-streaked firefighters sought momentary respite from the heat, then returned to the perimeter they'd established around the inferno.

The warehouse exploded with a terrible roar.

*   *   *

I stayed where I was, occupying myself by staring at the eerie patterns the firelight cast on the faces beyond the barricades. Earlier, when I'd tried to stand, my body had rebelled. I'd felt no urgent need to fight it.

I tried to care. I reminded myself that O'Neil was gone. I tried to worry about John. An unflappable interior voice replied that, at the moment, there was little I could do to remedy either situation.

Mustache and Blondie found me.

More accurately, I found them.

They were wandering along the barricades, staring out into the crowd. I watched them for a long time, convinced that they were searching for me. I stayed where I was, supported by the truck's massive fender. When they were exactly opposite me, I lifted my fingers to my lips and whistled shrilly to get their attention. They turned toward the sound, faces alert. I lifted my hand briefly.

They came forward slowly.

"Are you fellows looking for me?"

Blondie peered at me uncertainly, wrinkling his nose in distaste.

"Miss Nichols?"

I'd forgotten how I was dressed.

"Did you find your squad car?"

"It's her," Mustache said flatly.

Blondie squatted down, looked at my face closely. Apparently convinced of my identity, he spoke in a voice that betrayed complete bewilderment.

"Chief Callaghan wants to talk to you, ma'am. He said that if we found you, we *weren't* to arrest you. We are supposed to *ask* you to come with us."

"Well, Blon—" I began. I caught myself and said, "Exactly what *are* your names?"

Blondie seemed surprised that I didn't know.

"I'm Harris. This is Stevens."

I shut my eyes, leaned my head back against the truck.

"Well, Harris, I'm simply too tired to move. Why don't you go get Chief Callaghan while Stevens here stands guard?"

They consulted, found the plan agreeable. Five minutes later, Harris returned with Alex. Neither looked happy, but Alex's scowling, soot-streaked face was positively grim.

Harris sidled over next to his partner, apparently seeking moral support. For a moment, Alex ignored me to focus his attention completely on them.

"Damn it all, boys! There are two of you and only one of her. But not only does she wreck the phones right under your noses, steal your keys, and take off in your squad car, *now* she's giving you orders. I asked you to bring her to *me*."

Stevens and Harris shuffled their feet, managed to look acutely embarrassed.

"Sorry, Chief," Stevens muttered.

"Yeah, sorry, Chief," Harris echoed.

Alex waved a hand in dismissal.

"Ah, shit! Go back to the station, check at the desk, make sure that the phone company's sent a crew out to my house. Then write your report."

"Yes, sir, Chief!" Stevens and Harris cried in unison.

"And do me a favor, boys. Gloss over the details, okay?"

The pair looked relieved. Stevens hazarded a sheepish smile in Alex's direction before they beat a hasty retreat.

Alex shook his head slowly as he watched them leave. Then he turned back toward me. For a long time, he stood, saying nothing. His face was heavily shadowed, making his expression difficult to read. I turned my head slightly to stare past him, out at the crowd.

"So, Miss Nichols, was this what you were after?"

I didn't bother refocusing on him.

"No."

"But O'Neil was."

Surprised, I jerked my eyes back to Alex's face. But I said nothing.

"In spite of what you think of me, I *can* see what's here. We have Jim O'Neil, upstanding American businessman and international humanitarian, and Jane Nichols, team leader of a British anti-terrorist unit. And we have a warehouse that explodes violently and unexpectedly. Except that you *know* it's going to explode.

"The way I see it, either you set this fire or O'Neil did. Since you're supposedly one of the good guys, and I've just been told that O'Neil has stripped everything of value from his home and is nowhere to be found—I'm betting that he's the firebug. I've got an APB out for him."

"He keeps a speedboat tied up beneath the warehouse."

Alex nodded.

"The dock area's still intact, but there's no sign of any vessel. I'll alert the Coast Guard."

I gave Alex the boat's name and registry number, but doubted it would help. With plenty of cash, a head start, and an ocean to choose from . . .

"You'll never find him."

"Are you speaking from experience, Miss Nichols?"

I sighed, looked out at the crowd again. I had little to lose by telling Alex about O'Neil and his part in the smuggling operation. But the connection to Harrys was too direct. Smith and Jones needed time to escape. They'd get that time if I made myself the obvious target for an official investigation.

When it became apparent that I wasn't going to say anything, Alex spoke again.

"Something else interesting happened this evening. At Harrys. In fact, I was headed over there when I encountered *this* mess. Seems we have a double murder. Anonymously reported, of course. When Tommy arrived on the scene, he found both Harrys—one with half his face shot away, one with his throat slashed. He called me because it wasn't *just* a double murder. Someone dumped a sack of flour on the floor between the Harrys. Only it looks more like drugs than flour. And there are bricks of ice cream stacked in an open chest freezer. Only the ice cream didn't melt because it's actually plastique. Enough plastique, Tommy says, to level several city blocks."

"How ghastly. Though I don't understand why you're telling me."

"You don't, huh? Then I don't suppose you'd be interested in the third guy they found. Coincidentally, *he* was carrying a British passport. John Wiggins, businessman. An associate of yours, perhaps?"

"Thousands of British citizens visit your country every year, Alex."

He nodded.

"True. Very true. So I guess it doesn't matter to you that Mr. Wiggins is in pretty bad shape. Seems like he's been given a firsthand experience with a drug the military's developed. It's an experimental truth serum called acetylquaertox. The Harrys were using it to pry information from Mr. Wiggins when *someone* got the drop on them. Wonder who that someone could be?"

Alex peered at me closely. If he was looking for a reaction, he was disappointed.

"Of course, I could be wrong. Maybe Mr. Wiggins is nothing more than some strung-out addict who got himself caught trying to rip the Harrys off. Maybe the Harrys were just treating him to a new kind of high."

Alex paused.

I met his eyes squarely and waited.

"You're one tough cookie, aren't you?" he said bitterly.

Yeah, real tough, I thought. I couldn't stop thinking about John's drug-induced pain.

"He's a witness to a murder, you know. I'm tempted to send him off to the jail infirmary. Have them patch up those knife pricks, wrap him in a straitjacket, and hold him in a cell. Maybe wait for a few hours and see if this *stranger* comes down natural-like."

I didn't think he was serious. I couldn't take the risk.

"John's the kind of person you want by your side when you're walking down a dark alley."

Alex stared at me.

We both knew that I'd just given him the lever he wanted. If the quality of John's medical care was tied to my answering Alex's questions, I'd be hard pressed to keep silent.

Alex was a good man, I told myself. He wouldn't risk John's life.

Alex said nothing.

Alex was a smart cop, I told myself. He'd know that I would lie to him anyway.

Alex took a step closer.

"So you *do* have feelings. Your man's at the hospital. Doc Reinhart's taking care of him."

I almost sobbed with relief.

"Thank you," I said.

"Don't thank me, Jane. Level with me."

I owed him something.

"Everything I had—everything that you'd be interested in—burned with the warehouse. You've got the plastique. And the drugs. You should be able to make a connection between the two Harrys, some heavy-duty trafficking, and, perhaps, the shrinkage at Fort Stewart. Be satisfied with that, Alex."

"Both Harrys were murdered."

I shook my head.

"I know nothing about it. And I'm sure your torture victim was too delirious to have witnessed anything."

The look on Alex's face hardened. He slammed his fist against the fire engine's fender, glared at me with undisguised hostility.

"If you're so fucking clever, Miss Nichols, how do you explain knowing about the explosives in the warehouse which, I'm sure, will turn out to be plastique?"

"Coincidence," I said quietly. "I had an idea for a new novel—something involving street people as couriers for a smuggling operation. I was researching the topic when I noticed that a nearby warehouse was on fire. As I watched, an old wino—who I didn't get a very good look at—told me about something he'd seen beneath the warehouse one night when he'd crawled in there to sleep it off. I realized what he might be describing and I ran for help."

"You're lying. You—or one of your people—killed those two men."

I shrugged.

"I think you'll be hard pressed to prove it. But you do what you have to. I assure you, though, if you push too hard, you'll get a call from Washington forcing you to back off."

"I'll be looking forward to that call. In the meantime, I'm not going to arrest you. You saved some lives tonight. So I'm *requesting* that you stay in town until this investigation is over."

He braced his hands on the truck, leaned in close to me. His narrowed eyes and harsh, ruthless tone left no doubt as to his state of mind.

"If you leave without my permission, I'll have *your friend* arrested. He and his paperwork will be lost for a day or two. He'll spend that time in an overcrowded jail cell. His roommates will be told he's a cop."

I knew, perhaps better than he did, that his threat was an

idle one. Alex played by the rules. He'd proved that tonight.
But his anger was real. And justified.

"There's no need to threaten. I'll stay. You have my word."

He stared at me in disbelief.

"Your *word*? To an incompetent local cop? How much can
that be worth?"

He turned on his heel, walked back toward the line of firefighters.

I couldn't let him leave—not like that. I got up and staggered after him, resisting the urge to bend over and wrap my
arms around my viciously aching stomach.

I grabbed his wrist.

He stopped, stiffening at my touch. He didn't turn around.

"Alex, no matter what else happens between us, I want you
to know that I think you're a decent man and a *good* cop.
You'll catch your psycho. And maybe you'll get O'Neil, too."

He shook his hand free.

"Don't attempt to leave town, Miss Nichols."

Then he walked away.

I smiled crookedly at his back.

"Good night, Alex," I whispered.

I turned and limped slowly in the opposite direction, toward the barricades that kept out the thinning crowd. I concentrated on stepping carefully over the hoses that
crisscrossed the street.

It was okay, I told myself as I walked, for a bag lady to
bend over and stare at the ground. Okay, too, if she held an
arm pressed tightly against her stomach and cried a little, because of the pain. John would appreciate the authenticity.

I'd go back to John's suite, call Mac, report. Arrange for the
Feds to liaise with the local police. Perhaps between them,
they'd locate O'Neil. Or perhaps one of our people would. I'd
return to London and continue working for the organization.

It might take years, but inevitably O'Neil would resurface. In the meantime, there were others just like him.

I was halfway to the barricades when the agony in my stomach and back became unbearable. Very authentic, I thought grimly, as I doubled over and vomited painfully onto the street.

"Jane!"

Alex's voice. He sounded—concerned?

I couldn't straighten. My head was hot and heavy. I turned it slowly in his direction.

For a moment, I saw his running figure clearly. Then it blurred to a wavering shadow that smeared darkly across the glowing night sky. I groaned, shut my eyes, sank to my knees, slowly crumpled forward. I felt the cold, wet pavement beneath my cheek. Then, nothing.

37

Between phone calls, I considered the manuscript spread out on the kitchen table. Tentatively entitled *Jax of Hearts*, it was minus only a few chapters. At the moment, I wasn't laying odds on completing them. Inspiration had vanished. The dialogue was sounding forced. The characters were sitting in the margins with their feet up, thumbing their noses at me.

I'd moved to the kitchen seeking proximity to the coffeepot and the telephone, hoping that the change of scenery would help. So far, it hadn't.

The phone rang again. Why the hell had they repaired it so efficiently? I crossed the kitchen, answered it.

It was Alex. His voice was icy formal.

"Chief Callaghan here, Miss Nichols. I'm calling to let you know that I talked to your friend, John Wiggins, this afternoon. You were right. He doesn't remember a thing. And the Feds have arrived in force. They're right here in my office. You and Wiggins are free to leave any time."

"Thank you, Alex."

"I had no choice."

He broke the connection.

I held the receiver for a time, envisioning the man on the other end of the line, thinking about what I had lost.

I regretted so much.

Despite my protests, my fainting spell of the evening before had earned me a ride to the hospital. Alex stayed beside me as the paramedics loaded me carefully onto a stretcher. He rode in the back of the ambulance with me.

"Thanks for scraping me off the pavement," I said.

He avoided my eyes.

"Just doing my job."

"Well, thanks anyway."

I took some small comfort in the concern I thought I remembered hearing in his voice.

In the emergency room, he lingered nearby as an energetic Doc Reinhart examined me. Between tests and X-rays, Alex took me to John.

A sleepy-looking policewoman snapped to attention as he pushed my wheelchair past her and into a tiny, glass-enclosed room. John lay there. His eyes were shut. His breathing seemed regular, but he looked waxen and terribly frail. Monitors were hooked to his bandage-encased chest. An IV tube sprang from a forearm.

I pointed to the padded restraints that bound him to the bed.

"Are these necessary? He's not going anywhere."

"I didn't order them," Alex said.

"Please, ask that they be removed."

He looked at me with suspicion—analyzing my motives, I presumed.

I reached out, enclosed John's slack fingers within the shelter of my hand.

"Drug dealers seem to be John's undoing," I said slowly, thinking about Harrys. "Look at his hands and arms, Alex."

"I see them."

"This happened when a group he'd infiltrated discovered his identity. He was tied to a bed. Before he was rescued—"

I shook my head, driving away the images. I released John's hand, twisted in the wheelchair, looked beseechingly at the man whose trust I'd deliberately destroyed.

"John means as much to me as Tommy does to you."

Alex nodded curtly.

"Okay. I'll see what I can do."

Doc Reinhart ordered the restraints removed and pronounced my internal organs bruised but probably intact. He suggested I stay the night for observation.

I shook my head.

"I don't care for hospitals. If someone would be kind enough to call me a taxi, I'll pack my things and spend the night at a hotel."

Alex objected. He asked Doc Reinhart to leave us alone for a few minutes.

"I am conducting a murder investigation, Miss Nichols, in which you are a prime suspect. If you choose not to stay at the hospital, that is your business. But you'll remain as my house-guest."

I opened my mouth to object.

His stony look caused me to leave the words unspoken.

With a sigh, I hung the receiver on its cradle on the kitchen wall. I poured myself another cup of coffee, sat back down at the table, and tried to ignore a twisting ache in my gut that had nothing to do with physical injury.

*　　　*　　　*

We had returned to the house in the wee hours of the morning. Alex locked the door behind us. Without a word or a look in my direction, he left me standing in the foyer and went upstairs to his room.

Three hours of restless, hagridden sleep later, I awakened sore and exhausted. I wandered into the kitchen, found a new pot of coffee on the warmer and an abandoned half-cup of cold, black coffee on the table.

The note taped to the coffeemaker was as charming as the one Alex had left the day before. "Be here when I call." No salutation. No signature.

I'd called Mac immediately, let him know that the phone I was speaking from wasn't secure. Taking care not to imply any involvement on my part or John's, I outlined the events of the past twenty-four hours. I left it to Mac to fill in the details. He had a good imagination, too. I asked for immediate support from Washington and agreed to return to London as soon as the Feds had cleared things up.

Before disconnecting, he had echoed my advice to Alex.

"Be satisfied, Janie."

"I'll try."

I glanced at my watch, wondering who had sanctioned us in Washington. It was just past six o'clock on Monday evening. The Feds had arrived on Alex's doorstep in under thirteen hours. To get such a quick response, Mac must have rousted someone extraordinarily influential from bed at dawn.

Too late, I thought, to leave Savannah tonight. Besides, at the moment, I hadn't even enough energy to pull my clothes from the wardrobe. I'd wait until morning, perhaps manage one night's uninterrupted sleep. Then I'd pack my belongings and the contents of the suite, check in on John, and fly home.

In the meantime, I'd work on my stalled plot. Immerse myself in a problem I might actually solve.

I turned on the radio, fussed with the selector until I found a station I liked. I wasted a few minutes standing on the back porch. I looked out into another rain-drenched evening, wondered about the weather in London. I thought about John for a few minutes, remembered that he'd taken the back door off the alarm system, and made a mental note to reconnect it before I left. I considered washing the few dishes that were in the sink, then realized what I was doing.

I scolded myself for procrastinating, reluctantly settled back down into my chair. I began thumbing through my manuscript, resigned to rereading words that no longer held any appeal.

Early in my writing career I'd learned that when characters refuse to take another step, there was little point in forcing them. Instead, the astute writer reviews material already written, seeking problems within key scenes. The last time characters had been this uncooperative, I'd written a scene in which a wheelchair-bound woman had walked across a garden to greet Andrew Jax. I'd had to discard the scene, which I regretted. It had been extraordinarily well written.

I sat for an uninterrupted hour, poring over my chapters, hurrying my thoughts along by chewing on the end of my pencil. The phone rang again just as I discovered the flaw. Between rings, I made a quick note in the margin. Then I hurried across the kitchen and snatched the receiver from the wall.

A high-pitched, nervous male voice was on the line.

"My name is Joe, Miss Nichols. I saw your picture in the newspaper. I thought about it and thought about it and I'm sorry Miss Nichols but I had to talk to you."

Damn it all to bloody hell! I thought. I'd already heard

from half a dozen well-meaning strangers. Each had called to offer me—and Andrew Jax—information they'd been reluctant to share with the police. I'd conscientiously passed the information on to Alex.

I didn't want to talk with Alex again.

I tried not to sigh.

"All right, Joe. What can I do for you?"

"I just need to tell someone before . . . before . . ." He stuttered to a halt, drew a long, gasping breath, rushed on. "I want everybody to know. You tell Andrew Jax. Tell him for me. I didn't want to kill those girls. Tell him, tell everyone. I'm sorry. No more killing. No more. I'm stopping. Stopping the only way I can. The only way I know how . . ."

He was crying.

Over his sobs I heard a telltale metallic click. There was an explosion of sound, a moment of silence, a dial tone.

I phoned the police station, hoping the call had been some kind of sick joke. Knowing it wasn't.

The desk sergeant answered.

"Alex Callaghan, please. Jane Nichols, here."

"He took a quick trip down the hall, Miss Nichols. Can he call you right back?"

"Please. Tell him it's urgent."

I hung up the phone, stared blindly at it.

My stomach and back ached, and I was tired. Physically and mentally drained. Enough, I thought. I've had enough. I need to rest.

The crushing impact of a man's body propelled me against the wall.

My assailant grabbed my hair, slammed my face into the telephone's plastic cradle. The receiver fell from its hook, clattered hollowly against the wall. Blood burst from my nose. My teeth sliced into my lower lip.

I blacked out momentarily. Before I could recover, my

hair was released. The phone cord was looped around my neck.

A familiar voice whispered close to my ear.

"Game's over, Moura, me darlin'."

The cord was wrenched free of the cradle, pulled tight.

I lashed out with arms and legs, seeking to escape O'Neil's overwhelming weight, trying to claw my way free of the tightening cord. As I struggled, I cursed the blood that flowed from my nose, filled my mouth, gagged me, prevented me from catching my breath.

When bright points of light began exploding behind my eyes and my legs no longer supported me, I stopped struggling. I leaned into the wall, let the press of O'Neil's body hold me upright. I concentrated on dragging oxygen into my lungs and wished futilely for a knife to plunge into his body.

O'Neil's weight was replaced by an isolated pressure in the small of my back. The cord around my neck loosened.

I stayed against the wall, shifting my arms slightly to keep my wobbly body upright. I spat the accumulated blood from my mouth, moved my head so that I could blot my nose and mouth against the crook of my elbow. The pressure on my back, undoubtedly the muzzle of a gun, remained constant.

I held my position for a few more seconds, gratefully gulping for air. Then I coughed, spat more blood, and shifted again. This time, I slid my fingers closer to the cord around my neck.

"Oh, no, you don't!"

The cord was wrenched tight. The gun's muzzle slammed into my back. I moved my hand away from my neck. The cord relaxed.

"That's right, my girl," O'Neil said pleasantly, abandoning his brogue, "don't fight it. You're going to die. No choice in that. But the dying can be easy or it can be real hard. I'd suggest cooperation. Oh, just in case you're wondering, I have a .38 Smith and Wesson pressed up against your spine.

"Now, me darlin', let's go for a little walk."

We walked in silence across the garden, then along the flagstone path to the tree line. The rain had finally stopped. The clouds had parted, the moon was bright, the breeze felt cool and fresh.

"A lovely night for dying," O'Neil murmured as we reached the muddy path that wound down toward the river. "Especially when you're dying for the second time."

I said nothing. I continued to walk, moving as slowly as he'd let me. As I walked, I prayed that my phone call to Alex had raised an alarm, knowing that very likely it hadn't. My survival was in my own hands, as it had been so often in the past.

"The papers said Moura died," O'Neil said. "I felt bad. She was such a lovely Irish lass. So young. So sweet. I sent yellow roses to her funeral."

I had been drifting gradually away from the center of the path, looking for a tree trunk that would provide a barrier between me and the point of his gun. If I timed it right and flung myself sideways, off the path—

O'Neil yanked the cord backward, bringing me to an abrupt halt. He dragged the .38 painfully up my spine, continued upwards until its blunt muzzle rested along my right cheekbone, touching the right corner of my mouth. He used its pressure to steer me back to the center of the path. Then he moved the gun back against my spine and loosened the noose.

We began walking again.

"You won't escape," he said matter-of-factly. "You wouldn't have survived last time if I hadn't left the job to Tony. I should have taken care of you myself. Maybe had a little fun in the process. But perhaps it's not too late."

He gave my makeshift leash another tug.

I stopped.

"Take a step forward, into the moonlight, Moura, me darlin'. Now take off your blouse. And the bra. Remember, love, I can cut you in half by simply squeezing my finger. Now the shoes. And the shorts. And those cute little undies."

I followed his directions, knowing that he appreciated a submissive victim. I had learned that from bugging his mistress's house. If I behaved as she had, he might let his guard down.

I dropped my clothing into the center of the muddy path.

He grunted with satisfaction, kept the noose taut as he ran the cold tip of the .38 lingeringly up my spine again.

"Now, turn your head."

I did as he said, confirming my suspicions. He held the gun in his right hand, the strangling cord in his left. I gave him what he wanted. I stared at him with wide, frightened eyes and whimpered. When I could no longer keep the fury from my expression, I turned my head away.

O'Neil laughed.

"Ah, just as I thought. You don't look so pretty now. All bloody and bruised. Well, it doesn't really matter. I don't have time to play."

Keep it up, you egocentric bastard, I thought. Give me time. Sooner or later, I'll find an opening. Then we'll see who dies.

He prodded me with the gun. We continued walking. He kept talking.

"You and that incompetent little snake, Joe Green. I thought I'd gotten rid of you both and walked away clean. For years, it's been business as usual. Then some British bastard triggers the silent alarm and Black Harry catches him inside the restaurant, going through the merchandise. He's a friend of yours, isn't he, Moura. Or should I say, 'Janie'?"

I didn't answer. There was little point.

"Not real talkative, are we, darlin'? Well, your buddy wasn't, either. Not at first. He frustrated the Harrys. They take great pride in not having to resort to drugs. But after White Harry dropped off my payment, I phoned Black Harry. Suggested that he shoot the bastard up with some new stuff they'd acquired. Seems it's like having shards of glass pumping through your veins. Black Harry liked that idea. He likes hearing his victims scream. And your buddy *was* screaming. I could hear him in the background when Black Harry called to tell me that he'd spilled his guts."

You bastard, I thought. I clenched my fists, dug my nails into my palms, kept my anger under control.

"I'd already moved my boat to a safe place upriver. Just in case. It was a simple matter to torch my little operation and walk away. But I've always liked fires, so I was at the back of the crowd, watching, waiting for the explosion. That's when I saw you, my resurrected darlin'. Dressed like a bag lady and shouting in a snooty British accent for everyone to move aside. Funny, I don't think I'd have recognized you if you'd looked like you do now or like your picture in the paper. But you were filthy. I had to look at you real hard. Noticed the way you held your head, saw that profile. I tried to stop you, but you got through the crowd. Then I decided it didn't matter. No one was going to pay any attention to a derelict. But Callaghan comes tearing up and *he* listens to you. That's when I remembered the newspaper story about his houseguest—some woman writer from London.

"I began adding up my troubles and the answer was you. You, you fucking *bitch*."

O'Neil gave the cord a wrenching jerk.

I stumbled, fell forward onto my hands and knees. The cord bit viciously into my skin. The cold metal of O'Neil's gun was suddenly pressing against the base of my spine. For the first time, I felt a lurch of terror and despair. I tensed, waiting for the bullet that would tear through me. If I was lucky, it would end my life.

"Just who the hell are you, *bitch*?" O'Neil pulled backward on the cord until I was gagging for air. "The Branch? Interpol? Talk, damn you. Die easy or hard. You choose."

I had nothing to lose.

"British Intelligence," I gasped.

He didn't fire. He snickered. The cord relaxed. He gave it a quick tug.

"Get up."

Giddy with relief, I scrambled to my feet.

"Well, Moura, me darlin', we're back to where we were in Chicago. You've caused me considerable inconvenience, but my life and my business will go on. And because I don't want to give your people or that cop friend of yours any incentive to follow me, you—me poor darlin'—are going to be the strangler's latest victim."

No comfort in knowing that the strangler was dead, that Alex wouldn't be deceived.

O'Neil came up close behind me. His laughter was hot against my cheek. It grated against my raw nerves. Fed the panic I was already feeling. The whole situation echoed, too vividly, the endless forested paths and blood-soaked moonlit clearings of my dreams. I struggled for detachment, brutally dismissing thoughts of death. Cool, methodical thinking was the only chance I had.

O'Neil pushed the gun into my back to encourage me forward. We walked down the path another hundred yards. Then he tugged at the cord.

I stopped.

"This is where you die."

Once again he dragged the gun slowly up my back, ran its length along my cheek.

One chance, I thought. One chance.

I stepped down hard on his left foot, smashed my head backward into his face, drove my right elbow into his ribs. I grabbed for the snubnosed .38 with my left hand, caught it *and* O'Neil's hand, fought to wrest the gun from him.

I didn't succeed.

Overbalanced, unable to move his left foot, he fell backwards. He let go of the gun, dropping it onto the path. But he held onto the cord as he fell, wrenching me down with him.

We hit the ground together, me on top. The cord loosened. I tried to put my fingers between it and my neck.

Too late.

O'Neil recovered, yanked the cord tight, rolled us over so that I was face down in the mud. He straddled me, slammed his weight down on my back, trapped my body between his knees.

"You've been too much trouble," he gasped. "Far too much trouble."

Slowly, slowly, he twisted the cord tighter.

I struggled. I twisted my body, flailed my arms and legs, fought O'Neil, fought the mud that weighted my limbs, filled my mouth. I clawed the earth, tried to find a root, a limb, a rock. Something, anything, to give me leverage. Something, anything, to dislodge him.

I found his gun.

I stopped fighting, went limp.

O'Neil laughed. He gave the cord another twist.

"Goodbye, Moura."

I lifted the .38 from the mud, bent my elbow, brought the

top of the revolver against my shoulder, muzzle pointed upwards, towards O'Neil. I held it tight, fired. The noise beside my ear was deafening.

O'Neil stiffened, his weight shifting as if he was sitting upright. Then he collapsed forward on top of me. Warmth poured across my back and neck.

The cord was still tight around my throat. I let go of the .38, grasped the cord with my fingers, tried to pry it loose. It was hopelessly tangled in O'Neil's fingers. I tried to shift his dead weight from my back. Found that I didn't have the strength.

I couldn't breathe.

My world faded to red. A pulse hammered in my ears. Vague, disconnected thoughts buzzed through my mind.

I got him, Mac.

I miss you, Brian.

I love you, Alex.

Then, no thoughts. The beginning of darkness and peace.

Voices and footsteps in the distance.

Suddenly, O'Neil's weight was gone.

Fingers rough with haste pulled the twisted cord from my neck. They sought a pulse.

"Jane! Oh, God, Jane!"

Alex's voice.

He pulled me into his arms.

I opened my eyes, tried to speak, tried to tell him I was all right. Couldn't. I curled my naked body into the shelter of his arms, pressed my face against his chest, and breathed. Just breathed.

After a while, the world stopped spinning.

I peered through the darkness, saw Tommy standing over O'Neil's body, speaking into a portable radio.

"How?" I whispered.

"They said you'd called," Alex said. "That it was important. When I couldn't get through . . . All I could think about was that I'd left you by yourself. I grabbed Tommy, and we drove to the house. I saw the kitchen, the blood . . ."

His voice broke. His arms tightened convulsively.

Tommy's radio stopped crackling, went silent. He stepped over to us, stripped off his shirt, waited as Alex wrapped it around me.

"The ambulance is on its way," Tommy said. He hunkered down, brought his face closer to mine. "Looks like you got our strangler."

I shook my head, swallowed. Liquid fire traveled down my swollen throat. Didn't matter. I was alive.

"Strangler's already dead. Suicide. Why I called."

"Then who the hell is this?"

I tried to speak, coughed instead.

Alex hugged me closer.

I swallowed, tried again.

"Jim O'Neil. Terrorist. Murderer. His gun."

"Well, you got him. Close range, center of the chest. Not bad for an *amateur*, right, Chief?"

"No, Tommy. Not bad at all."

No humor in either man's voice.

A message, I thought. Whatever I was, whoever I worked for, my rules or theirs—we were still on the same side.

Tommy stood.

"I'll go meet the troops."

Briefly, I watched the beam of his flashlight bob its way down the path toward the house. Then I closed my eyes, snuggled deeper into Alex's arms.

"Tommy's wrong," I croaked. "Max Murdock's no amateur."

Then Alex laughed.

He held me tight, rocked me in his arms, and laughed.

Though, to be honest, it sounded more like he was crying.

Andrew Jax sat up in bed and reached for the pack of cigarettes on the bedstand. Beside him, Millicent stretched and sighed deeply.

"Nice," she murmured.

"I don't usually take the help to bed," Jax muttered through a cloud of smoke.

"Yeah, I know." Millicent closed her eyes and snuggled in close to him. "That's most likely been your trouble all along."

Then she drifted off to sleep, leaving Jax alone with his thoughts.

AUTUMN

Twenty minutes had passed since I'd received the phone call.

Twenty minutes. Like a sleeper caught in a nightmare, I couldn't move fast enough. No matter that I drove with a terrible disregard for traffic signs and speed limits. It still took me twenty minutes. A lifetime.

The emergency room was crowded with men and women wearing indigo blue uniforms. They stood apart from the hospital staff, murmuring to one another in hushed voices, their hands moving over their utility belts, lightly touching leather holsters, walkie-talkies, and polished nightsticks as if they were charms to ward off violence and death.

Conversation stopped when they saw me.

I paused in the doorway, searching familiar faces for some sense of the news to come. I saw only shock edged with fear.

They saw a slim, hazel-eyed woman with curly honey-brown hair who hadn't taken time to change from cutoff blue jeans and a sloppy T-shirt. But if they saw in my face a mirror of their own emotions, it was because I allowed it.

Pretty lady authors, even ones who write hard-boiled detective novels, are supposed to show their feelings.

"How is he?" I asked no one in particular.

Suddenly, no one would meet my eyes. Bodies shifted, clearing a path between me and a large, uniformed black man at the opposite end of the room. He sat in a chair beside closed double doors marked Hospital Personnel Only. His face was buried in his hands.

"Sarge," someone said. "Jane's here."

Detective Sergeant Tommy Grayson raised his head, his hands folding around themselves in a gesture that looked like prayer. Blood, nearly dried, dulled the smooth skin of his arms, stained his hands a rusty brown, smeared raggedly beneath his right eye and across a cheekbone.

Alex's blood.

Before Tommy could stand, I slipped into the chair beside him, wrapped my hands around his big wrists and gave them a gentle shake.

"How is he?"

He shook his head.

"I've called Joey. She should be here soon."

Joey was Alex's younger sister. Tommy would not have called her unless—

An aggressive female voice interrupted my thoughts.

"Sergeant Grayson. We heard that Chief Callaghan's been shot. Tell us what happened."

I looked up. Reporters and camera crews were crowding in through the entrance, jostling with one another for position. A young woman wearing the insignia of a trainee was trying to block their way.

Tommy sighed so quietly that I doubted anyone else heard.

"Let 'em be, Jamison. They're just doing their job."

He stood, confronted the cameras.

The lights on the minicams blazed to life.

"I'll give you a statement, folks. Then I'm going to ask that you move outside."

Tommy straightened his shoulders, delivered the information as if it were a routine report. As if his best friend had not just been shot. He chose his words carefully and delivered them precisely. Even his deep Southern drawl, so much like Alex's, lent no warmth to the statement.

"At approximately eight forty-five this evening, Chief Callaghan was the victim of a drive-by shooting that took place in front of the Calvary Baptist Temple on Water Street. No suspects have been apprehen—"

"Hasn't Callaghan been working with rival gangs in that area?" cut in one of the television reporters. Before Tommy could answer, another reporter asked, "Was the attack random or was Callaghan the target?"

"We have no reason to believe that this incident was gang-related. As to whether the attack on Chief Callaghan was deliberate, it is too early in our investigation to determine that or to speculate as to the cause of the attack."

"How is Alex?"

The question came from the pudgy, balding crime beat reporter from the *Savannah Morning News*. He was a frequent visitor to the squad room. In his voice, I heard sympathy.

"He's in surgery." Tommy looked away from the reporters before adding, "We'll keep you posted."

He turned his back on the cameras.

Jamison ushered the reporters from the room.

Tommy sat back down beside me, leaned forward, rested his elbows on his knees, and stared down at his hands.

"The shooter was parked, waiting." His voice was toneless, as if he was filling in each line of a police report. "We'd just come out of the church. I heard a car start, then heard shots . . ."

I didn't care about the details. I wanted to shake him, to shout at him, to make him tell me, *now*, about Alex. Instead, I sat quietly.

"I dove for cover, drew my weapon as the suspect vehicle accelerated past us. The car sped around the corner."

I knew what he was doing, had often done it myself. The trick was to ignore the pain, to focus on the details.

"It headed east on Lincoln, toward the highway. A late-model Ford Taurus. Dark blue or black. Four-door. No lights."

Tommy's voice faltered. His Adam's apple moved as his neck tensed. He gulped, struggling to control his emotions, trying—and failing—to remain detached.

He hadn't my training. He didn't need it. For him, Vietnam was decades in the past, and Savannah wasn't a particularly dangerous town. He didn't expect those he loved to die violently.

I did.

Sooner or later, everyone I loved—

I dismissed the thought. Alex was still alive.

Tommy took a deep breath and began speaking again.

"I didn't get a license number. Didn't see how many were inside. Couldn't get a clear shot."

He began rubbing at the dried blood on his left palm with his right thumb.

"Alex hit the ground behind me. So at first I didn't realize . . ."

He noticed what his hands were doing and curled them into tight fists.

"I thought, 'Thank God he wore his vest.' Then I looked closer. The bullet'd gone right through. I called for assistance, then I tried to stop the bleeding. Pressed my hand against the wound. Alex was conscious. He tried to laugh. Told me they lied to us in boot camp. 'See, Tommy,' he said, 'Marines *do* bleed.'"

Tommy lifted his head. His eyes glistened with unshed tears.

"I rode in the ambulance with him. The hospital was five minutes away. Only five minutes, I kept telling him. You lasted a goddamn fucking week in the jungles of 'Nam, and you were hurt worse than this. So you hang on, man. You hang on.

"His heart stopped as we pulled into the driveway. They rushed him inside, and I've been waiting . . ."

He shifted his attention back to his hands, unclenched his fists.

His nails had cut crimson crescent moons into his palms.